D1527543

# THE
# WOLF
## AND THE
# *Wildflower*

# THE
# WOLF
## *Wildflower*
### AND THE

*USA TODAY* BESTSELLING AUTHOR
# STACY REID

Entangled Publishing, LLC
644 Shrewsbury Commons Ave
STE 181
Shrewsbury, PA 17361
rights@entangledpublishing.com

Amara is an imprint of Entangled Publishing.

Edited by Stacy Abrams
Cover design by Bree Archer
Cover photography by Killion Group Images
leonello/Getty Images

Manufactured in the United States of America

First Edition February 2023

AMARA
an imprint of Entangled Publishing LLC

*At Entangled, we want our readers to be well-informed. If you would like to know if this book contains any elements that might be of concern for you, please check the book's webpage for details.*

*https://entangledpublishing.com/books/the-wolf-and-the-wildflower*

*Du'Sean, always and forever.*

# Prologue

*Sheffield, 1860*

The heat in the bedroom was stifling, the pain twisting through Mrs. Miranda Southby's more brutal than the last few times she'd been in the childbed. Despair hitched through her, burying the pain in her body but rousing the one in her heart.

Despite her long and fervent prayers for a healthy babe, yet again, this one had come early. A scream clawed its way up her throat as pain scythed through her and terror filled her heart. She writhed atop the sweat-soaked bedding, twisting the sheets beneath her with such strength that it was indeed a miracle she did not rip them to shreds.

She heard the echoes of her husband's frantic pacing. Clearly, he waited to see if this child would be alive and, most importantly, if it would be a boy. They did have a lovely daughter who had reached her second year only yesterday, but it did not matter to her husband they already had that wonderful blessing. He *needed* a male child to carry on his legacy. The desire was so strong in him that he had ignored the doctor's orders after Sarah's birth.

*I do not recommend Mrs. Southby to fall with child again. This birth was difficult, and she bled a lot. I fear the next time, the outcome might not be so favorable.*

Her husband had stared silently at the doctor, eventually seeking other opinions. Only a few months had passed before he climbed back into her bed to exercise his husbandly rights. Miranda had tried to protest, saying she had still not recovered from the last ordeal, but he had been seductively persistent, and she hadn't been able to keep refusing her duty or deny her love for him.

Now, not only pain cleaved her body in two, but a ripe fear sat heavy in her belly and coated her tongue with bitterness. She was only six and twenty, and she might die today. A swell of resentment rose inside for the man she loved with her whole heart.

"One more push, Mrs. Southby," the midwife muttered, wiping the sweat from her brows. "I can see the head."

Hope burst inside her chest like fireworks. "Truly?"

The midwife's eyes crinkled at the corner. "Yes, ma'am. Only one more push and the babe will be here."

Miranda nodded weakly and pushed with all her strength. *Please let this babe be a boy.*

"Come, ma'am, you need to push; it is not out yet!"

She started to cry, and even that came out as a weak, pitiful whimper. "I can…cannot. I…I am so *tired*. Perhaps I might rest for a few minutes, and then we can start again?"

Determination flashed in the midwife's eyes. "I know you are tired, ma'am, but I also know your strength. This babe needs you, so please, *push*!"

Sitting up on her elbows, Miranda inhaled deeply and bore down with all the strength left inside. It felt as if something tore her open, and she screamed.

A wet rag pressed against her brow. "You are an

extraordinarily strong lady. You can do it, ma'am!"

Her entire body shaking, Miranda squeezed her eyes and pushed with the little remaining strength she owned, knowing she could do no more. A great pressure seemed to expand through Miranda's entire body, and then it was as if she floated on air.

A thin wail sliced through the room. A burst of joy filled her heart, and she struggled to rise. The child lived and had a healthy pair of lungs, too. She started to laugh and cry and was barely aware as the after birth eased from her body, and the midwife and her assistant hurriedly cleaned her.

"Is it a boy?" her husband yelled through the door, hope and excitement vibrating in his tone.

She could feel his impatience, but his gentlemanly honor would not see him barging through that door.

"It is a fine, healthy child," the midwife said.

"Let me see him," Miranda said hoarsely, unable to stop crying with her joy and relief. "Let me hold my son."

Miranda was propped on a pillow, and a swaddled bundle was placed in her arms. "Oh, my little love, you are so beautiful."

"I have a son!"

She snapped her head up at that joyous shout. Miranda hadn't realized her husband had come inside. Charles hurried to her bedside and sank onto one of his knees. His beautiful blond hair was mussed, a testimony to how often he must have raked his fingers through the strands. Even his glasses seemed perched on his long nose haphazardly. His lashes were damp as he peered at the babe in her arms.

"We have a boy," he said gruffly, reaching out to touch the baby's cheek. Charles looked at her, love and gratitude naked in his dark green eyes. "I shall teach him so much. Thank you, my dearest, *thank* you!"

Her husband leaned forward and pressed a tender kiss

to her forehead. Miranda sobbed, the relief in her heart too profound for her to restrain her emotions.

*Dear Lord, thank you.*

"No more after this one," she whispered. "We have two beautiful blessings, and I implore that they will be a sufficient joy to our lives. We *must* take precautions to ensure there are no more children. I simply cannot do this again, Charles."

He dropped his forehead to hers and closed his eyes. "I have been a right fool to lay so much pressure on you, my love. My heart is guilty. I am guilty. Forgive me."

Charles held her tightly for several seconds, and she basked in his reassuring embrace. A few minutes later, the door closed gently on his departure, and she heard his bellow for their servants to fetch the port; there would be a grand celebration tonight. Miranda glanced up, and her smile dimmed, the gladness inside her chest growing cold.

"What is it, Mrs. Garrick?" she asked at the midwife's unusual somber countenance. "Is all well with the child? Is he well?"

The portly midwife bustled closer. "It all happened before I could say anything, ma'am. The baby cried, and I placed her in your arms, and you were saying you had a beautiful boy, and the door opened, and I was afraid…"

Something heavy and frightful pressed against Miranda's belly. *"Her?"*

The midwife sat on the small chair before the bed, her face creased with worry, her dark brown eyes glowing with compassion. "The babe is a girl. A beautiful, healthy babe."

For a precious moment, Miranda could not speak. Swallowing down the tight, uncertain lump forming in her throat, she carefully parted the blankets with trembling fingers. "A girl," she whispered. "He'll be so disappointed."

Miranda looked up at the midwife, seeing her face through a blur of unshed tears. "He'll want to try again."

*Soon.* "I do not think I could bear for it to be so."

Mrs. Garrick sighed heavily. "You labored for two days, milady. The entire household thought you would have gone on to your rewards and kept vigil with grim visages. You cannot take to the childbed again, ma'am. There are remedies I could suggest, but they might not work for long."

A raw sob tore from Miranda's throat, and it felt like her heart broke into pieces. "I cannot do this again. Oh God, what am I to do? How do I reach my husband and let him see reason?"

Mrs. Garrick remained silent for long moments before another heavy but resolute sigh slipped from her. "In my experience, ma'am, even the poorer class husbands do not bathe their children, dress them, or have need to know of their sexes. Not even you will be expected to feed and nurse this child. It is just not done."

Alarmed confusion jolted through Miranda. "I beg your pardon?"

The midwife lifted her chin. "Mr. Southby needs not to know this child is a girl. No one needs to know. My oldest daughter will be more than happy to be your nursemaid. It would be a secret we would take to our graves."

"But my husband...surely, he would eventually know," Miranda said, wondering why she was even indulging in the madness of such talk. "I *cannot* lie to him and surely I wouldn't be able to deceive him in such a manner forever."

"Aye...not forever," Mrs. Garrick said kindly. "But it will give you some time to recover. I've tended to you five times in as little as seven years, ma'am. Yer husband claims to love you, but a boy child is more important than your health."

Miranda flinched at a truth she had long acknowledged and wept for. Her husband was the second son of a viscount, and they had fallen in love and wed eight years prior. Their romance had been fast and passionate; in Charles, she found a man she admired and trusted with her emotions. She knew he loved her. But it pained her that she did not understand his desperate desire for a male child. He was a second son and was not likely to ever inherit unless a terrible tragedy befell his older brother's family.

Her husband owned a comfortable estate in Sheffield and an income of two thousand pounds a year, and while it was a tidy fortune that allowed them to live comfortably, this was not an accomplishment that demanded an heir and spare. Yet he continued to insist he needed a male heir to teach his craft and inherit the legacy he was determined to build.

The child fussed in her arms, and Miranda peered down into that small, wrinkled pink face, profound tenderness filling her heart.

"I love you so much already," she whispered. "So very much."

"Forgive my boldness, milady, but Mr. Southby will have no cause to ever see this child in the nude. As per your station, a nursemaid will see to this child's most intimate needs, and my daughter will keep this vow of secrecy for however long you desire. You trim her hair, give her a boy's name, and most importantly, treat her as a son in every way. Then hope and pray that when you eventually inform Mr. Southby of the truth, you will be strong enough to weather that storm and perhaps the birthing bed again."

Miranda shook her head in denial. "This is a deception that could ruin my family. I cannot imagine the scandal should it ever come out. My husband's brother is a viscount, and our family is a part of the *haut ton*. Our reputations would be forever lost. I...I would lose the love and trust of my husband."

"It is a deception that is necessary to save your life. Unless you believe Mr. Southby will stay out of your bed."

A blush heated Miranda's cheeks. He would not. Her

husband did not only come to her bed to ensure she got pregnant. They had a passion between them that flared at the slightest touch. She could keep him away by stating she was not yet recovered, but his need for a male child had proven to override his good senses. "Perhaps there is a way to prevent… to prevent me from falling with child?"

The midwife grimaced. "Those are not methods fit for a lady, and I fear he would uncover them. Some are also quite grueling to the body, and you are very weak, ma'am. I believe you need at least five years' rest from the childbed. Perhaps then you could inform your husband of the truth and hope for his forgiveness. Perhaps his affection will not have him beat or banish you."

The midwife stood and went about her business cleaning the room. Miranda stared down at her child, wondering if she could possibly tell such a terrible falsehood to her husband. He was an emerging physician of the mind, one of the most notable in society. She, too, was a viscount's daughter, but not much in society, at least not since her come out several years ago.

*How would it ever be revealed if it is a tightly guarded secret?*

She closed her eyes, tears trailing down her cheeks. Miranda had fallen in love with Charles the minute she had seen him at the midnight ball, and she had never stopped once. How she had prayed that she would finally give him a son.

But even now, she could feel the weakness in her body, and the thought of Charles climbing back into her bed again soon after this birthing ordeal made her want to cast up her accounts. Miranda did not enjoy pregnancy and certainly not childbirth. The constant vomiting, pain in her feet and lower back, the dizziness…and the tearing pain of losing that child before it was ready to come into the world.

However, now that they had a daughter…and a son, their lovely family was complete. Charles would happily give her several months to heal before expecting passion between them, and after, knowing he already had a son, Charles would honor her wish and take the proper precautions to ensure there was no pregnancy. But if there was no male child, he would want to attempt another pregnancy. A fierce determination flowed through her body. Lifting the child to her chest, she kissed the babe's forehead. "Welcome to the world, my darling Jules."

Miranda prayed that she had made the right decision.

# Chapter One

*23 years later…*
*England, Derbyshire.*

> *"Ten years ago, the Duke and Duchess of Wulverton tragically lost their son, little Lord James, and their little Lady Felicity at sea. London has been buzzed with the news that two persons matching the description of Lord James and Lady Felicity have been found by an archeological team in a jungle near the border of the Congo. It is reported they are no longer recognized as humans but are feral after years spent amongst all manner of creatures with no human interactions!"*
>
> *The Daily Scandal, 18 April 1884*

Jules Southby lowered the newssheet with an inelegant snort befitting something an annoyed gentleman might have made. That was the third account she read of a most extraordinary discovery, and once again, the facts were obscured, the news stated outlandishly. Reaching for another newssheet, she found the section that spoke of the gossip that had all of society abuzz and reportedly even the queen out of sorts.

*"Good news at last! The duke has been found! After missing from England and his family for more than ten years, credible reports have been submitted that missing Lord James, the new Duke of Wulverton, has been found deep across the Great Norton Sounds of the Bering Sea. Reports suggested he was found in a cave, dressed as a beast and barely recognizable as a human. Many in society, especially among the medical and scientific community, recall the incredible discovery of feral children in the Norwegian wilds and their sad demise, never imagining such a disaster could ever befall one of our most distinguished families."*

*The Morning Chronicle, 18 April 1884*

Jules sighed. The stories grew more fantastical with each printed report. Even yesterday, while traveling from Manchester to town, the passengers on the train had been buzzing with news of the lost duke and the whispers of his feral insanity.

"I have read all the papers and the scandal sheets, and they each have something different to say about this duke and his family. If it is the Duke of Wulverton who has been found. They should be ashamed for pandering to the masses and not getting the correct and truthful story."

Jules's mother, Mrs. Miranda Southby, who had been laboriously eavesdropping on her husband's conversation, straightened and patted her prettily coiffed strawberry blond hair.

"You did not lose a feather while bent to that keyhole," Jules said, grinning. "Mama, your actions are insupportable. Father discusses a private matter. It is not correct in any regard that you are intruding upon it."

"I cannot credit that your unruly inquisitiveness has been tamed during your time abroad," her mother said with a touch of acerbity, flushing to her hair roots. "I am dreadfully curious as to who has called so secretly upon your father. The lady wears a veil, and her carriage crest is covered with a black cloth. Are you not at all wondering what is happening?"

Jules glanced at the varied newssheets and scandal rags scattered about on the rococo table. It was indeed a simple deduction as to who might have called upon her father, a notable doctor of the mind in their society. "I suspect it might be the duchess."

Her mother's eyes widened. "I beg your pardon?"

"A duchess, Mama," Jules repeated patiently.

"A *duchess* in my home, and I am not aware of it? What duchess?"

Jules held up one of the papers. "Her Grace, the Duchess of Wulverton. I might be mistaken, but I strongly suspect it is the duchess meeting with father if there is any veracity to these numerous reports about town."

"Upon my word, you cannot be serious!"

Jules wrinkled her nose. "I am."

Though she wanted to believe it, the reportings were all too...imaginative and sounded like a tale from a storybook. The duke and perhaps his sister being lost at sea when their parents' ship sunk over ten years ago were alive? Or even that they had instead been lost in the great ice-capped mountains of Canada, how were they alive? *How?* Her curiosity stirred as the impact it would have on their minds and personalities would be far-reaching.

Were they indeed feral? Could they be successfully socialized back within society? How old had they truly been when they were lost?

"Are you familiar with this, Mama?"

Her mother looked ready to faint. "I have some knowledge of it, but I have never paid any keen attention to the yearly reminder of the lost duke by the newssheets. Every year on the anniversary of the tragedy, the London papers run a piece offering the reward for any news of the young duke. Even the local paper here in Derbyshire writes something around the anniversary. Quickly summon Helga. Tea and the best pastries need to be immediately prepared."

"Mama," Jules said softly, pushing off the desk. "I believe we should wait for father's meeting to conclude. I daresay I should not intrude with offers of tea and cakes."

"*Pish!*" Her mother whirled around to bend and peek through the keyhole once more. "It would be an incredible boost for this family if it is known the duchess was here at our humble manor. Your uncle would be most appreciative."

Jules said nothing to that because her uncle, Albert Southby, Viscount Ramsey, was indeed most concerned about his family's standing and connections within the *haut ton*.

"Uncle would be appreciative indeed," she murmured drily.

Her mother cast a baleful glare over her shoulders. "We've never had such an important guest call on us before. Are you not at all curious, my dear?"

"I am, but this is not a social call, Mama." Jules folded her arms across her perfectly bound chest and rested her slim hip on the large oak desk. "I cannot see how peering through that tiny keyhole is a good thing."

Her mother straightened with a sheepish grin. "Wouldn't it be most fortuitous if Her Grace hires your father when you are just home from university? This would be a terrific opportunity to show your father that you are more than able to continue in his footsteps and work beside him in ensuring his legacy. You know that has been his dream for so exceptionally long."

Jules smiled, raking fingers through her short-cropped strawberry blond hair. She had spent the last four years in Austria, studying in the field of psychology at the University of Leipzig in Germany, where she had recently graduated with distinction. It was there, in the friendships she had formed with her professors and peers, that she had learned to accept the lie her life was meticulously built on, even if she did not fully understand its construct.

For four years she had avoided returning home to England, and she'd bitterly accepted that if she were not considered a gentleman by society and by most of her family, such a freedom would not be allowed. Jules had promised herself upon her return home, she would break down the wall of deceit that had been carefully built around her entire life to better understand herself, the past, and the hopes for her future. She had allowed for the pain and damage it might do to her family and had braced herself to shoulder the responsibility of it all.

Except...now that she was here, the memory of her mother's desperate pleas and tears the last time Jules wanted to reveal all to her father eroded that decision until only doubt weighed like a boulder atop her shoulders.

How could she bring such distress and uncertainty to her family, who were for all intent wonderfully happy? Worse, by telling her father everything, Jules risked giving up the life and freedom with which she had lived for twenty-three years. Would her father even ask her of it if he knew the truth? Or would he continue helping her to deceive the rest of their family and society?

Her mother waved an elegant hand before Jules's face. "My dear, cease your woolgathering and answer me. I do so loathe this habit both you and your father own. To stare off in retrospect as if you were alone! Do you not think this would be a wonderful opportunity to join your father's team?"

"You know it is one of my dreams to work alongside Father, Mama," Jules said softly, staring at her mother's wary expression. "I am more uncertain if he would wish for me to continue his legacy if..."

Fear flashed in her mother's eyes, and she held out a hand. "Jules, *please*...you must not..." She took a deep breath and smoothed her palm over her dress. "Why must you wish for your father to know the truth? It has been years. And are you not happy?"

"I cannot defeat the questions that haunt me when I wonder if Father would love me the same...if he would have the same pride and hopes in me if he knew I was of the female persuasion, Mama," she said softly. "Would he understand I am the same person even if I wear a gown?"

Her mother paled, and the misery naked in her eyes brought that awful lump to Jules's throat.

"How is Sarah doing, Mama? I have not heard from her since her marriage. My sister's last letter a few months ago declared she was desperately in love with Viscount Halliwell and adapts to life well as the new viscountess."

*Desperately in love*...an inconceivable concept to Jules.

Relief flashed in her mother's eyes at the shift in conversation, however, before she could answer, the door opened, and her father framed the doorway. His angular face was composed, but his dark green eyes, a perfect replica of Jules's, were eager and excited.

"Jules, if you would come into my office for a moment. I would like you to meet an important guest."

His wife sent him a hopeful look, clearly wanting to be a

part of whatever was happening. Father winked at her, and though Mama pouted, she smiled her encouragement and made her way from the drawing room in a swish of colors. Her father stepped back and waved Jules to precede him into his office through the connecting drawing-room door.

Jules's fingers instinctively fluttered to the moustache she wore and patted the soft curls. She straightened her neckcloth, squared her shoulders, and swept inside the room. Immediately her gaze arrowed in on the imposing woman sitting in the chair normally reserved for her father, with another gentleman hovering by her arm. The woman was not old or young. In truth, she seemed ageless in her beauty and cold rigidity. The lady was arresting, with lustrous dark hair that showed no gray. Her features held a unique blush of youth; her blue eyes still sparkled with vitality.

"Your Grace, Mr. Williams, please allow me the honor of presenting my son to you, Mr. Jules Southby, recently returned from Austria where he completed his studies in psychology. He graduated with distinction," her father said proudly. "He also speaks French, German, Greek, Russian, and Latin fluently."

Jules dipped into a quick and elegant bow to the duchess. "It is a pleasure, Your Grace." After standing, she glanced at the gentleman. "Mr. Williams, it is good to meet you."

"Mr. Southby," Mr. William murmured, his shrewd gaze skipping over her face and lingering a beat longer than appropriate.

He was not able to conceal the widening of his eyes upon seeing her full countenance. Jules was much used to it, and people often commented on her fair complexion and fine bones for a "gentleman." Even at university, there had been a few who teased her for being a "pretty lad." She discreetly lifted her hand to her upper lip, to ensure her fake moustache was firmly in place. The stage makeup applied to her face to give it a sterner appearance had been expertly done, and she had perfected her low pitch way of speaking over the years. Confident all was in place, she said, "Thank you for including me in this meeting, Your Grace."

Pleasantries aside, there was a charged moment of silence.

"How does meeting this young pup help with my concerns?" the duchess demanded in clipped accents of impatience, her eyes narrowing in on Jules. "Dr. Southby, your services were recommended to me by Sir James Reid, and I made the journey here, though I am still uncertain how your newfangled ideas can help my family."

Disdain and skepticism dripped from the duchess. Jules did not take offense, she was very much used to others dismissing issues of the mind. It was one of the reasons she had chosen to study in Austria, where their field of passion was talked about with more seriousness. There were those in England who did not understand why one would want to study the maladies of the mind, or how their knowledge could even help one so afflicted.

"The study of the mind is not newfangled, Your Grace," Jules said politely, moving to sit on the sofa closest to the duchess. "The study of the mind and behavior dates back to the ancient Greeks, who created provable science to help those interested to understand certain patterns of behavior, and even to influence behavior."

Jules waved toward her father. "My father is one of the best doctors of the mind there is in England. I am certain you came to him because you are worried about your son and daughter...and it is important that you do everything possible to help them, even if you yourself do not believe in the methods."

The duchess stared at Jules for a long time before releasing a shuddering breath.

"Your father came highly recommended by Dr. Grant

who operates the…that institution in Reading for those people with unsound…thinking."

Her lips trembled and Jules spied the dark fear in the duchess's eyes.

"Are you afraid that…that your children suffer from unsound thinking, Your Grace?"

A harsh breath sawed from the duchess's throat. "My son…*only* my son."

Jules smiled gently. "Forgive me, Your Grace, for assuming."

"Someone…a man was recently found in the Alaskan wilds by a trapping team. Or he found them. That man appeared on my doorstep exactly four weeks ago. I *know* he is my son, not like those charlatans who have shown up over the years claiming to be the duke, seeking wealth and rewards. He…he is the very image of his father."

The duchess fell silent, and Jules and her father patiently waited for her grace to find her equanimity. There was a pleading look in her eyes when she glanced at Jules's father. It prompted him to ask, "Did this man recognize you?"

"Yes. I immediately saw that recognition in his eyes, but he did not rush into my arms or even show his relief and happiness to be back with me…with his family."

Jules shifted on the sofa. "How does he refer to you?"

The duchess's shoulders stiffened. "Your Grace…since his return only 'Your Grace' or 'Duchess.' The newspapers are having a whirl with the news of his return. The queen sent her personal physician to Hertfordshire and my son, he…he barely responds to Sir James Reid, who understandably has a lot of questions. How can he give a good report to the queen?"

"Is it your hope the duke will be more forthcoming with his experience to us?" her father asked. "Or do you fear that he has been hurt…mentally?"

The duchess flinched. "I cannot see why he would speak

with strangers instead of his family. I am his *mother*...and I...my heart cried and ached for him every day he had been missing. *Every day*."

And there it was, the rough edge of guilt in her words, the haunted look in her eyes. Guilt was a terrible chain to wear around one's neck, and the duchess seemed to be burdened with the coils around her.

"My son is not the same...and that is why...that is why I might need your help, Dr. Southby. How can he step into the role he is duty and honor bound to fulfill if he is thought of as eccentric and addlepated? My son has very decided and odd mannerisms not fit for *haut ton* life. He is the Duke of Wulverton. He *is* the *haut ton*."

A bit arrogant to Jules's way of thinking, but in many respects the duchess was correct.

"Now that my son has been found, he must be presented to the queen and society as a gentleman of sound mind and fortitude. He is to meet the queen's representative in as little as three weeks at the first ball I will host for the season, then he will eventually visit the Queen at Windsor Castle. There can be no doubt that he is fit. *None*."

*Three weeks?* The desperate fear in the duchess's voice tugged at a cord inside Jules. She understood that fear. The queen had the power to consign the duke to an insane asylum should she deem him a threat to himself or others. Or if her father declared him to be mentally unfit.

More threatening and problematic, the queen had the power to remove the duke as the heir if the crown did not believe in the duke's mental stability. There were not many private mental hospitals, and even recently a baron had been committed by the order of the queen to The Bethlehem Hospital for the insane in Moorfields, north of St Pauls, and the City. The scandal of it still lingered in the drawing rooms of society, though it had been months.

Was the duke competent enough to worry about such matters befalling him? Or was this the duchess believing the duke did not fit the current mold of society?

"My father will be able to help," Jules assured the duchess with calm confidence. "He is considered by many to be a brilliant alienist, Your Grace."

The duchess pinned her father with a probing stare, the hope and fear naked on her face for them to see.

"I will entrust my hopes to you, Dr. Southby. I have only a few weeks to prepare my son to show the world he *is* the Duke of Wulverton. I feel such a goal to be *impossible* and I despair."

Her father stepped closer. "Your Grace, if you'll be comfortable with this suggestion, I would like my son to accompany me down to meet the duke and to remain with me for the duration of my assessment."

Shock and a surge of excitement traveled through Jules, and she worked to present a calm composure. It would be such a privilege and honor to work alongside her father. He was one of the most noted and respected doctors of the mind in Britain, even though their society still struggled with accepting psychology as a valid scientific tool that helped people. The awareness that he wanted her with him on a matter so important filled her with rich pleasure and warmth.

"Father?" Jules had to clear her throat, which had thickened beyond the low pitch she'd achieved over the years. He could take any one of his estimable colleagues, but he wanted her with him.

*No, not me—his son.*

With an inward, irritated scoff at herself, Jules tried to shrug aside that insidious fear that should her father know his only male child to be a young lady, he would be bitterly disappointed, and her father, in light of the deception, would no longer love, honor, and respect her as he did.

So many nights, Jules had tossed restlessly in bed wondering, should she sit and speak in a forthright manner with her father, what would she discover? Shame and outrage that his Jules was of the female persuasion and his wife had deceived him for twenty-three years? Pain and disgust that his child had joined in that deception years ago when she herself realized the truth of her own circumstances? Would it irreparably break their family as her mother feared?

Or would Jules see knowledge and peace? Had he discovered at some point his child was of the female gender and had maintained the ruse to protect his family's reputation? If all were to be revealed, would her father expect Jules to shed the only identity she knew to assume the mantle her older sister carried with such pride, but one Jules might never understand or accept?

It took incalculable effort to shut those thoughts out and to concentrate on what was important now.

The duchess leveled her probing gaze on Jules. "Your son is frightfully young and seems quite wet behind the ears. I do not see how Mr. Southby could be of much assistance."

Jules silently groaned, seeing this exciting opportunity slipping from her grasp.

"Your Grace, my son has been exemplary in his studies and many of his professors wrote to me detailing his performance that has been nothing short of incredible," her father said solemnly. "If it is your wish, he does not have to interact directly with the duke, but my son will assist me greatly with note-taking and his empathic insight."

The duchess stared at Jules, and she returned her unflinching regard, breathless with the need to plead to be there.

*Do not be carried away with the science*, she reminded herself harshly, and forced herself to look upon the duchess's pain and humanize the duke instead of seeing him as an intriguing subject.

"Your Grace," Jules said gently. "Will you share more with us about His Grace? What is his name?"

A soft look entered her gaze. "My son...he is James Leopold Winters, the Duke of Wulverton, and the Earl of Lydon. This horrendous experience has greatly and undeniably altered him," she said, her lips trembling before she firmed them.

The duchess stood, walked over to the fireplace, and held her hands over the wavering flames. "I want...I want back the gentle boy who would mend the broken wings of birds, play the pianoforte with me and sing in that beautiful voice of his. I want back my son who allowed me to hold him close and kiss his cheek even when he grew a sight taller than myself. He has not allowed me or anyone to touch him. I..."

The duchess lowered her hands and faced them. "My son is not the same. I *need* him to be as how he was."

"The newssheet said he was lost at sea for a number of years?"

A faraway look entered her dark blue eyes. "How wrong they are. My son was almost eighteen years old when he became lost in the Yukon Territory in the Canadian wilds. For ten years and four months he lived in the emptiness of the great mountains of Mount Logan without any other human interaction."

Her throat worked on a swallow as emotions brimmed in her eyes. "*Ten years.* We knew he was there...all the experts that were hired to track him when he went missing said it *was* possible. My husband...before he passed, we hired dozens of men to search the area, but all reported on the impossible task we set before them. And I assure you, many tried because we offered thousands of pounds as a reward for James's return home to us. Even if only a body so we could lay his remains to rest properly and as befitting of the heir to a dukedom."

The duchess's steps were agitated as she made her way to the windows overlooking the small garden of their town house. "Mount Logan is the largest and highest mountain in Canada and has a subarctic climate. Do you have any idea what that means, Mr. Southby?"

Jules chose her words carefully even as her heart pounded, and questions swirled in her head. "Yes. He...your son lived in a place characterized by long, cold winters, and incredibly brief periods of warmth. To survive there..."

Jules could not imagine it, to be surrounded by endless miles of trees, hills, mountains capped with snow and bitter coldness with little food to hunt. How had an eighteen-year-old boy done it for years?

"Such a feat would have taken extraordinary resilience." *And luck.* "Your son is most incredible."

The duchess sent her a quick astonished glance. "You sound as if you admire the duke, Mr. Southby, without meeting him."

"I do, Your Grace."

*Survival of the fittest*, an expression coined by psychologist Herbert Spence in his book *Principles of Biology,* and one she had extensively studied rose in her thoughts. Jules had devoured that book on many occasions and the pages opened in her mind, the theories on why some survive insurmountable odds while others faltered swarmed through her.

She wanted to meet the duke...now. God, the excitement burning inside her chest felt surreal.

"When...when the trapping team encountered my boy... he had a weapon, a curved-like dagger made from the bones of creatures they claimed he fought. Wolves...bears..." The duchess clasped her gloved hands tightly together. "He still has that weapon. In our *home.*"

The fear in her voice had Jules canting her head. "That weapon was his means of protection in the icy wilderness—

perhaps it comforts him to have it now."

"In our home?" the duchess repeated, incredulity ringing in her voice. "There is no danger there. Only people desperate to welcome him home and *love* him. People he refuses to see or connect with."

Jules carefully chose her words as she held the duchess's stare. "Gentlemen of our society carry a weapon, Your Grace. Almost all gentlemen travel around with walking sticks which hide swords, and some even have daggers in their boots. I, too, in some instances travel with a rapier in my walking stick. In some parts of America, it is said men walk openly with guns hitched onto their hips, and fight in the streets at the slightest provocation. The fact the duke holds on to his weapon of bones which aided his survival in his world is normal and not something to fear."

The duchess's eyes widened, and her father sent Jules a swift glance of approval.

"I…I never quite thought of it in that manner." Her Grace frowned. "It is a fearsome thing to behold. I have asked him to discard it and…he has not."

"Does he say why?" her father asked, reaching for his notebook. He then sat in an armchair, peering at the duchess over the wire-rimmed spectacles perched on his bony nose.

"The duke does not speak. And this is one of the many reasons I require your brand of specialty."

Her father frowned. "This has been determined to be by choice?"

Her gloved hand fluttered to her chest. The motion delicate, almost ethereal, yet Jules suspected the duchess had a spine of steel.

"I perhaps phrased it incorrectly. The duke *barely* speaks. Mostly grunts for affirmation and silent stares. I've yet to hear a full sentence from his mouth. It is as if…he finds the world around him tedious. He…" The duchess took an audible deep breath. "I cannot begin to describe how my boy is altered but still appears the same."

"Tell us," Jules breathed, unable to halt the need blooming through her. "Please, Your Grace. If it is not too difficult to recount."

"My son had always been slim in youth. Now his build is not that of a gentleman, more of…of a common dockworker, rendering his presence when he stands almost intimidating."

The duchess moved away from the windows and resumed her pacing, her agitation once again emerging in sharp relief. The vision that leaped to mind was someone with powerful muscles…*everywhere*. An unexpected image of a naked man delineated with sinews on his shoulders, back, buttocks, thighs and calves flared in her mind.

The duchess continued, "After much pleading, the duke conceded to take a few baths in milk then rosewater to soften his skin. I daresay it did not help. His teeth have been cleaned with lime pulps, salt, and then dental powder. The doctors reported his teeth were all miraculously well intact with none missing and gave the appearance that the duke had somehow tended to them in that icy wilderness. Though my son has allowed his hair to be groomed and untangled, he will not permit it to be trimmed. It flows past his shoulders, though he thankfully ties it in a queue."

"Why try and force him to cut it?"

The duchess appeared astonished that Jules had even asked.

The duchess's lips thinned. "I am certain you understand it is terribly inconvenient for the duke to appear so in society. His appearance will fuel the gossipmongering, but he is immune to those reasonings from myself, his grandmother, his sister…well, from *everyone*."

"Is the duke amused by your suggestions?" Jules asked, trying to craft an initial impression of the duke's character.

"No, further from it. He is…at best indifferent."

"May I have more of his description?"

A fond smile crossed her lips. "His eyes are a perfect replica of his father's…an arctic color of such unusual beauty, more gray than blue. They no longer gleam with laughter or gentleness. They are unfathomable except for those moments where I see the savagery behind the veil. He spends most of his time outdoors deep inside the forest of his land, but I cannot imagine what he does out there. I *love* my son, but I find his manners barbaric and unacceptable."

*Savagery.* Jules didn't understand the odd manner in which her heart jerked or the shakiness of her fingers. The picture drawn by the duchess…it did not repel her senses; in truth she was compelled…fascinated. And an odd part of her wasn't sure if it was the budding scientist inside her or the hidden woman.

She recoiled from the thought, lurching to stand, almost stumbling to the mantle and the decanter of brandy. *Why would I even dare to think such a ridiculous thing?* Any sort of relationship for Jules was unthinkable. Her entire life was an elaborate deception with unimaginable consequences should it ever be uncovered.

A few years ago, she had thought about finding a way to reveal to society the truth of her existence. She had spent months pondering the benefits of living a life as a lady, of knowing about wooing, about kissing a gentleman, of falling in love, of having children, and of needlepoint, playing the pianoforte and all the other delicate arts her sister attended to with such keen joy.

Then Jules had thought about the life she enjoyed, the freedom to enter a tavern to drink a pint of ale, to walk without being watched by a chaperone, to ride astride, to be…free—and she had decided to take her ruse to an even greater level and attend university.

All desire for those fleeting feminine yearnings had been buried and had never once resurfaced. Not even when her schoolmates had tried to convince her of the wonders of kissing and tupping. They had thought her a man, but the woman in her had not been curious.

Why now, and for a figure that was so ephemeral?

*It is ridiculous, and I am giving it too much importance.*

The duchess's gaze swept the room. "Will you take this case, Dr. Southby?"

Her father hesitated slightly.

"I am willing to compensate you quite handsomely," the duchess said, lifting her chin. "And the Queen herself mentioned you in conversation, of course."

Jules's heart pounded and she understood her father's pondering. The entire situation was unusual and of high significance. It was her father's head and his family on the executioner's block should his expertise yield no result.

Her father fiddled with the pen clutched between his fingers. "Does your son understand he is the duke, your hopeful expectations of him, and his duty to his title and to this realm?"

"I cannot tell," the duchess said, her eyes growing teary, "and it is a question the entirety of society, the queen, and his family need to know the answer to. In short, Dr. Southby, it is a question which must be answered without any doubt. "

Her father stood and bowed. "It will be our pleasure to offer assistance in any way we can, Your Grace."

An odd and unknown sensation jolted through Jules. It felt almost like fear. The notion was laughable, but Jules suddenly felt should she travel to Hertfordshire with her father, something about her life might be forever altered.

# Chapter Two

*"A marriage is a necessity at this critical juncture. Surely you see that, Uncle Hubert!"* Cousin Eugenia said in a dramatic whisper.

*"Can we really not convince him to cut his hair? He has been home for a month now. It is quite unfashionable, and I declare he is as close to a savage as possible! Everyone will be speaking about this, whatever are we to do?"* Aunt Margaret replied in a tone laced with despair.

*"Surely a dance tutor,"* said Cousin Eloise. *"Nothing says everything is well as dancing. Should he stand up with a few ladies, I am certain society would see all is well, indeed."*

James Winters, the Duke of Wulverton, had never heard anything so ludicrous. Yet he did not turn from his position by the balustrade, as he overlooked the night, ignoring the facile chatter echoing in the drawing room of his country manor. A small part of him wondered if his family did not perceive his presence or if the stillness that he'd learned to cloak himself with to survive made them pretend he was not there.

*No, not them, my family.*

Still little to no feelings wafted through James at the thought of the dozen or so people crowded in the drawing room. News of his arrival in Hertfordshire had somehow preceded his presence. James had only been home for a few days before they had descended on the stately country home, all cackling over themselves to "help" him find the essence of himself. They flocked to his home to study him, to dissect his every thought and action.

His family seemed to watch him keenly as if to ensure he was not a raving lunatic who might one day murder them in their sleep. Or so Uncle Hubert had muttered upon more than one occasion, pinning James with a gimlet and almost challenging glare. His mother regarded him with pain, guilt, and worry in her expressive eyes.

Weatherby, a cousin he'd never met, sent him bitter scowls, for he was no longer the presumptive heir. Felicity, his sister, could hardly meet his gaze, and whenever he moved too close to Cousin Eloise, she scuttled away like a frightened crab. His grandmother merely matched him, her expression inscrutable until her eyes would pool with tears and she would hurry from his presence.

There was nothing James could say or do to assuage his family's anxiety, for he admitted he had long stopped feeling. It was in those complex sensations which lingered and twisted in the heart that he could lose a sense of his self. How did he then identify and connect with the myriad emotions and expressions that he saw in the eyes of his mother, sister, cousin, and aunt?

James could not. Still, the most pertinent truth gleaned from his family was that he *must* become James Leopold Winters, the Duke of Wulverton, cloaking himself in the skin of a man who knew his power and position in the world. They all depended on him, his sister and the duchess more than all the others.

*A duke.* A title and honor he had not thought about in years.

*"There might be a need to hire many other tutors, one might assume. When did the boy stop learning? At fourteen years?"* Aunt Margaret muttered with a sigh.

The varied voices rushed over themselves to contribute to the current discourse.

*"I believe it was seventeen summers. He did not get the chance to study at Cambridge like all the previous dukes of our line. It is a terrible disgrace to the family."*

*"Is it too late for him to enroll?"*

This voice he recognized as Uncle Hubert.

*"To attend university at eight and twenty? It is absurd, Uncle Hubert. Why, I cannot imagine the scandal of it!"*

*"A wife is what he needs, I say! A wife!"*

*"We can scarcely hope he might achieve more than a respectable alliance."*

His uncle's wife, Aunt Clarissa replied, *"He should be able to find a most excellent match. There are many mothers desperate to catch a duke in their matrimonial net. Do you deny it to be so?"*

A huff sounded, and then contemplative silence lingered only for a few moments.

*"Who will marry him? He…"*

That unfamiliar voice dipped so low he barely caught the words "savage, inelegant, and unrefined."

Ah, so they were fully aware that he stood only a few feet from them but only thought it necessary to be careful over some words which they were afraid for him to discern.

*"He is a bloody duke, a rather wealthy one! Who will not have him?"*

*"Well, I for certain would not take him! We've been here almost two weeks and he has not deigned to speak with us. I do not think it arrogance but…"* A great huff of annoyance

sounded, then an affronted sniff. "*Something unseemly must have happened out there in that mountain. It is rather frustrating that he will not tell us about any of it.*"

Something warm tickled James's chest and rose inside him. With a start he recognized it as amusement.

*Something unseemly indeed.*

The darkness of the forest and the wide-open space called to him, and he sensed the heralding rain on the air. His skin felt tight and unusual, and James wanted to get out of the clothes which felt as if they choked him. He vaguely recalled a time when he had been much concerned with the style of his hair, the complex and fancy knots of his cravats and neckcloths, and the cut of his coat. He'd even had a man who helped him get dressed and scrubbed his back if needed. But everything seemed different now—even the fashions for men had changed, felt more restricting and looked drabber and more pompous.

Now the very idea of having a valet was inarguably laughable.

The scent of jasmine wafted on the air, and an elusive sensation trembled through his entire body. The duchess approached. James did not remove his gaze from the distant tree line in the forest when she stopped beside him, the top of her head barely brushing his shoulder. His mother did not touch him, and he was careful not to step away from her.

That mattered. At their very first meeting after so many years, she had rushed toward him, and James had avoided that embrace, unable to bear the weight of her touch. Wounded eyes had pooled with tears, and he had stepped forward, recognizing a woman he'd never thought to see again in his lifetime. She'd attempted to touch him again, and his recoil had been dangerously instinctive. He did not like anyone too close to him, and that extended to the duchess.

She had not hugged him then, and since, had been very

careful in the distance she placed between their bodies. James slowly permitted her closer, but he had not given any thought to allowing the duchess to wrap her slender, elegant arms around him. They stood in silence for several beats of his heart, the inane chatter of his family like busy magpies circling in the background.

"I apologize if I've overwhelmed you with tonight's gathering. The doctor…" She hesitated and cleared her throat gently. "We thought a familiar setting might be helpful."

Familiar…another fleeting memory of a large family outing on the sprawling lawns, much laughter and joy wafted through him.

*Helpful to do what?*

James did not voice the question, nor did he make a reply. There was simply nothing to say. Whatever they needed to feel comfortable, it was his duty to provide it. That much he understood, even if executing it was another matter entirely.

"You are always standing at a window or on a balcony looking toward the woods. What is out there?" his mother asked softly.

"Peace," he murmured, mildly surprised at the answer.

"Is it so chaotic here with your family?" she asked with heightened color. "We are your family, and we all *love* you. Very much, James. Please do not act as if we are strangers!"

He turned slowly and stared at the mix of family members all heatedly discussing what to do about him, as if he were a rare creature that had upended their world. Uncle Hubert, his wife and two daughters were huddled in a corner furiously whispering and casting him quick glances. Other cousins and aunts were conducting their own meetings and his sister pounded away at the pianoforte with none of her usual skills.

"They are very…busy."

*Chaos.* They represented chaos when he needed stillness.

"They only want the best for you…and that is what I also want."

James looked down at her, noting the glistening of tears in her eyes. She clearly fought not to cry, and another odd and quite unfamiliar sensation wrenched inside him. "What does the family perceive that is best for me?"

A glint entered her eyes. Hope perhaps. He didn't converse much with her, or anyone. Most of the time the family said too much and then waited for his replies to questions he had no wish to provide. The past had happened. He had left it behind him. Yet they wanted to wrench him apart to know what his life had been like for the last ten years. Those memories belonged only to him, and he did not owe it to anyone to share his private torment and endless unavailing hopes.

James owed the world nothing but the proof that, somehow, he had survived. In the place he'd lived for years, there hadn't been any room to think about anyone else. Memories of another life; hopes and dreams had only been instruments of torture. A weakness to overcome, which in itself had taken him years.

His mother had many expectations and fluttered around him with constant reminders of what the world expected, of what she and his illustrious family expected without stating specifically what she desired. The duchess watched him daily with an air of fragile hope and hardened determination. James did not understand it, nor did he like it. "What do you want of me…Mother?"

"Thank you," she murmured, smiling brighter than he'd seen since his return.

"For?"

"I never thought I would hear you call me mother again." That bright smile remained on the duchess's mouth. "The season has started. It is most important to find yourself a wife, and we must get you ready to go into the marriage mart."

*A wife…*

This time his heart jolted. James had not thought of his future in such an explicit regard. The past existed in a tightly guarded space inside his mind and heart, and he did not want to visit it or share it with anyone. The present was a place he existed in now, and that space was merely to endure living as he came to terms with being back in a life he had long given up on.

It was each moment of the day that counted. Nothing else. A wife bespoke of a life that did not belong to him, a future that could vanish like wisps of smoke under the gust of a gentle wind. A deep cold wrapped around him. "Why is this important?"

"To marry?"

How aghast she sounded.

"Yes."

"You are the duke!"

"I am aware of this. What does that have to do with a wife?"

Her swift inhale echoed in the space between them. "All of society knows you were missing for years. Though you have returned to us, and I have declared you are my son, our family will still dwell under the scrutiny of the *haut ton* and the queen. We…*you* must pass muster, and no one must be allowed to doubt that you are my son and the Duke of Wulverton. Especially the queen. Under the circumstances, it is perfectly permissible for you not to sit in this season's parliament. You will be ready for the next one."

There went that odd tug again. "It is fine to miss attending the house of lords, but it is not permissible to miss…"

What did they call it? His mind searched for the answer to only draw a blank.

The duchess nodded and supplied it for him. "The

marriage mart—lavish balls, and dances, the theatre, and the opera, promenading down Rotten Row, or even visiting the amphitheater. Those are *perfectly* normal, and I assure you, the first step in reclaiming your standing in society."

"And if I have no wish to reclaim any sort of standing?"

An accusing look entered her gaze. "How could you say so? This is most important and that, my dear son, getting society to accept you, will not happen while you sit silently in the house unable to comment or debate on any matters of the realm. They will only seek to capitalize on your ignorance, and that will not do."

*Ignorance.* The chill in his gut went deeper, as if it would pierce his bones. He understood nothing of the past and current political climate of the realm. His family had always been Liberals who supported bills and motions that advanced the poor and stabilized the economy of the realm. What those bills have been for the last decade he did not know. If wars had been fought and won, he did not know. He had no connections. He was a duke without political power. A restless energy shifted inside of James, and he turned to the dark of the forest, wanting to escape into its peaceful confines.

His family was desperate for him to be normal. To perhaps revert to the youth he had been before that fateful adventurous trek through the Canadian wilds with his friend, who had returned to his family safely. James did not remember that free-spirited boy, in truth he hardly recalled himself as a young gentleman on the cusp of discovering himself.

"We must present a united front to the world," his mother continued earnestly. "When you visit the court, the queen must not be in doubt that you are the duke. Cousin Weatherby might be silly enough to cause a scandal of the decade by challenging your right to your inheritance by casting doubt on your capacity and identity. Society might look down upon our family if they believe it to be so. Your dukedom is blessedly a wealthy one, but we are not infallible. We *can* be ruined, and the duke behind Wulverton must be impeccable."

She paused to take several sips from the flute of champagne she held in a too tight clutch. "It might not seem like it now…but the best thing to do is to secure yourself a wife. One of estimable lineage, reputation, and connections. You cannot…I am not sure any young lady would be amenable to your suit should you approach her now. So, we must get ready."

Her voice trembled and the tears she'd tried to suppress brimmed over. An embarrassed flush reddened her cheeks, and she turned away from him to brush the offensive tears away with a delicate flick of a slim finger. Memories he had long suppressed in his loneliness rose in the forefront of his thoughts—of the duchess kissing his cheek and leaving rouge behind. He a boy of about six years, laughing and smearing her perfume on his skin, and her snuggling her nose into his neck.

"You spend a lot of time in the woods…that must stop—"

"No," he clipped.

She snapped her spine straight. "My son, you cannot act in a manner contrary to your position—"

He shifted, slashing his gaze down to her. "No."

She flinched and subtly moved back from him. An answer welled inside of James, but to voice the peace he found in the emptiness of the woods and nature eluded him. He craved space, and since his return to his family, every day he had been bombarded. The forest and whatever time he spent there was not negotiable. His mother fell silent, her gloved fingers tightening on the railing to the point they must pain her.

"What do I need to be ready?" This he could try to give

to her.

She whirled to face him, her mouth trembling with repressed emotions. It was clear she had not anticipated his response. James knew he was the duke. Duty and honor had been stamped in his blood and bones at an early age, and *nothing*...not even the biting cold of the Northern Sound, the echoing deep of loneliness could erase that. His mother needed him to reclaim the part of him that she felt lost. The way he wanted to do it...to simply be alone...to be given space to acclimate to his new surroundings did not seem acceptable to his family.

"What do I need to do, Mother?" he repeated, holding her stare with his.

"A doctor...see a doctor of the mind," she said with a slight, but unmissably combative lift of her chin.

He schooled his expression.

"A doctor of the mind?"

The duchess searched his face almost frantically. "Yes."

*"Savage. Possibly insane. He is different. Wild and unrefined. What he must have done to survive..."*

Those words from his family, each one had stabbed deeper and deeper, even though he did not understand why. They should be irrelevant. Life had shown itself to be harsh and uncompromising. Mere words should not be able to rattle his mettle. "Will you be reassured for me to speak with this doctor?"

"Yes," she said, her hands fluttering to her chest to press over her heart. "I would, James. Very much. He might help you...prepare for the world."

He tried to imagine this doctor, a portly fellow perhaps, poking and prodding at his intimate thoughts, trying to decide if he was insane or well enough of the mind to be the duke. James thought it laughable...yet he acknowledged there was an echoing hollowness inside that not even the woman before him and the bustling family behind him seemed to be able to fill.

Was it insanity that resided in this distance that he endured?

The emptiness had formed six hundred and ninety-five days after he had been lost. It was in that hollowness, away from emotions, he had maintained his sanity. It was in that emptiness he had found safety. He would never willingly leave that space, that much he knew about himself. What was there to really talk about with a doctor? "What else would you need of me?"

She folded her arms demurely at her waist. "Dancing tutors."

He slightly jolted. "Dancing?"

His mother smiled, as if finding humor in his start of surprise. "Yes...it is most necessary. I am to hold a ball in a few weeks. It is a most sought after event and you *must* be in attendance, James. Even Gladstone, the Prime Minister will attend, and his acknowledgement of you...society's acknowledgement of you will set the tone and expectation of everyone going forward."

It was nonsensical at most, certainly not a necessity. "When is this ball?"

She lifted her chin. "A little over three weeks."

Somehow those words scythed unknown feelings deep inside his gut. "Change the date," he said flatly.

"It is not done, not after invitations have been sent. I... our family has held one of the first balls of the season for years. All those plans were put in place before...before you came home, but now that you are here you *must* attend. And you must...dance and interact and show the world who you are. The duke."

How much she needed from James slapped him like a brutal fist. He did not like it and he bit back the snarl rising up to swallow him down. "I will...try."

The tension eased from her shoulders and that hope in her eyes burned like one of the stars winking down at them. "A tailor to fit you in the latest fashions will be summoned immediately."

That was said with a pointed look at his throat, bare of a neckcloth. Earlier it had felt like a noose, slowly strangling the breath from his body. He'd removed it, and his family had all paused eating to stare at him as if he'd grown horns. Their priorities made no sense to him. He did not bother to inform the duchess he would never wear it around his throat again.

The duchess took a careful step closer, and James stepped away. The duchess attempted a small smile, one that did not reach her eyes.

"A study of Debrett's and the top families in society," she murmured.

"I will make myself available to learn." James bowed. Some courtesies he did remember. "If you will excuse me."

"Where do you go?"

He glanced toward the pitch-black woodlands.

Her lips flattened. "Of course, you go into the night... *again*."

The soft rebuke and confusion in her tone did not deter him. James made his way from the drawing room outside into the night. He tipped his head to the sky, and as he inhaled the cold air into his lungs a modicum of peace infused his veins.

He walked away from the house, his shoulders tingling. A glance behind him showed all fifteen of his family members bundled on the balcony, watching him stroll into the forest. James couldn't help thinking he didn't belong.

Right at the edge of the forest, a thick blanket of grass covered the land. He shrugged from his jacket, dropped it to the ground, and then lay down with his laced fingers behind his head. This was where he slept sometimes. Out in the open, staring at the vastness of the sky, feeling the smallness of self, and conquering the fear that came with the realization of how insignificant one was when compared to the power of the natural world.

He closed his eyes, hoping sleep would come quickly. The forest noise, the sound of the grasshoppers, owls, and other animals did not soothe him as they had done the previous night. James felt an emotion that he was wholly unfamiliar with and could not name. That lack of understanding of himself gave the restlessness a sharper edge, and it dug into his gut, twisting like a blade. For years he'd hungered to be back with his family...and now that he was here...it was clear he did not fit. His perspective of the world had changed. James knew he wasn't addlepated, but he *was*...different.

The path stretched before him, and he accepted that for his family's sake, he needed to become the duke. Perhaps in that transformation, he might once again understand life and find a purpose for himself that went beyond merely just surviving. Another odd sensation kindled within his chest, but he crushed it before it could fully form, knowing that a state of not feeling must be maintained.

It was in feeling that one could lose one's sanity and sense of self. James blew out a slow breath and rotated his shoulders, using the emptiness to soothe the restless edge. After a few moments, nothing lingered within his thoughts but icy purpose. The best step forward was to study in private...and also procure himself a duchess.

*A wife.*

He stared at the night sky until his eyes ached and the stars blurred.

*A wife.* A woman. An image of pale skin and soft curves rose in his thoughts. A wife meant a lover...and intimacy. The cold bit even deeper into his bones. James inhaled the night, and the scent of the forest filled his lungs.

He barely recalled the experience with his only lover right before he'd set off on his ill-fated adventure. The memory flared through James's mind—a younger, softer version of himself tumbling into bed with a young widow from the village, the shape of her body, the lush scent of her skin. She had been a few years older than him and a skilled lover and a charming conversationalist.

He remembered kissing her dewy skin, driving his cock into the wet tightness of her body, savoring her gasps and moans, reveling in the way she'd clung to his body and wrapped her legs high around his back. How he'd enjoyed the flushed satisfaction on her pretty face, and her heavy-lidded eyes. They'd been lovers for a few weeks, but when he tried to think of giving and receiving that pleasure now, no sensation or ache or need followed behind those visceral images.

If the truth of how he had lived for so long came out, his family would be terrified, society would be appalled. His father… James could not imagine what his father's reaction might have been to his son's emergence. He still recalled those lessons from his father on the importance of the role he would one day undertake. His duties and responsibilities had been impressed upon James at the age of five. And he had never forgotten the pride and honor of his father.

A memory of walking with his father along these very paths before him wafted through him.

*He is gone without knowing I am alive.*

A piercing sensation burrowed under his skin, clawing, and digging deep into that place he did not allow much and an aching wrench caused a hiss to slip from him.

*You must be a man of courage, strength, and shrewdness. Always, my son, it is a part of being a duke.*

Those early lessons imparted from his father had succeeded in helping James pull himself from the brink of the pit that had yawned before him.

*You must be a man of courage, strength, and shrewdness.*

It was not in James to ever give up on anything without attempting to scale those insurmountable odds. If he had been that type of man, he would have been dead within days of being lost. He would try to fulfill this duty even knowing it might damn well wrench him apart, knowing he might not even succeed.

*I'll become the Duke of Wulverton. I'll damn well learn to dance, I'll learn politics from the best masterminds of the political arenas. And find a suitable wife to make my duchess.*

Only as he stared into the dark, mesmerizing beauty of the night, the vows echoed without a sense of truth in that empty place inside.

# Chapter Three

"Utter rubbish," Jules muttered, lowering the third scandal sheet she'd been reading on the uneventful journey from London to Hertfordshire to meet the new Duke of Wulverton, who had earned the moniker of Wolfe in his earlier days at Eton. Or so the scanty report the duchess had put together for their study claimed.

The carriage lurched on one of the ruts in the country road and she scowled. For a man who believed in progress, her father still did not trust traveling via train. If he had, they would have arrived at least four hours ago. Jules and her father had been traveling for the better part of the morning and afternoon.

She was more than ready to meet the duke and direct the nameless energy inside her into something more worthwhile. She did not like being confined in the carriage with her father. The temptation to try and probe his mind and past was too pressing. At times she caught him watching her, and more interestingly he would quickly glance away once their gazes collided. Perhaps much had changed in the years she had been away at university.

"What are they saying now?" her father asked, jutting his chin to the newssheet. "Is there anything new, or is it the same nonsense?"

"London has chosen to recall the famous case of the boy found in the woods after supposing he had been lost for over fifteen years. He was christened Peter by King George I and was paraded at court for the amusement of others. This newssheet dares to wonder if the duke might entertain them by walking on all fours as Peter had done! How disgraceful they are!"

Her father pushed the spectacles up his nose. "Is it not possible?"

A jolt of shock went through Jules. "I hardly think it might be, Father. Surely the duchess would have mentioned such observed conduct."

"If I recall it correctly, Peter also walked upright at times but under extreme circumstances devolved into the behaviors which had enabled his survival for many years. The duke has been lost for a similar period of time. We have no notion of his mental capacity. If he had been alone all this time and what he had to do to survive. All those probabilities will have had a significant impact on his development and behavior going forward."

Exasperation and concern rushed through her. "The duke was lost at eighteen years of age. It should not be possible for the character which had formed since birth to that age to disappear. This situation would either build him or break him, and that he is here now…he was not broken. Father, it is the theory of survival of the fittest."

Her father nodded thoughtfully, his eyes gleaming with thrill and speculation. "We must tread with care at all times. Keep a careful distance but assess him keenly."

"The queen expects a direct report from you, Father,"

Jules murmured, brushing aside the carriage curtain to peek at the impressive manor they approached.

An avenue of beech trees lined the long driveway, and in the far distance behind the lake, the sunlight dappled through the thick leaves. The forestry to the right was dense and lush, and the four-story house as it came into view was simply breathtaking. The exquisite mansion was surrounded by lawns, rolling down on one side to a large lake. A massive woodland lay beyond the lake, carpeted with dark moss, and a thick foliage of the trees where the sun would no doubt penetrate in uneven patches.

"I do not want you alone with the duke, Jules."

Her gut tightened and she turned her regard to her father. "What are you thinking?"

"Do you recall the case of Victor Aveyron?"

Jules frowned. She and her peers had intensely studied that case in her final year of studies. "I do. He...he was violent and given to aggressive outbursts. He did not speak, rejected all physical contact and attempts to re-civilize him into society."

Her father folded his arms across his chest, a thoughtful frown on his face. "Yes, Mr. Aveyron was considered quite feral and beyond redemption by the best doctors of the mind. Reports indicated that even those Mr. Aveyron allowed some closeness, he attacked at the slightest provocation."

"Is this a concern of the duchess?" Jules asked, recalling the long private meeting her father had with Her Grace. A conversation he had not mentioned to her in any detail, and Jules had respectfully not pried. "Has the duchess said anything more, Father?"

Her father reached into his breast pocket and pulled out a letter, handing it to her.

Jules quickly read it. "The duchess anticipates results in time for the duke to present at her ball in London, but also asks for you to stay longer if necessary."

"Yes. She fears it might take months."

"Surely Her Grace cannot expect us to be her guests for so long. You have other obligations that need your attention, and mother will miss you."

He agreed with a slow, thoughtful nod. "However, if the duke needs us for that length of time, we will have to compromise. Do we have any choice but to?"

Jules arched a brow. "The duchess promises a very generous compensation."

*Five thousand pounds.* It was a fortune they could not afford to refuse. Jules had noted the threadbare cushions in the drawing room, the simple way they ate of late, and that her mother wore dresses from at least two seasons before. The estate Papa earned his living from was not as profitable as it had been before. Nor did he make much money from the practice of aiding those with mind maladies, and he was far too proud to ask his brother for a loan. "We cannot afford to look down on the duchess's generosity, Papa."

"I am more interested in finding out how the duke survived in such a harsh environment for over ten years. It… it is nothing short of incredible, Jules. The duchess's aim is to find her son a wife this season. It seems to be most important. Her Grace stressed repeatedly that he must be ready to enter the *haut ton*, meet the queen, and secure a respectable and influential lady to walk by his side."

Jules's heart ached for the duke. To have possibly been isolated and away from human contact for several years and to now be bombarded with such demands. Did he long for a wife himself?

"Is the duke of the same mind?" she softly asked. "Does he too wish to marry?"

"Her Grace seemed to believe he is amenable." Papa cleared his throat. "Have you…given any thought to that state yourself?"

Jules's heart twisted. "I beg your pardon, Papa?"

Her father smiled slightly, pushing his spectacles once more up his nose. A habit which meant he was fiercely concentrated on the conversation while attempting to appear nonchalant. His spectacles were also an object which helped him center his emotions. At times she wished she could stare at her papa and not see him through the lenses of the knowledge she held. Perhaps she was overthinking the matter. Perhaps the touch of his glasses was simply an endearing habit and not a sign of anything more serious.

"Have you given any thoughts of marrying yourself?" her father replied calmly. "Is there any young lady you have an attachment with?"

Jules swallowed the laugh bubbling in her throat. It was not a light matter, but if she did not see the humor in the deceit, she would weep with pain. "Father, surely you jest. I have only just returned to England. I've not been out in society much."

Thank heavens they were not forced to attend all of the events which the viscount and viscountess invited Jules and her parents to. It had been easier to discourage her uncle's numerous invitations by implying she had little time to attend balls and the theatre because of studies. Now that Jules was back home in England and had yet to meet her sister's new husband, she would be harder pressed to be able to ignore or deny those invitations.

Sometimes it was...exhausting having a family that belonged to the *haut ton*. Though she was not about town much Jules was still painfully aware that her actions could affect the entire family, especially her sister, who was so gloriously happy as the new Viscountess Halliwell.

A sly glance from beneath his bushy brows. "You did not meet anyone while you were studying?"

She glanced through the carriage door. "A few cherished friends. I am only three and twenty, Father."

"Your uncle believes he has the perfect match for you. A young lady who has recently become his ward. Her father had been his friend, Baron Irving. I have not met her, but Albert writes that she is good-natured and lovely."

Her heart thumped. "I have years before I will think about taking a…partner." *Good heavens, this is getting even more ridiculous.* The continued deception burned inside her belly like she had swallowed the bitterest of poison. "Uncle Albert has not mentioned Miss Irving in his letters, and please do not encourage him, Father."

"You did not visit home for the holidays for four years," her father murmured, an amused smile about his mouth. "Your mother missed you fiercely."

And in his tone, she heard the echoed sentiments that he too had missed her presence terribly. Regret clutched at her throat, and she brushed aside the emotion. *What's done is done.* There was no sense in looking back with sadness, only to look forward.

*Would you love me the same if you knew I was a female, Papa?*

The coach drew to a halt, and Jules breathed a sigh of relief.

She alighted from the carriage and was greeted by an enormous four-story, endless Georgian-style house built to dominate the landscape and certainly intending to be impressive. But the surrounding landscape was no wilting flower in the face of this stately home. Rolling grasslands with flowering gardens housing myriads of colors designed in intricate patterns were placed artistically. At the edge of it all loomed thick forestry, teeming with birds and wildlife, for as she surveyed the land, a fox scampered across her view while a few birds glided above the treetops.

They walked toward the entrance where a man, possibly the butler, awaited their arrival. He introduced himself as Mr. Campbell, the chief steward of the estate. He escorted them inside the manor, and Jules handed over her hat and overcoat to the butler before caressing her moustache. "Gentlemen, the duchess, and a few other family members await you in the drawing room," Mr. Campbell said. "The duke is also there, and His Grace is keen to have this meeting underway."

Her father frowned, and Jules understood his thinking. It would probably be best if they met privately with the duke and the duchess for their first meeting. Father, however, did not object, and they followed Mr. Campbell down the long hallway. Jules's heart raced, and it vaguely stunned her to know that inside her gloves, her palms sweated.

*Why must I be nervous to meet this gentleman?*

Upon reaching the drawing room, Mr. Campbell knocked once and then opened the door. Immediately Jules saw that there were six occupants, and their animated cheer was a carefully constructed pretense. The duchess's lips were pinched, and a strained expression appeared around her eyes. The young lady playing the pianoforte did so a bit too vigorously, oftentimes striking a discordant tune. The other two ladies beside the duchess taking tea appeared as if they wanted to be elsewhere. And there were two gentlemen playing chess by the fireplace.

A cold gust of wind blew through the room, and Jules lifted her gaze to the wide-open windows. A gentleman stood there, with his back turned to those gathered in the room. She hadn't seen him in her initial assessment of the occupants. His stillness had set him apart and had not immediately registered.

His body was perfectly motionless, the clothes he wore—tan trousers fitted into knee-high boots and a dark blue superfine jacket—clasped his frame with elegance and perfection. Though his hair had been caught at his nape, it flowed past his shoulder blades and even lower to his upper back. The way he stood apart from everyone spoke so much about the man.

*He finds comfort in isolation.*

"Dr. Southby!" the duchess said, hurriedly lowering her teacup and saucer to the small walnut table before her. She stood, glancing behind her and then back at them. "I do believe you are a day early."

The rebuke in her tone did not deter her father. He stepped forward with a courtesy bow. "Your Grace, I had sent a note ahead and I believe your man, Mr. Campbell, received it, since he greeted us earlier."

An interesting flush rose on the duchess's cheeks before her expression shuttered. Everyone in the room stared at Jules and her father, and even the young girl's fingers hovered over the pianoforte keys as she glanced between the man at the window and the duchess.

"Wulverton," the duchess said brightly. "Do you recall I mentioned Dr. Southby will be visiting?"

The duke turned to face the room and Jules's thoughts crashed. He was...*beautiful*. It felt wrong to describe him so when his raw masculinity was undisguisable. The sharp slant of his cheekbones, his elegant nose, full sensual lips, dark winged brows set above brilliant dark gray-blue eyes. He wore no cravat or neckcloth, and she spied the strong column of his throat. The pit of her belly dipped, and an acutely unfamiliar sensation tightened low inside. Jules had a momentary sensation of complete bewilderment before she worked to school her face into a polite mask.

The duke's gaze scythed indifferently through her and their party. Their regard did not connect, nor did his eyes linger on Jules or her father.

"Your Grace," her father said bowing. "It is a great

pleasure to meet you."

"Dr. Southby," the duke replied with indifferent civility. "It is best we get acquainted in privacy. We shall remove to my study."

His voice was deep and smooth, controlled, perhaps a bit disinterested, and Jules sensed that he had not agreed to this meeting for himself. The duke nodded gracefully to his mother, then made his way from the room. Jules hurried to the side, and he walked past without looking at her or her father. They followed, and Jules glanced at her father to try and guess his thoughts.

He had a frown on his face as he observed the confident, rolling strides of the duke. They came upon a rather impressive door which the duke unlocked. The duke stepped inside his domain and made for the chair by the fire which faced the door. The one where he could see all the avenues of entry and escape from that one position.

Jules glanced around. The room was bare save for two large armchairs by the roaring fire. Between the chair rested a table with a chess set in play, a book, and a glass of something golden. The splash of color came from the beautifully woven blue carpet and the matching drapes with silver tassels. Jules glanced around, feeling the echoes of the emptiness in her body.

The duke liked space. But where did he write his correspondences? Where were the rest of the books, the paintings, the desk, and globes and scrolls? The space did not invite comfort and relaxation—it was cool and intimidating. It suggested distance between him and this world. Worse, it was a place he liked. There was no tension within him, just a predatory awareness as he watched them observe his room.

*How truly fascinating.*

"It is important to my mother and family that we meet. Hence, I am allowing it. You must state your purpose here today and let me understand what it is my mother hopes we might achieve with this meeting. Do be concise."

Her father shot her a quick frown and gripped his black satchel before relaxing his fingers around the leather. "We appreciate your time, your Grace."

"Do you?"

"Yes, Your Grace."

"Good. Endeavor not to waste it," the duke murmured.

That soft, insouciant reply threw Jules for precious seconds. This man was not addlepated as the dowager duchess suggested. He was…terribly, icily composed. Seated in the chair with one of his hands resting against the armrest, and the other casually resting on his knees, the duke did not fidget, nor did his gaze wander restlessly. There lingered a faint cynicism in his expression, a hint of self-assurance, and an awareness of the power he owned.

Somehow, she had expected a duke handicapped by his circumstances. The duchess's fears seemed to have been rooted in the hopes and expectations she had for her son. Not in science or anything evident. Jules frowned. Perhaps the duchess's fear was provoked by the indifferent composure of the duke. But what did that suggest but a strength of purpose and will that was not detected in most men?

*He is the most extraordinary creature after all.*

Something unspoken lingered in the room, and she felt uneasy. *How unusual.*

"Your Grace," she said, stepping forward with a slight bow. "I am Mr. Jules Southby. My father and I would like the opportunity—"

The duke's gaze landed on her and, for the second time that day, white noise filled the space in her head. The reaction was outrageous *and* embarrassing.

*He seems so elegant…intelligent and cunning.* That impression felt stamped onto Jules's awareness, making her feel silly for even noticing.

He unfurled from the armchair, a slight frown flickering on his face. "Who are you?"

Her steady eyes met his unwaveringly. "I am Mr. Jules Southby. I am here to take notes for my father, Dr. Charles Southby, and to assist him in his assessment and report, Your Grace."

"A gentleman scholar," the duke said softly, his gaze lingering on the moustache above her lips. "How old are you?"

Her father stepped forward. "Your Grace—"

His gaze slashed to her father, and whatever Papa saw in the duke's eyes made him falter.

The duke's regard returned to her. "Have I made some social gaffe by requesting your age?"

"Some might consider it impolite."

He canted his head. "But not you?"

Jules allowed a small, reassuring smile to tip the corner of her mouth. "Not me. Some have said I am more the unflappable sort."

A calculating glint entered the duke's eyes, and with a sense of astonishment, Jules realized her attempt to reassure him had done the opposite. He now found her suspicious. She carefully glanced at her father and deduced he had drawn the same conclusion. "I am three and twenty, Your Grace."

"You are young."

"Many gentlemen complete their studies at this age."

Oh, bloody hell, she hoped he did not think this was a reminder that he had not done so. The duke's expression only remained mildly curious, and the tension in Jules's shoulders eased.

"What exactly was your pursuit in University, Mr. Southby?"

"Psychology."

"Ah, a science that studies the mind and behavior of others."

"That is one aspect of it."

His Grace studied her with an air of boredom for a few moments. Jules felt it important to remain unperturbed by his assessment, even though there was something about the duke's intensity that made it impossible to look away, even now under the sharp and critical gaze of her father, who observed too keenly.

The door opened and the duchess bustled in, an air of agitation and impatience about her.

Her father turned toward the duchess. "Your Grace?"

"My nerves would simply not settle! I do not like waiting." She took a deep breath. "Is all well?"

The duke regarded his mother. "It is."

The duchess did not seem assured by that brief reply.

"Mother, if it will calm your nerves, you are welcome to stay."

The duchess smiled at her son. "I would very much like that. Should I call for the servants to bring a few more chairs?"

"No."

His mother's spine snapped taut. "It is not polite to keep your guests standing."

His gaze returned to Jules, and she felt the weight of it like an anvil. The duke waved to the chair beside his, and she hesitated.

"One will not do," the duchess said crisply.

"It will," the duke replied, his tone soft yet unbendable.

Why had he invited her to sit and not her father or his mother? Perhaps Jules was more agitated than she'd realized, because as she stepped forward, the front of her boot jammed on the curled edged of the lush carpet. Jules stumbled and before she could try and balance herself, the duke moved with unnatural, shocking speed and caught her in his arms.

The difference in their bodies, his strength to her smallness, immediately registered against her senses, startling Jules. The duke felt as if he was surrounding her, all hardness to her softness. She gripped his arm, aware of his firm clasp on her hips. He flinched and instantly, Jules knew he loathed being touched. She released him, painfully aware that he was still holding onto her. Was he aware of it?

His regard rested on her face with bored indifference.

"I might have fallen flat on my face if not for your swiftness. Thank you, Your Grace."

A slight movement of his head was his only response. She felt the easing of his gloved hand, suggesting he was about to release her, but then he stilled. The slightest frown touched his brows, and his gaze swept over her face in a searching glance. The duke leaned forward, and a startled sound left her throat, for he followed even as she arched away from him until she was bent backward.

*Good heavens! What is he doing?*

He dipped his head, inhaled deeply and audibly, slowly running his nose close to the curve of her neck up to her temple.

"Your Grace!"

A choked sound came from her father and the duchess gasped. This was beyond outrageous conduct. For a moment, Jules was utterly dispossessed of all rational thought. The duke had *smelled* her. Nay, he had inhaled her into his lungs and held his breath, his inky eyelashes fluttering closed.

An odd sound lifted in his chest...like a purr, and it vibrated deep inside Jules. Her mouth dried and she stared up at him in appalled shock. The duke had yet to release her trapped fragrance or her body.

"Release me," she hissed softly, only for his ears.

His eyes snapped open, the movement sharp and piercing. Heart pounding a brisk tattoo, she peered into his gaze and espied something in the duke's eyes she had never seen on another gentleman—shattering awareness. Her skin prickled with a depth of realization that shocked her into rigidity.

"Wulverton!" the duchess cried. "Dear heavens, I implore you to release Mr. Southby at once! This is most unseemly!"

The duke lowered his hand, his expression inscrutable. Jules hurriedly took a step back, then another before inhaling a deep breath. Another fraught silence blanketed the room, thick and impenetrable.

"Your Grace, thank you for that timely assistance, I fear without it I might have fallen…"

*Oh, hell, I am rambling.*

It was her turn to falter as she noticed the minute shifts in his body that had only been infused with stillness. His nostrils flared slightly. Nothing else changed and she scanned him quickly, trying to ascertain the change in his demeanor and the reason for it. Anything that had the power to impact the countenance he showed to the world was most important.

This time he wasn't looking through her…but right at her face. The duke stared at her as though no one else was in the room and those icy gray-blue eyes were no longer cold.

No…they were curious, cunning, bright, and extraordinarily beautiful. With unconcerned slowness, his eyes caressed over her curly strawberry blond hair worn in the *croup de vaunt* style. That gaze lingered on the bridge of her nose, on her moustache, her throat, shoulders, waist, knees, then her shoes. Then he lifted his eyes to her face once more. An infinitesimal smile touched the duke's mouth, and Jules felt an uncomfortable and unfamiliar rush of physical awareness. Why did the duke suddenly appear so… intrigued? Stunned recognition nearly knocked the breath from her lungs.

*The duke knows.*

The shock that tore through Jules rendered her to a

marble statue. Her mouth had gone dry, and her heart was already pounding. Could the duke truly have seen through her disguise? Her own wits seemed to have taken flight. What an asinine thought to have; surely he could not be aware that…

Jules's thoughts withered. The duke canted his head, and now amusement and something far more elusive shifted in his eyes. A desperate feeling of unreality crept through her.

*He really knows…*

The impossibility and enormity of Jules's supposition strangled her breath. How could he know with only a look, when the entire world had been deceived for years? The very air she breathed felt as if it were trapped inside her lungs. Jules felt faint…until finally the breath shuddered from her chest. She breathed again, and she retained her composure. That mattered greatly, especially given the cool cunning that stared back at her.

How could the duchess believe his intelligence diminished in any regard? The very idea was preposterous.

"Everyone out," the duke said without removing his regard from Jules.

The duchess stiffened, her eyes widening.

"Your Grace—" her father began.

"Except Mr. Southby," the duke added, then turned away and prowled to the large windows overlooking his estate.

"I do not agree," her father said stiffly. "We must both remain in this room, Your Grace."

"Then you may both leave. This meeting is over."

His mother gasped. "Wulverton!"

The duke remained unmoved at his mother's cry, and the duchess cast her father a desperate glance. This peek into his will informed Jules that nothing about this man would be easy. Her father took a deep breath, nodded to her once, and lifted a finger to indicate he would be right outside the door. The duchess hesitated for a moment, before squaring her shoulders and leaving the room. The door closed with a soft *snick*, that sound an echo in the space.

Jules exhaled slowly and softly, staring at the duke's shoulders. He had not turned around at their evident departure and she did not prod him. Instead, she dipped into her satchel and removed a notepad and pencil. She went to the chair and sat.

Then she waited.

*Your move, Your Grace.*

# Chapter Four

A hint of sea wind…the fresh scent of morning after a heavy night of rainfall, the sweetness of the forest, the musk of pinewood…the smallest discernable touch of lavender and caramel. This creature was all of that. This scent was inconceivable, yet James had never inhaled anything so lovely. The varied fragrances swirled together in some sort of alchemy until they shaped into one distinct scent that in all his life had never before wafted beneath his nose.

How could there exist such a delectable fragrance?

The essence of it was so exceptionally delicate, yet it sliced through the amalgamation of all other fragrances in the room (lavender, sandalwood, bergamot, ambergris, beeswax, jasmine, pine, and lemon) with the precision of a scalpel. Yet it was not an overpowering aroma; it was like the gentle stirring of a breeze, the hint of frost before the snow storm. It was a distinct fragrance he could give no name, yet it tugged at a place deep inside James that was wholly unfamiliar. It was a scent he could get drunk on; it was a scent that could distract him from any purpose; it was a scent that could inspire anyone to feel.

*It is singularly dangerous, for it is a bewildering anomaly.*

It felt like a dark, slowly moving current, this fascination wending itself through James's heart. The power of heightened senses had become his survival tool within months of trying to live in the vast icy wilderness. He hadn't realized the full value of his altered senses to him in this world, but he was most certain that without it, he would have allowed himself to be deceived like everyone else around this person.

The extraordinary creature in the room with him was a chameleon. A human one.

*How...singularly interesting.*

James could not say how long he stood there, feeling the call of the wild as he stared at the woodland, but it was at least several minutes. The person did not stir or ask him any questions. James frowned. In truth, this might be the first time in weeks he was in a room with another person who did not rush to fill the space with discourse or pierce him with their endless curiosity and ridiculous questions. As if he were a feral creature on display in a menagerie. Truly, there were times when his family acted shocked when he replied.

James turned around, leaning a shoulder against the wall. Mr. Southby was staring at him, and this chameleon did not look away as if having been caught. There was no guilt or mortification...no wariness. James had always been able to understand an animal in the wild from how they held his stare. This creature had a steady gaze that looked fearlessly out at him and on to the world at large. There was no fear or apprehension in that regard, only bold curiosity that made no apology for its nature.

The chin was very decided. Stubborn almost. The mouth wide and covered with a stiff moustache that curled at the sides. It was a ridiculous little thing, that moustache, but it revealed this creature might have a hint of something whimsical in their character. The gentleman's eyes were a dark green, mysterious, and lush like the forest.

James supposed this person *could* be a young gentleman, but he had spent years being silent and observant, for the slightest give in his attention could have cost his life. Could a gentleman have such a soft, pink skin tone? Such delicate cheekbones and nose? Such pretty, lush pink lips?

*Perhaps.*

He canted his head and stared at this unexpected intrusion into his life. The creature merely stared back.

*Some say I am the unflappable sort.*

James prowled over, uncaring that he might seem savage or unrefined. The gentleman did not jerk away or act skittish, merely arched an unconcerned brow in question. James moved in even closer, stopping when he was a scant inch away. Lowering his head, he inhaled the unique scent wafting from this person into his lungs. Something almost obscene pulsed through James as his body reacted with a slow stretch to this supposed gentleman's provocative fragrance.

The shock of it punched him in the gut, and he slowly drifted from Mr. Southby, putting a respectable distance between them. James had the feeling someone extraordinary had stepped into his awareness. He had felt off balance since setting his feet back on the land of civilization. However, for the first time since his return, James felt another sensation that did not reside in remoteness, or aloneness.

Despite this newness, despite that it was different and wholly unique, he did not like it. Anything unfamiliar was dangerous. And there was nothing remotely known in the sensations prickling over his skin.

"It is a most remarkable disguise," he said, keeping his tone low and careful.

The odd creature opened the notebook, pencil poised to write. "In what way, Your Grace?"

*Unflappable.*

Those bright green eyes met his unflinchingly.

*Audacious.*

The mouth smiled as if in challenge. Or was it a taunt?

*Daring.*

Those brows arched in a challenge.

*Foolish.*

A smile tugged at the corner of his mouth, surprising James. "Why are you dressed as a gentleman?"

"Why do you stand so close when you must know it is socially scandalous?" Southby asked, eyes gleaming with decided mystery and cunning.

That look of calculation had James staring at Southby intently. "No denial?"

Those lips quirked. "Have you considered I might be an extraordinarily attractive gentleman?"

"You have a very complicated neckcloth knotted at your throat."

"Most men do." A shoulder was lifted in a shrug. "Some have called me a dandy. I do not allow it to prick my vanity or assurance. I daresay I am simply too confident."

"The tie of the cravat is no doubt a bid to hide the softness of your skin and the distinct lack of Adam's apple. Your scent is of ripened peaches…and the fresh, crisp air after rainfall…a wildflower."

Curiosity and what he perceived as a glimmer of admiration lit in those lovely, expressive eyes.

"Which wildflower do you perceive I smell like?"

"All of them." James stepped even closer, forcing Southby's head to tilt back to regard him.

"There is a trickle of sweat on your temple." James inhaled again, noting the heat that flashed through him this time seared.

"That merely signifies I am a trifle warm, Your Grace."

How challenging Southby sounded. James recalled the first time he had smelled the fetidness of a bear's breath, the wildness of oakmoss, the murky, elusive fragrance of a rotted tree, the decay of death, and the crispness of new life. The fragrance emanating from this person was indeed something wonderful and different. That uniqueness repelled his senses yet also drew him dangerously closer.

"There is a softness to that scent in your sweat...a hint of musk that is not derived from soaps or perfumes. A scent that seems to be natural to all women I have encountered." And James's sharpened sense of smell had not failed him in years.

Southby's eyes widened slightly before those lashes lowered. The pencil scratched over the notebook, and he glanced down to read what the creature had written.

*The duke must learn to not smell people in public or even in private. He must <u>absolutely</u> learn this.*

"Your sense of perception is astounding, Your Grace. Would you say this was a skill you had before you became lost?"

"I spent several weeks in a cave bereft of even a sliver of light. I relied on..." He stilled. James did not share how he had lived with anyone, and he had just done so effortlessly.

Southby's head snapped up from the notebook. "You must have suffered."

Those soft words were filled with deep empathy, and he did not understand why it made him feel...discomfited. "Everyone suffers, Southby."

"I am truly sorry, Your Grace."

James went over to the windows and stared out into the woodlands.

"Would you tell me about that experience, Your Grace?"

His sense of smell was what he had learned to survive with first. Not sight or touch or even hearing, though those had been sharpened by circumstances. Those experiences would never be available for someone to dissect.

At his silence, Southby murmured, "I implore you to share only what you are comfortable with."

Suddenly, James was damn annoyed. "I have no plans to share anything. My lived experiences will not be fodder for drawing-room gossips. It is simply the past, and it will stay there. Do you understand?"

The words came out on a growl, and he hissed in a sharp breath, tempering himself.

"I hear your words, Your Grace."

Yet this was not an acknowledgment they would be heeded. That dark restlessness surged through his veins once more. James turned around to stare at Southby. "You are an unexpected mystery. I do not like things that are unexpected."

The pencil scratched over the pages. "I daresay we share similar sentiments, Your Grace."

They stared at each other for a silent minute, the air cracking with an odd sort of challenge.

"Why are you here in my home, Southby? Only the truth."

Those eyes glinted for a moment and then were swiftly veiled.

"The duchess hired my father to speak with you. I am here to assist my father to the best of my capabilities."

"What does your father want of me?"

"More conversation, Your Grace."

He arched a brow. "What would you and your father like to talk about?"

"You, of course." This was said with a small smile. "The duchess…your mother is very worried about you."

Those words dug into his gut and twisted. "She does not need to be. I am home and I know my duty."

*If I am capable of doing that duty in the time she needs is only my damn business.*

"You are home; however, you are different to the son she recalls. I believe it causes some distress for her."

"I am certain everyone evolves the older they get. I am not a raving lunatic, and I believe that is easily proven. Is it not?"

The words were almost a hiss and wariness leaped into Southby's eyes. The unseen tension in the room tightened and prickled over James's skin. Southby was not unaffected because the pencil was gripped so tightly, it was a wonder it did not snap.

"It is true that our experiences shape us. I believe that is what the duchess fears. You were missing for over ten years."

"I am here now. Nothing else should matter."

Empathy gleamed from piercing green eyes and Southby leaned forward in the chair. "You were alone for over *ten* years, Your Grace. That knowledge eats at the duchess, every day, in slow tormenting increments. Though she should now feel whole that you are alive, the guilt that she somehow failed you will not be conquered unless she believes you are now happy and well."

Pleasure ghosted along James's cheekbones as though this rarity before him had brushed fingertips along his face in a reassuring caress. The power of that inherent stare beguiled him, and instantly he did not trust the creature before him, for he had never before encountered the like.

"She presumes I was alone," James said, looking away into the forest for a brief moment.

"Were you not alone, Your Grace?"

*Painfully so.* Yet James would never admit that. Instead, he murmured, "I had the ice-capped mountains and the trees. At other times I had wolves and bears. I had nature and the call of the wild. Those were enough."

• • •

The duke had indeed existed alone for ten long years. That shattering knowledge brought a harsh ache to the back of Jules's throat and calmed the odd sense of fright that had filled her at his intensity. There were so many times she had felt an aloneness that ravaged her, for she truly felt like she did not belong. Despite being surrounded by friends and family, Jules had not been able to confide her uncertainty and hopes to anyone. As she grew older she had kept a careful distance from her sister and acquaintances lest they discovered the truth. Eschewing deep bonds and friendship had bred a sense of aloneness that had eaten at her, and more than one night she had buried her face in her pillows and wept.

How had it been for the duke? Everyone needed a measure of contact, and he had been deprived of it for years. How had he endured without the comfort of a hug or a lover's embrace? To touch others and be touched was an imperative biological need and necessity. It was a language without words that he might hunger for without knowing it, for touch was far more powerful and stronger than verbal or emotional contact. There had been no gentle touch, a kiss against the brow...a lover's touch, the reassuring slap of a friend across his shoulders. The latter years of his life had become directed by a survival instinct. A part of her ached for him and another part found him endlessly fascinating.

"You stare at me as if I am a creature like none you've ever seen."

She closed the notebook and rested it on the small table beside his chess set. "You are no creature, but a nobleman."

The duke's gaze flicked over her with some interest. "I am heartened that you know it. Tell it to the queen and the duchess so we can be done with this nonsense of dissecting my every word and action," he said with icy civility.

"I admit you are not like any gentleman I have ever met," she said with a careful tilt of her head, unable to understand why her heart pounded so. With each word exchanged, the tension did not lessen, but tightened until she could feel it crackling over her skin.

Jules shifted and the way his eyes tracked that infinitesimal move reminded her of a predator. *Who are you, Your Grace?*

"Society can be outrageous at times, and you are the current topic of fascination. There are many newssheets' speculations about how you've lived for the past decade. Many expect that you have lost all the grace and accomplishments you learned as the heir to a dukedom. They are looking for a *beast* to present to the world. I cannot simply *tell* them that you are no feral animal, Your Grace. My father and I are here to ensure that what they *see* is the gentleman."

The duke tilted his head back, returning her regard with one of amused cynicism. "Is that so?"

That dark, mocking drawl rippled over her skin, and jutted her chin and held his gaze. "If you will allow it, yes, Your Grace."

A considering look touched in his eyes and he held her regard for several moments. "I will speak only with you, Southby. That I will allow."

Her heart jolted. "Your Grace! My father—"

"Only you."

She shook her head sharply. "Why?"

"You have something to hide, Southby. Hence you will tread with utmost caution when you peer beyond the veil into my life and in what you share with others. Won't you?"

It felt like a threat. Or perhaps he believed they had common ground. Did the duke feel as if he had to hide his true self? "I shall discuss it with my father. The decision lies with him."

"You will both leave if he does not agree."

She rose and stepped toward him. "I am not at all certain the duchess will agree. I do not have the experience or knowledge of my father, Your Grace."

"My mother is well meaning, however, this decision lies with me."

Jules canted her head and stared at him. "I sense your discontent."

He lifted a brow. "The duchess hovers and stares at me with wounded eyes. I do not like it."

"Your Grace—"

"My mother wishes to present a duke to the world in a few short weeks. That is the reason I will allow you to remain here. You are clearly adept at deception. A skill that will be invaluable to me, Mr. Southby."

Something sharp stuck in her throat and her heart twisted. "You wish to deceive the duchess?"

An emotion she could not identify shifted in the depth of his brilliant gaze. "Do I sense your disapproval?"

The mocking way he looked at her pricked deeper at her chest. She could not escape the feeling he would be quite complicated to understand or handle. "Your Grace—"

"I wish to give the duchess and the world what they want to see."

"But not what is real?"

The small smile that touched his mouth felt sharp.

The duke took a single step closer. "They'll see a refined duke with a polite and respectable manner. One who will be able to tolerate their…idle chattering, balls, and social gatherings. My mother and my family must stop believing me a savage, and so as not to shame the duchess and her standing within society, the *haut ton* must also believe and accept it wholeheartedly."

*So it would all be a pretense.* "You could really try," she said with bite.

"I know who I am and know what I cannot be," he said, those words low yet piercing.

*Who are you really, then?* she silently asked, feeling that sense of doubt because pretenses never lasted forever. "What do you want to be, Your Grace?"

"Only concern yourself Southby with helping me present the image that I am conformable and dignified, as you know a duke must *never* appear discomfited," he said. "I must learn the art of allowing necessary touches and then move along as if it was not unpleasant. Especially with the lady I am to select to be my wife."

How cold and indifferent he sounded.

Jules canted her head. "Your wife?"

His gaze gleamed. "It is to be one of my main priorities for the upcoming season."

"I see." A powerful and well-connected wife would go a long way in smoothing his acceptance back within his society.

"You do not like being touched?" Though she sensed it, Jules wanted to know his thoughts.

The duke flinched, and if Jules had not watched him so closely, she would have missed the reaction.

"You do not have to answer until you are ready," she said softly.

"Disabuse yourself of the notion that you will receive a reply to every question asked. I doubt you will ever get answers to intrusive questions. I value my privacy. Recall it."

*Then how are we to help you?* she almost questioned. "I will, Your Grace," she said with careful patience, thinking he would not have to re-learn arrogance and superiority of self. Those seemed to be stamped upon his bones.

She also couldn't escape the sense that the duke was rather intelligent. Jules wondered if he allowed any touch from his family. The science said no. Being alone for so long, learning to survive against nature and creatures of the mountain that would kill within seconds would have brutally honed the duke's instincts. His response during any confrontation would have been more fight than flight.

"My future wife might find me a bit difficult," he said. "Your task here is to help me assure her comfort within limits. I do not wish to hurt her."

Her heart tapped against her breastbone, and Jules recognized the duke was not a gentleman who would easily allow his personal space to be invaded. He would naturally be more aggressive because of the survival mode he had lived with for so long. From his perspective, innocent behavior might be perceived as a threat and his reactions could be unpredictable. His lady wife might very well find him too savage.

What would he be like in an intimate relationship?

He would not be talkative. Very stoic. Possibly inherent to his nature from a child but his experience would have deepened that stoicism as he learned only to rely on himself to live.

The easiest thing for the duke might be to relearn himself and his limits in privacy, apart from the maddening crowd and desperate family. As she observed the muscles of his shoulders, the calm, controlled way he watched her, Jules realized he would find it extraordinarily difficult with social cues and situations. The duke would have a hard time processing the marriage mart. The closeness involved with dancing and chatting. It must have been painful…and continued to be painful as he adjusted to the bustle of life from his varied sensory deprivation.

"I will assist you, Your Grace," she softly said.

Though his mouth did not smile, she sensed the tension leak from his demeanor.

"That we are not exactly as we present to society will be our secret."

*Our secret.*

Denial finally hovered on her tongue, but the words

would not spill from her. Jules did not want to lie to him. The realization burned through her in a fiery wave. She wanted a connection that was...honest, even if that connection would be for a few weeks with no lasting attachment. Dukes and those who serve them never became friends.

"My father is the doctor, Your Grace. He will need to speak with you a few times to assure the duchess and even the queen that all is well. Please allow this."

He did not reply but turned away and went back to the window.

Jules almost chuckled at his rudeness. "Good day, Your Grace."

She did not wait in vain for a reply but made her way from his sanctuary. Once in the hallway, Jules breathed easier, a tension she'd not been aware of seeping from her body. The duchess emerged from another room as if she had been listening at the keyhole. The duchess beckoned Jules forward with an imperious wave of her hand. She hurried forward and entered a smaller sitting room, tastefully furnished in warm oak and pastel colors.

Her father set down a cup of tea and stood, reaching for the notepad. Jules swallowed a groan and handed it over. She had barely written anything on it that he could assess.

The duchess appeared to be a bundle of nerves and hope. "*Well*? Did you learn anything, Mr. Southby?"

Carefully, she chose her words. "I do not believe the duke is affected by any malady of the mind, Your Grace. However, that assessment is best performed by my father."

Her Grace's eyes widened. "My son spoke with you at length?"

"When it mattered to the duke, Your Grace."

The duchess made a hopeless gesture with her hands. "What is your prognosis on the state of his mind?"

"Your Grace...your son...the duke, he is not insane."

Only cold, watchful, and dangerous. He would not be malleable, and her father might fail in all his attempts to reshape the duke. Still, she kept the observation to herself until she understood him more.

The duchess gasped. "Truly?"

Jules frowned. "Did you really believe him to be, Your Grace?"

The duchess's eyes glittered with emotions. "My son is very different from the boy I knew. *Very* different."

"Being different or even altered does not make the duke not of sound mind, Your Grace," her father said. "That is what my son is inferring."

Jules nodded. "His Grace is very much aware of himself and his surroundings. He understands his duties. While he has been indelibly changed in respects you might not understand, I truly believe he only needs time to reacquaint himself with his life."

"How much time?"

"Months...years, Your Grace."

"We do not have months! We have weeks at best, Mr. Southby!"

"He has been alone for over ten years," Jules said quietly.

The duchess briefly closed her eyes. "He confirmed that he was alone?"

"Yes. No one can expect him to be the person they recall in a matter of weeks or even months. He needs more time," she once again stressed.

A shudder went through the duchess as she processed this. "That we do not have, Mr. Southby," Her Grace clipped. "The season is upon us and my grand ball in barely a month!"

Jules looked to her father for support, and her heart lurched at the wariness in his gaze. She tried to read what he was thinking. Was he worried about the loss in income if they could not help the duchess? Or how the potential failure might affect his reputation in the field and overall practice?

Jules shifted her regard to the duchess. "The duke means to find himself a wife this season and wishes to present himself as the duke to society. That is what the entire *haut ton* and the queen seem to be anticipating, his arrival in society."

"Yes, for all his words and actions to be taken apart and dissected! There can be no misstep in his conduct."

She smiled reassuringly at the duchess, even as uncertainty pierced her chest. If the duke only meant to pretend how could Jules guarantee there would be no misstep? "Perhaps with frequent meetings, my father and I will be able to assist the duke in this regard."

"Surely it *cannot* be that simple," the duchess said, shaking her head. "*All* of his elegance of mind and manners have been lost. There must be a deeper, malevolent reason for this!"

"The duke is a gentleman of superior senses and willpower. He is a man to be admired, not feared."

The duchess appeared fleetingly bereft before she smiled. The transformation was rather breathtaking as the air of anxiety seemed to peel away like a layer of skin.

"It is good you believe my son a gentleman to be admired, Mr. Southby, and I am heartened to hear of the duke's willingness to marry."

The skirt of her gown swished over the carpeted floor as she moved to stand before the large bay windows. "I hope for my son a genteel lady who is well-educated and a model of propriety to be his wife. In truth I will accept no less. There must be no scandal attached to her name or her family as she must be the anchor to his precarious place in society. Though she must be virtuous, dignified, and submissive, his duchess should wield enough influence to see that whatever flaws society perceived will be overlooked. Nothing less will be accepted," the duchess crisply said. "Do keep those points in mind as you guide him, Dr. Southby."

"Yes, Your Grace," her father said. "Most assuredly."

The duchess nodded regally. "Dr. Southby and Mr. Southby, remain my guests for as long as needed. I will also send the invitation for a small house party immediately."

Her father frowned. "A house party?"

"Yes, Dr. Southby. Invitations were already made, inviting seven of the *haut ton's* most eligible families with their daughters for a week here. A ball will be held at the end, and many lawn games will be organized. This will aid in Wulverton's foray into London and hopefully prepare for the larger ball there."

"I was not aware house parties were held at the beginning of the season," Jules murmured.

The duchess was certainly pushing too hard; however, the inherent strength Jules had just spied in the duke informed her that he was not easily breakable or changeable. Yet that could be a faulty assumption it was best not to rely on until she learned more about his character.

The duchess's expression grew reserved. "It will be a simple gathering for a few days. I am the Duchess of Wulverton. Many will clamor to attend, but I will only be inviting those worthy to align with my son. I will not have him tossed to those circling sharks in town but allow him to become acquainted with a few ladies here, and then Wulverton can continue his courtship in town. A brilliant set up, if I might say so."

"It is, Your Grace," her father said with a respectful bow.

When the door had closed on the duchess's retreating form, her father ambled closer to Jules.

"Are you well? You seem out of sorts."

"Do I?" Jules said with a deliberately dismissive air, quickly drawing on her mantle of professionalism.

She gave her father a concise report of what happened,

carefully omitting matters about her disguise. "The sense of smell is our most primitive sense, yet the duke's own is extraordinarily developed. He is a *most* interesting specimen."

A frown pleated his brow. "Is that all you think? That the duke is interesting?"

For an infinitesimal moment, Jules's breath quickened along with her pulse. "Whatever do you mean, Father?"

An unusual smile touched his mouth. "I have never before seen you so animated about anything."

"Papa, he is *extraordinary*!" Jules said with a laugh.

"Oh?"

"The duke is able to distinguish the biological predisposition between a man and a woman in terms of their natural scent. Think what this means, Papa. To have honed his sense of smell in such a superior manner must have been daunting. Can you imagine what environment His Grace must have endured for it to sharpen so? He would have at least been deprived of sight for a very long time."

Her father stared at her, and Jules's pulse tapped a brisk tattoo as the implications of her words sank in. *Please do not ask, Papa*, she silently pleaded. Though she could quickly provide an arbitrary explanation of how the duke had come to reveal knowing the difference between the scent of a woman versus a man, she did not want to lie. Her heart felt laden as she waited for her father's question.

"Do you truly not think the duke feral?"

The tension unknotted. "There is nothing feral I could see. The duke is cold and calculating and...intelligent," she murmured. "But he is *not* senseless. I am certain you will form a similar opinion."

"He could be pretending."

The thought astonished Jules. "If he is...that would suggest a capacity for deception that is rather alarming and even proves more his sanity is quite intact."

Her father nodded thoughtfully. "The duke seemed rather taken with you. The duchess mentioned it was a great irregularity that he wished to speak alone with you and did so for a few minutes. She was equally perturbed and elated at this development."

Her heart skipped several beats and settled into an erratic pattern. "Perhaps the duke feels some sense of comfort, as we are close in age."

. "You are three and twenty and the duke is eight and twenty."

"Five years is a minimal gap."

Another smile of amusement touched her father's mouth. "The duchess mentioned his university education was blighted. She fears the wild gossiping should he go to Oxford or Cambridge at his advanced age. We should suggest private tutoring to help with the gaps in his education. This must be done in a delicate manner so he is not offended."

Somehow Jules did not think he would be affronted. The duke was…an enigma. It would be foolish to ascribe the usual notions to his character, and it was better to study him before forming an opinion. A few minutes later, Jules parted from her father and was escorted to a guest chamber. It was a beautiful room overlooking the southern end of the estate. Glancing through the window, she spied the duke strolling across the lawn with a large dog at his heel. They walked in some sort of companionable harmony, and then headed off deep into the woodlands of the estate.

Jules rested her forehead against the coolness of the glass. "Is the duke's chamber on this floor, Mary?"

The servant busily packing away her clothes in the armoire paused. "No, Mr. Southby. His Grace sleeps alone in the west wing."

She turned to face the maid. "How many rooms are in the west wing?"

"Twenty-five, sir."

*More isolation.* "I will also move to the west wing."

A rather risky move, but her instincts warned her to, and while she should follow logic and science, Jules allowed that innate sense to guide her decision.

The maid's hazel eyes rounded almost comically. "Move you to the west wing, sir?"

Jules hid her smile. "Right away, Mary. Please ensure my chamber is directly across from the duke's. There is no need to update anyone on this matter. I shall inform the duchess myself."

The maid bobbed and hurried to finish her tasks. Jules would not inform the duke that she was relocating to the west wing. However, should he discover her presence and object to her being in his wing, she would remove herself immediately.

*Or not.*

Moving closer to the duke would allow also her a greater chance to observe him and understand who he was. It was also necessary to gain more privacy for herself to maintain her secret. Thankfully her menses had ended before she traveled down with her father and would not likely return before her departure.

*I shall be able to protect my secret from the servants and the duke's family hidden in the west wing.*

# Chapter Five

A few hours after requesting a servant to discreetly move her to the west wing, Jules deftly slipped inside the duke's chamber, closed the door, and leaned against it, her heart pounding. The duke had been gone from the main house for some time, and from what she gathered, he would spend the rest of the evening in the woods. The duchess had seemed angry and defeated when she informed them of this habit of the duke. Jules had shared with her father that she would take the opportunity to try and learn about the duke by observing his space.

It was a very risky and dangerous move on her part, but it felt entirely necessary. There was a niggle of discomfort at invading his space that she squashed, sensing he would not allow her close enough for them to truly help him, and they only had a few weeks. Jules straightened, glancing around the shadowed room.

"You are so alone," she whispered, frowning at the emptiness of the room.

A four-poster bed was positioned in the center of the

palatial room. There was no carpet for comfort, writing desk, or chaise. Half of his walls were large windows covered by dark, billowing drapes. The room was dreadfully cold, and the fireplace remained dark and unlit. Jules stepped forward, the flash of an image snagged her attention, and she turned toward it.

A large painting leaned against the far wall left of the bed. She moved closer, a peculiar feeling of awe and fright thumping through her. It was a dark, powerful, and majestic painting of a forest bathed in gray-blue snow and wolves blended in the background. Some of the wolves were vivid, and others were predatory silhouettes in the background. She stared at the painting, shocked at how alive it felt. A few brushes were on the ground with some oils. Jules stooped before the large canvas and delicately brushed the tip of her finger to the corner.

"You painted this," she murmured. "How incredible you are." Yet somehow, even through his painting, she felt his aloneness.

A soft sound had her lurching to her feet and whirling around. The room still felt empty. There was no one here with her. Jules gasped, realizing it was the echo of footsteps growing closer.

"Bloody hell," she gasped, hurrying over to the large drapes and dashing behind them as the door opened.

She gripped the edges of the drapes until her knuckles ached. It was the duke. Why had he returned when all the reports said he spent each night in the forest? Her heart pounded, and she waited, keenly listening for his movement about the room. There were a few rustles and then stillness.

Jules tensed, straining to discern what was happening. A deep silence lingered, and shifting as slowly as possible, she peeked around the drapes, grateful for the darkness of the room.

The duke was standing before the open windows…stark naked. Her lips parted, but no sound emerged, and Jules could only stare as the silvery beam from the moonlight painted itself over his body. His thighs and calves were thick and powerful, stomach and buttocks lean and delineated with muscle. Though they stood several feet apart, she was all too aware of the breadth of his shoulders, his height, and the inherent power in his body.

*You are so beautifully formed, Your Grace.*

Alarmingly, her cheeks went hot, then her throat and belly. He was so compelling she stared helplessly, absurdly grateful for the darkened room. Jules drew a soft breath, trying to calm the wild pounding of her heart.

The duke tilted his head, baring to her gaze the strong column of his throat. She refused to look lower than his shoulders, not wanting to feel that baffling heat stabbing her belly. He inhaled, and it came on a soft growl when he released his breath.

She bit into her lower lip, hard, for that thumping heat low in her belly responded viscerally to that low growl. The corner of the duke's mouth curled upward and seemed mocking and cynical. Still, she was struck by the incredible sensual beauty of that small smile. Unexpectedly he turned his head and stared directly at her.

Jules froze, even her breathing suspended. Though she held herself astonishingly still, her heart jerked with more erratic force. Surely he could not see her. *It is impossible.* Yet she felt way down inside her, every nuance of his stare. Perilous tension coated the air, and she waited for him to move closer to her, but he turned away and padded over to the bed, the darkness hiding him from her entirely. Jules could not say how long she waited, listening for sounds that he slept. It could have been a few minutes or an hour. She heard nothing, and again she couldn't escape the feeling the duke knew someone was in the room with him.

*But why did he not say or do something if he suspects it?*

She closed her eyes and drew strength for calm, allowing that she might be panicking in vain. There was no peril, and she only had to leave his chamber without being noticed. Jules waited a few more minutes before softly moving from behind the drapes. She paused, then lowered herself to her knees and crawled on her hands and knees to the door. She almost smiled at her absurdity but marshaled her reaction and ventured forward as fast as possible. At the door, she reached up and gently eased open the latch, grateful the hallway was also dark. Perhaps if the duke was awake, he might not notice the slight opening of his door. She crawled through the small space created, and once in the hallway, she lurched to her feet and hurried toward her door.

Jules deftly entered her chamber and stood alone in the center of the room, her palm pressed against her chest. She slowly took off her disguise, removing all of her clothing until she stood naked in front of the large cheval mirror, save for the bindings across her chest. Unknotting the strings, Jules unwrapped the bindings and casually tossed the thin strips of linen on the chaise. She stared at her naked form, the smallness of her breasts and the roundness of her hips and buttocks. Her thighs and calves were toned and well-shaped from her many physical activities, and her stomach almost hollow.

Resting a hand on her belly, a soft breath shuddered from her. Jules had never really *looked* at her body, and she did so now, for she was painfully aware that earlier it had somehow betrayed her mind and composure. There had been a reaction to the duke that had been wholly unusual, and Jules had felt that odd stirring way down inside of her. Trailing her fingers to her navel, she watched her hand in the mirror as if it was a stranger who touched her so and not herself. Those fingers were slim and elegant, hesitant yet also bold and curious as they ghosted over the dip and hollows of her body, for the first time feeling the softness of skin beneath her blunt fingertips.

Resting those fingers right above her mound, she whispered, "*Here*...this is where I felt that heat."

To her wonder, a soft pink blossomed over her skin, painting her body in delicate shades of roses. Dropping her hand as if she had been burned, Jules took a steady breath. Padding over to the large bed, she dropped her body onto the mattress and stared at the ceiling. She had never before wondered about carnal relations between a woman and a man. Never hungered or even owned a fleeting touch of curiosity.

Was that burst of heat desire? Why was she even thinking of it now after one fleeting encounter? She closed her eyes, recalling the feel of the duke surrounding her, the fleeting touch of his fingers against her hips when he caught her...the provoking brilliance of his dark gray-blue eyes. The way he had smelled her, as if she were a thing he could consume. *Just now, in your room, did you also smell me?* Jules laughed in the emptiness of her room.

*This is preposterous.*

The duke was merely an interesting specimen to analyze, and the unique reaction experienced at his nearness was...

"Nothing," she whispered. "Nonsensical, and it has no relevant bearing on the situation here."

*I must never forget that.*

• • •

Jules and her father had been at Longbourn Park for three days and had not met with the duke alone since. He was adept at simply ignoring their presence nor had he given any indication that he suspected Jules had been in his chamber.

The duke extended no invitations for a private meeting and whenever her father tried, he was politely rebuffed with a reminder that His Grace was busy.

Jules was amused but also chagrined. They had limited time to help him in whichever way they could, yet the duke locked himself away in his study for hours, and everyone seemed hesitant to interrupt. Whenever that imposing oak door opened and she had a glimpse inside, it was to see the duke seated in his chair, a book in his hand, an air of intense concentration about him. He was a voracious reader, and she gathered he was consuming the written word, hoping it would adequately inform him about the years he'd been missing from society.

Her father was frustrated by his lack of interest. However, Jules was patient, and she did not press the duke's forbearance. What she did was to carefully observe him whenever he met in the common rooms or the dining hall with his family, all fifteen of them—his mother, sister, aunts, uncles, and several cousins.

The duke appeared notoriously ill-disposed toward long conversation. He preferred to listen and gather his thoughts before speaking. Whenever he did speak, he did so in single syllables and did not elaborate, to his family's evident ire and frustration.

He displayed a complete lack of interest in the activities his family organized—cards, croquet, charades, and even cricket on the lawns. Not only was his sense of smell superior, but the duke also had exceptional hearing, for he always seemed to know when someone approached long before Jules saw anyone. And he never permitted the familiarity of anyone touching him.

"I have never in my life seen anything so uncivil," Viscount Hayfield, also known as Uncle Hubert, muttered when the duke pushed back his chair and walked out of the dining room without any sort of announcement.

"Perhaps the meal is not to his liking," Aunt Margaret said, casting a frown at her nephew's retreating back. "He barely eats!"

Everyone seemed anxious that the duke had left the dining table and the savory feast laid out for their pleasure. And it was a grand feast indeed of roasted duck, roasted pork, stuffed quail, prawns in creamy garlic sauce, wild rice, and an assortment of vegetables.

"He always leaves, Uncle Hubert," Lady Felicity murmured, lowering her fork, and staring after her brother.

There was an air of pained sadness about her, but Jules had observed that Lady Felicity always avoided the duke's presence. Unlike his mother who always attempted to engage him.

Sadness flashed in the duchess's eyes, and she cast a desperate glance toward Jules. "Perhaps His Grace might appreciate your company, Dr. Southby, and you, Mr. Southby."

Truly it was a command to follow the duke. Jules eased back her chair and stood, her father quickly following suit.

"It would be our pleasure to see if the duke is amenable to some company," her papa said.

The duchess nodded once. "Thank you, Dr. Southby."

Her father hastened after the duke, but Jules kept a comfortable pace, thinking about his indifference. His family tried too hard, and though she saw their love and concern, there was a strain to their interactions, a careful pretense of cheeriness, as if they wanted to show that all was well.

*But show whom?*

The duke would perhaps only see hypocrisy in their behavior and not his family's uncertainty.

Jules rounded the hallway to see the duke exiting a side door through the drawing room into the gardens. He ripped at the cravat around his throat, a frustrated snarl echoing from him. The carefully cultivated boredom had slipped, and in its place stood a man clearly ill at ease.

Her father gripped her hand. "Wait, Jules!"

"Father—"

He pushed the glasses up on his nose. "I have been discreetly observing His Grace for days and making notes on his temperance. Until now he has not betrayed himself to any emotion, not even by the flicker of an eye lash. I was rather impressed, for I had never encountered anyone so icily controlled. Look at him now, Jules. *Look*!"

The duke stood, his feet braced apart as if he tried to hold up some unfathomable weight, his head lifted to the sky, fingers pinching the bridge of his nose. His shoulders were tense, his expression savage and stark.

*What do you think of?*

"He is not controlled now," her father excitedly murmured. "I cannot tell if His Grace is angry or merely frustrated. Even in displaying other emotions, there is a measure of control that is rather admirable."

Jules stared at the hint of torment cut into the duke's features, an ache twisting inside her chest. "The duke's control and indifference are a mere facade. He perhaps feels most keenly but denies himself those feelings. Perhaps to spare his family from worry...or there are reasons that are known only to him."

"I am rather astonished. I never would have guessed it to be so. We must follow and watch him, instead of making our presence known."

Something inside Jules viscerally recoiled from the idea and she frowned. "It does not feel right to intrude on his privacy in such a manner." Somehow this felt more intrusive than entering his chamber without an invitation. "Let us make our presence known or retreat, Papa."

Her father stared at her in clear surprise. "It is not unethical to do so, Jules."

"Father—"

He waved a hand in dismissal of her concerns. "There are no boundaries being crossed. A part of our job is to make observations and form helpful conclusions about his behavior. The duke will not even be aware of us."

"I understand, Father," she said, taking a steady breath. "But it feels *wrong*. I...I do not think His Grace would be pleased if we were to see him in a manner that he did not permit."

He frowned. "That is the problem, Son, he will not allow us to see his real self. How are we to assess him then? The veil must be pierced so we can get a detailed picture of what happened to the duke these past years."

"Papa—"

"Come now," her father said, walking forward in a clandestine manner. "I will suffer no more of these ridiculous objections from you. Do not let me believe I was wrong to ask you to accompany me on this trip."

The duke surged forward and disappeared from view. Her father rushed after him as quietly as possible, beckoning her to follow. Swallowing down her protest and trying to trust her father's instincts and experience, Jules went toward him. They rounded the pathway, and it was to her papa's credit that he only gasped to see the duke standing in their path, clearly awaiting them, his expression inscrutable.

"Your Grace," her father said with admirable composure. "It is a pleasant night for a stroll."

"No one is owed the experiences of my past," the duke said with chilling civility. "Most certainly not you."

His clipped, direct confrontation seemed to startle her father.

"The duchess expects—" he began with a grimace.

"Not even my mother is owed it," the duke smoothly interjected. "I will not avail myself to your expertise. I do not trust you, Dr. Southby. I do not work with those I do not trust."

Jules stiffened, a heavy sensation settling low in her belly. The duke was going to turn them away, and she knew the duchess would blame her father for this. *Bloody hell*! Though she did not fully understand the duchess's character, it would never be good for her father's practice and reputation if she deemed him incapable of helping. Certainly, a good report would not be provided to the queen.

Her father stepped forward, lifting a hand in apologetic entreaty. "Your Grace, I made an error in judgment and I hope—"

"You are dismissed," he said with icy civility. "You may depart Longbourn Park at your leisure."

"Your Grace," Jules said, surging forward to stand beside her father. "Please forgive my father. He meant no harm or disrespect."

An indefinable expression flickered in his gaze. "I have already informed you, Southby, of the capacity in which your presence will be allowed here. Did you somehow misinterpret my meaning or fail to convey this to your father?"

"I did not." Jules met his gaze without flinching from his austerity. His stare was unnerving, intense, and far too perceptive. "The scientist in my father cannot help being fascinated by your experiences, Your Grace. He is rather curious about you. I must admit I am, too."

An inexplicable expression briefly shifted in his eyes. "Are you?"

"I am, Your Grace. I also respect your need for privacy, and I am sorry yours was violated."

Mocking humor danced in his eyes at this, and she bit back a groan. He did suspect she had been in his chamber.

*How curious.* "Perhaps in time, Your Grace, if you wish it, we might…share stories of our lives these past few years."

Jules held her breath, hardly daring to believe she had said those words, but recalling that flare of raw curiosity in his gaze when he had seen through her disguise so effortlessly. Perhaps he needed that connection, a mutual sharing of secrets to allow anyone close.

His gaze gleamed, those piercing eyes like that of a hawk upon her person. "An exchange of truth, Southby? Of our past experiences?"

*Truth.*

Not mere stories meant to entertain or put one at ease but an unveiling of their souls. Nerves pricked hotly at the base of her spine.

"If it pleases you, Your Grace," she murmured, aware of her palms sweating in her gloves. Jules shifted her gaze to her father, then back to the duke, hoping he understood the need for secrecy she silently communicated.

An imperceptible frown touched the duke's forehead, and his gaze flicked between Jules and her father.

"Tell me more, Southby."

"I would offer an exchange of truth, of our varied experiences and perhaps hopes for the future."

"It pleases me," the duke said.

Her father had stiffened beside her, but he wisely held his counsel.

A small, rather enigmatic smile touched the Duke's mouth. "By all means let us converse with only honesty between us."

Jules dipped into a quick, respectful bow. "Thank you, Your Grace."

The duke's regard shifted to her father. "Dr. Southby, I am sure your associate will share all pertinent information with you about our…meetings. You are free to convey whatever you believe necessary from it to the duchess and the queen."

Her father's eyes widened. "Your Grace, I cannot solely rely on—"

"This bargain is between myself and Mr. Southby," the duke said, pinning her father with his unrelenting stare. "I very much doubt Dr. Southby has any truths to exchange that I might find valuable. If this cannot be agreed upon, you may both leave."

How polite yet cutting the duke sounded. Somehow it made the uncertainty clawing inside her belly dig deeper. What would it be like to be so alone with him? Allowing him to see pieces of her existence that she dared not share with anyone else?

A calculating expression appeared in her father's eyes. "Of course, if this is what makes Your Grace comfortable."

"You are welcome to continue staying at Longbourn Park. I will tolerate your presence for the sake of my mother."

How could the duchess doubt in any regard this man was not the duke?

Her father bowed. "Thank you, Your Grace."

Jules watched as her father stiffly walked away, returning inside the main house. She sensed his pride had been injured.

"How long will I be tolerable for?" Jules asked without looking away from her father's retreating figure.

"Do you regret your bargain already, Southby?"

Those nerves once again raked at her insides like clawing talons. "I never regret once I step forward."

A small silence lingered, then he said, "Walk with me."

The duke did not wait to see if she would obey his command, strolling out into the night. The moon shone faintly in the dark sky, and in the distance woodland creatures chirped. Jules fell into step beside the duke, ambling with him for long minutes in silence.

"I am not insane, Southby. I hope that I would sense that

I had taken leave of my mental faculties."

His tone had the edge of anger, causing a ripple of discomfort to course over her skin.

"I know you are not, Your Grace."

He sent her a sharp, assessing glance. "Do you truly know it?"

"Yes."

"However, your father does not believe it, thus he decided it was necessary to intrude upon a private moment to spy upon me?"

She winced at the stinging rebuke. "I think Papa knows it, but he must be certain of it himself and cannot only rely on my assessment, Your Grace."

"Why not?"

"I have not his skills or experience of this world or medical matters. For the world...or more like England and the Queen, you are a curiosity...a marvel...a *miracle*. My role here is to assist my father to provide a good report to the queen and to reassure your mother that all will be well."

"I can do that myself," he said smoothly. "My mother is eager for me to travel with her to town in as little as three weeks for her grand ball. I am certain I will find your presence fairly tolerable until that time."

Jules chuckled, surprising herself. "Thank you, I shall endeavor to not make a nuisance of myself."

The duke stopped at the edge of the woodland, peering into the inky blackness. They stood there for immeasurable minutes, the silence cloaking their presence distinctly unfathomable.

"Will you return inside, Your Grace?"

"No."

"I am by no means an expert on social etiquette and proprieties," she murmured, "but I do believe it is considered abominably rude to leave in the middle of dinner with your family."

An odd sound came from the duke, almost like an irritated grunt. "Am I to account for every action of mine?"

"Sometimes it is necessary with those who love us."

"I find I do not enjoy the rich taste of the food. I am going to hunt for my dinner."

"Hunt?"

"That is what I said, Southby. Would you like to join me?"

Jules was so astonished by the invitation, she nodded.

The duke had that odd smile at his mouth again, pushing her to wonder about his musings. She followed him into the woods, thankful for the moon slicing through the thick leaves overhead. They walked for several minutes in silence, the only sound her trampling boots echoing in the forest. She could barely discern the tree line and kept her gaze pinned on his broad shoulders, allowing him to be her guide. The duke walked with incredible stealth, his prowl predatory.

Jules almost tripped over her feet when they emerged in a clearing, the pathway lit with lanterns. In the distance, an owl hooted, and the duke lifted his hand over his mouth and replied in kind. They walked along the dirt pathway, and Jules stopped, staring up at a sight she did not understand. It seemed as if it was a cottage, built high into the trees.

There was some sort of roped ladder hanging down from the large opening to the foot of the trunk. The building was rather magnificent, and intricate. The tree house seemed to be a part of two majestic oaks, rising to the skyline. It felt almost impossible for such a thing to have been built. Lanterns were hung suspended on tree branches that were attached to the cottage itself. Immediately the forest felt quaint and enchanting.

"The cottage is *in* the tree," Jules said faintly, peering up at the structure. "What is that thing hung between those thick branches?"

"A hammock. It is a thing to lie in if one wishes to."

She cocked her head to the side. "You have no fear you'll topple off and fall to the ground?"

"No," he said, his tone warmly amused.

"Permit me to ask who designed and made it?"

There was a momentary silence as if the duke considered if he should deign to answer her curiosity.

"Several local builders at my direction."

"This was done since your return?"

"They were handsomely rewarded for their discretion, skill, and the timeframe in which they accomplished what I needed."

Jules recalled then the duchess's frustration that the duke spent many hours in the woods daily away from the main estate. This was the duke's place of comfort. A sanctuary. Jules suspected this space was not empty but filled with the things he might consider essential.

*And he is sharing it with me.*

Was this his first exchange of truth? Her heart lurched in the oddest manner, the ache spreading from that unfathomable organ to her entire body. Odder even, Jules felt warmed and extraordinarily pleased. She cast him a sidelong glance to note that he was intently watching her.

"It is beautiful," she said softly, holding herself still underneath his bold appraisal.

"It is peaceful."

"It is also lonely."

"Being alone does not mean one suffers from aloneness, Southby," he drawled. "Should you of all people not know this?"

"It has been my experience they are more often than not the same and—" She stopped herself abruptly, wondering at her ease at revealing herself to him. Jules flushed at the sudden intent way he stared at her, glancing away from his probing regard.

"I am interested in your experiences, Southby. It is one of the reasons you are here at this very moment."

Jules drew in a slow breath. "I—"

From the forest came the unmistakable sound of footsteps, forestalling the need to reply. Boots trampled closer and she whirled around to see a lad of about ten years walking toward them, a pheasant hanging from his grip. It was cleaned and ready to be cooked. Jules stared as the lad reached into a bag tied to his belt and rubbed the large bird with what appeared to be crushed herbs. The lad then spitted the bird and began to build a fire beneath the pheasant on the stick.

"David here is my attempt at civility," the duke murmured, a hint of amusement in his tone.

"What do you mean?"

"He is my valet and my man of affairs."

"David cannot be more than ten," she said drily. "How can he be adept at such roles?"

"He is twelve, very discreet, efficient, and clever. A good lad for the jobs I need him for, and he is handsomely compensated. He provides for his family of seven."

"Is David your only valet?"

"Yes."

Jules almost smiled thinking of how out of sorts the duchess must be at that. "You might need to procure another helper, Your Grace. A proper valet."

"Because a duke must have people to dress him, bathe him, make his bed, put on his shoes. It is a damn wonder I am even allowed to even clean my own arse."

This bit was drawled with mocking cynicism. Jules choked on the air, hurrying to slap a hand over her mouth.

His gaze gleamed. "Why stop your laugh? It is a lovely sound."

*Lovely?* That strange sensation once again kindled inside

her chest. "It is very unprofessional to do so."

He lifted a brow but made no comment on her lapse. "David is my helper, and I need no other meddling around."

The little boy's chest puffed with pride.

Jules stepped forward and bowed. "I am very pleased to meet you, David."

For a moment, the little lad was not certain what to do with himself, but he straightened his shoulders, then bowed so deeply he almost pitched on his face. "Please to meet ye, too," he replied, straightening. "I am going now, yer grace," he said.

"Very well, David."

The duke dipped into his pocket and removed a sovereign. He flicked it in the air and David deftly caught it before sprinting away deeper into the woods. The duke shrugged from his jacket, dropping it on the thick, verdant grass, and rolled up his shirt sleeves to reveal muscular forearms. He removed the already loosened neckcloth, tossing it beside the jacket. Jules could only observe in silent astonishment as he removed his boots and stockings.

His feet bare, the duke strolled over to the bird, sat on one of the large boulders before it, and turned the bird over the roaring fire.

"Are you to stand there the whole night, Southby?"

Jules walked over and lowered herself to the boulder beside him. "Do you come to this space each day, Your Grace?"

"Yes."

"You could order simpler fare from the kitchen."

He made a low sound in his throat that she supposed could be a grunt. After a few more moments of silence, Jules looked at him. The duke seemed to be thinking on his response and she did not prod, already knowing it to be a rarity to be in his space with this much conversation.

"Requests for simpler fare have been sent to the kitchen. The duchess was displeased with the staff when they followed my instructions. A duke wanting to eat roasted bird and some potatoes. *Ghastly*," he said drily.

She snuck a quick glance at him to see that the duke watched her rather intently, a smile about his mouth, his eyes gleaming with provoking humor. Jules swallowed and swung her regard to the flickering flames.

*Despite everything, he appreciates the humor in life.*

"I know I can remove whatever power she has in countermanding my order...yet I find I wish to treat her gently," he said gruffly. "I see her strength, but I also see her fragility."

"I understand."

He said nothing more, and several minutes passed in a silence that she dared not interrupt. This was the duke's space and he had welcomed her here. If he had no wish to speak, she would be respectful of that silence. Jules looked around, realizing how incredibly enchanting the forest was, and the majestic beauty of the cottage built amongst the twisting limbs of the large trees was indeed a sight to behold. She wanted to climb the trunks of the tree and explore the world he had created up there.

The fire crackled, the wonderful roasting fragrance of the bird rose on the air, and her stomach chose that moment to alarmingly rumble. Jules grinned sheepishly when the duke glanced pointedly at her belly. "I walked away from dinner to chase you, Your Grace. I am famished and your bird smells divine."

"Worry not, Southby, I shall share my pheasant with you."

"My stomach is already deeply appreciative of your kindness."

There went that smile at his mouth again, setting off

those odd sparks low inside her belly. "Do I amuse you, Your Grace?"

"You...interest me, Southby."

"So you have mentioned, Your Grace. Am I to gather that is a remarkable thing?"

The fire popped and sparked as fat drippings landed on the wood.

"Little interests me—that you do is a curiosity."

*I assure you it is entirely mutual,* she silently replied.

Jules waited for him to ask her probing questions about her disguise and was rather astonished when he remained silent, turning the stick to ensure their fare was evenly cooked. It was his restraint and patience that was interesting. She couldn't imagine anyone else suspecting her secret and being this restrained. Though for the duke he would accept it as an irrefutable fact given his superior senses.

"Is there any dish prepared by the cook you enjoy?" she asked, recalling how little he had eaten each night at the dining table.

"The duchess swears as a lad my favorite was braised pork belly in sweet sauce. I find it...revolting."

A savory dish that had been a part of their dinner course since Jules had been in residence. No doubt the duchess added it to the menu so that he might have some comfort in the familiar.

"You should let her know you no longer have a taste for pork or sweet sauces."

Amusement sprang to the duke's eyes and his beautiful smile appeared. "When I did the very next day, a larger haunch was presented on the center piece, with three different complementary sauces."

"I believe the duchess is merely eager for things to return to how they were."

"Life changes and we adapt."

"It is normal to seek comfort and reassurance in the familiar," she said softly.

The duke reached behind and removed a large knife from somewhere off his body and sliced the bird a few times. "I've indulged in a few bites each evening. The duchess seems happy with it."

"Do you find the notion of explaining yourself to the duchess unpleasant?"

The duke stilled. "Explain what?"

"That you find comfort in the woodlands and in being alone because you have existed so for a long time. That your palate has changed, and it might take years for you to eat such rich cream and sauces again. Perhaps she does not understand it in full because you have not taken the time to explain it to her."

The duke's expression was inscrutable as he stared at her for long moments. "You are perceptive, Southby."

"Does that scare you?"

"I am afraid of nothing," he said with a touch of arrogance. "Lest a small thing like yourself that barely clears five feet. My thoughts alone can swat you away, Wildflower."

*Wildflower?* Jules's heart shook, and she lowered her head to hide her expression. "Is this to be my new moniker, Your Grace?"

"It suits."

*Do not ask, it is unimportant.* "Why does it suit?" she said, ignoring the voice of logic.

"Wildflowers grows in places least expected. They are resilient, determined, some might even say unbreakable, their scent myriad and inexplicable."

*Is that how you see me*, Jules silently asked. She took in a breath, feeling absurdly shy. "Very well...*Wolfe*."

The way he regarded her almost pushed Jules into squirming. She stilled the reaction and held that unflinching regard, knowing it was very important to not be perceived as easily intimidated or stirred. She had the conviction that if she showed the slightest weakness, he would dismiss her from his thoughts. Somehow Jules knew he valued strength…and she wanted to exist in his awareness.

It was an innate impulse that guided her and not science, yet Jules obeyed that silent drive urging her to match his intensity. His instincts were clearly honed to predatory…and he must never believe her to be prey.

"I should also inform you I am incapable of being *swatted*," she drawled.

The space between them crackled with challenge. Those brilliant eyes skipped over her face as if he searched for depths he was certain remained unsounded. The grimness left his mouth, and he smiled. She felt that small smile way down in her belly, an unanticipated curl of heat that blossomed outward and set her heart to racing.

*Five times since entering the woods, he smiled*, Jules absurdly thought.

"I'll ensure I am gentle with you, Wildflower, so you do not break."

Her heart stuttered hard. "What do you mean?"

"You'll discover."

"You do not like explaining yourself to others, do you?"

"I know it to be an existence unsuited to a man of my temperament."

She made a gesture with her hand. "What temperament is that?"

The eyes looking down into hers were suddenly bored and a little cold. Jules couldn't help feeling as if she prodded a wounded beast who had no notion it was indeed injured. She held his regard, knowing it was very important that she did not shy away from him or act scared in the face of his grim visage.

*How strange this dance between us is.*

"The stillness that I've lived with seems to have gone," he murmured. "I liked that stillness."

"Would you tell me about it?"

A short, taut silence pulsed.

"Inside of it there are no expectations, only existence," he said, once again turning the bird over.

Those words slammed inside her chest and pierced her with an awful sensation. "I see." A part of her did, and for a wild moment Jules felt afraid that she might never be able to touch the parts of him that were mysteriously obscured. *How do I help you, then?*

"I cannot tolerate the facile chatter or the high-pitched laugh of Lady Eloise."

"I've only known your cousin a few days and her laugh does exacerbate the senses."

The duke smiled again, and Jules's belly flipped. He used his oddly shaped knife and cut into the bird removing the leg. He handed it to her. Jules tugged off her gloves and took it, the heat of it slightly stinging her fingers. "Thank you."

She bit into the drumstick, almost moaning at the wonderful taste exploding on her tongue. The blend of salt and spices were the right combination. The thyme-infused fat dribbled on her chin and between her fingers. She licked it away, conscious of his eyes upon her, aware that he suspected her to be a lady and not a gentleman. Somehow, she anticipated a remark on the vein of her unladylike graces, but the duke said nothing, merely removed the next bit for himself and bit a chunk of his own drumstick.

"Is it good, Wildflower?"

She swallowed a piece. "Very."

That small curve touched his mouth again, pushed Jules to acknowledge she really liked when he smiled. They ate in companiable silence for several moments, the chirping of the forest creating a lush ambiance.

"You will inform no one of our conversations."

Frustration surged through her. "Your Grace, my father—"

"No one. If you cannot honor that, Southby, you may leave."

"How am I to help if you are so decided and obstinate!"

"You'll help in the confines I permit or not at all."

Tension crackled in the air, and Jules stared at him, feeling the beat of his will against hers. Jules was also so very conscious of the way his eyes touched every part of her. She bit into another piece and chewed before answering, "I will only reveal what you wish."

The duke nodded once. "There are days I feel quick tempered and out of good humor with the world around me. There are other days I am tranquil, and nothing ruffles my composure. I do not like it. Tell me, do you think this a malady shared by many?"

"I share it."

"Do you?"

"Yes. I daresay others do, too. I believe it is quite normal to feel the ebb and flow of living through our emotions. It does not make you afflicted but…alive."

He said nothing to this, however, an introspective air lingered around him.

Jules cast her gaze around. "Do you sleep in these woodlands?"

"Many nights I do."

She took another bite of her roasted pheasant, chewing slowly and thoughtfully. "That you do so will not be perceived as gentlemanly conduct. Your family does not understand it nor will society if it becomes known."

"There is comfort in being a savage then, hmm?"

Those low, provoking words had her looking at him. The

duke appeared...amused.

"Your family does find your manners barbaric," Jules murmured.

"I know."

"Your tone is unapologetic and uncaring."

"I know."

"Your Grace—"

"There was no room for softness in the mountains. There were days it was so cold, if I had closed my eyes for rest I would have slept to my death. There are times when the sun does not penetrate the foliage of the towering trees, and the vast emptiness is endless and beautiful and cruel. There are days of no food...of avoiding those creatures that would make me the food. There are days of no sleep or rest. Tell me, Southby, should I have been reminding myself then about the nicest manners that come with being the heir to a dukedom?"

The hint of amusement in his tone felt like a trap. "You are no longer living in the wilds, Your Grace."

"My waking moments are threaded with ghostly wisps of the Northern Sound."

She was suddenly aware of an aura of ruthlessness surrounding him that was intimidating. Worse, his eyes seemed hollow.

"You must be careful that when you peer at the past, you do not look too long," Jules said softly. "Those ghostly echoes will be with you for a lifetime, but the present is also here. A life that should once again become familiar if you allow it, Your Grace."

There was something curious in his stare but also calculating. "Is that so?"

*Yes.* "Your mother said you sang once, beautifully, and you often sang for her as a lad. Do you still sing?" she asked, hoping to remind him of the moments that bonded him to his family.

"That voice is now gone."

"Is it?"

"Broken by my screams of despair in those first months."

That painful hitch darted through Jules's heart. "I am sorry, Your Grace."

Silence fell, and without speaking, she felt the duke cloak himself in indifference and reserve. She moved away from the past, sensing the impenetrable nature of the walls he had erected. "The duchess informs me a dance tutor will attend on you tomorrow."

His grunt was decidedly annoyed, yet he made no comment.

"Will you see those lessons through?"

The chill in his gaze grew pronounced, and she suspected he wrestled internally.

"Is it a requirement to be a duke?"

Jules smiled. "Perhaps in finding a wife."

"How so?"

As she watched him, Jules couldn't help thinking there was something about the duke that seemed too stark and ageless. "Ladies do love to dance, and they see it as an important expression of courtship. Gentlemen share the same viewpoint and are quite eager to dance with ladies they admire and woo."

"Do you enjoy dancing, Southby?"

She lifted a shoulder in a shrug. "Though I have received the appropriate lessons, I've never taken a partner to the dance floor. I have no notion if I would enjoy it or not. I have observed that it looks remarkably freeing."

He chewed for a few moments. "I find our conversations pleasant."

"I am pleased given that your family seems to think you have lost the ability to hold any sort of discourse, Your Grace. You should engage with them more."

"Call me James."

A soft breath rushed out of her. "I cannot—"

"I grow tired of this incessant 'Your Grace' business."

"Very well," she said a trifle pertly.

His gaze sharpened. "What is this?"

"What?"

"Your cheeks are rather flushed and your eyes suspiciously bright." He leaned slowly, deliberately, almost leisurely toward her, and her heart kicked a furious rhythm. The duke ran his nose across her cheeks. "It is quite fascinating how your scent changes. Earlier you smelled like the forest itself, now you smell like caramel and lavender."

"You should really learn to keep your nose to yourself," she said, painfully aware that she *was* blushing. *How bloody ghastly!* "That will be a requirement for when you are about in society."

His aristocratic nose flared, and the provoking gleam in his eyes deepened.

"You are free to smell me in return. I shall not object."

A faint feeling of surprise stole over Jules at that terribly improper invitation. "What is a little nose between us partners in deception? Is that your reasoning?"

Appreciation lit in his eyes. "You are of a teasing disposition."

Jules's muscles were knotted with terrible tension and her heart trembled. "It must be something in the woods," she drawled, giving him a slightly mocking stare.

"I am never teased."

"I shall endeavor to tease you every so often, Your Grace. It should make for interesting encounters." *And perhaps make you more comfortable.*

"James," he said. "I shall anticipate these encounters, hmm?"

His unwavering gaze was filled with things that made

her chest stir and ache with sensations she had little hopes of understanding. Reason and caution were slowly slipping away from her, and Jules frowned. "I shall try—"

Jules almost choked when he reached out and pinched her chin between his thumb and forefinger. Her breath audibly hitched, and her awareness contracted to that single improper touch. Then the dratted man smelled her again. Jules felt as though she couldn't drag enough air into her lungs. "You must *never* do this in public, Your Grace!"

"I assure you the inclination only seems to descend on me in your presence. Is it not interesting? I have *never* smelled anything like you, Wildflower."

Jules narrowed her gaze thoughtfully, leaned closer to the duke, quite aware of how perilously close their lips were. Then she dragged his scent deep into her lungs, already sensing she was making a most dangerous mistake.

# Chapter Six

"What do I smell like?"

*You are unknown to my senses.*

"Like roasted chicken," Jules murmured, swallowing down the tightness rising in her throat and flicking her glance up to his.

Dark humor gleamed in the duke's eyes. "Let me remove my drumstick." He held his hand far away from his body and arched his neck. "Go ahead, try again."

Jules bit inside her lip to prevent the urge to smile. Surely he was also teasing her. Perhaps he did not expect her to follow through. "I—"

"Afraid?"

That soft word was caustic, the indifferent look in his eyes at odds with the controlled way he held himself still. She scoffed, not liking that he might perceive her rattled nerves. "I fear *nothing*, Your Grace."

His mouth twitched but he made no reply. Jules leaned forward, dipped her nose close enough to where it brushed against his skin. She expected his flesh to be chilled…but the duke's skin was heated. He stilled even more, and an odd sort of awareness flowed over her skin and settled like a sharp kiss of warning along her nape.

"Your nose is cold," he said with quiet intensity.

"Is it?"

A soft sound rumbled in his throat, but he did not move away. "Go ahead…smell me."

The command crackled through her body in the most peculiar manner.

*Why is it important*, she silently asked him. She could not read any answer in his eyes or decipher any hint of his thoughts. Curious as to what the duke's reaction would be, Jules sucked his scent deep into her lungs, shocked at the instant weakness that seemed to pool low inside her belly and to her knees. His scent was…unknown to her, warm yet cold…a hint of oak moss and something far too elusive. His inexplicable fragrance invaded her nostrils, tightening her stomach and warming her most feminine place. The strangest heat darted through her body, and her heart quickened. Jules let the scent wash over her like the cool glide of wind.

She shifted, lifting her nose from his throat, still aware of how close they were. His face came into view, and his expression was carefully composed. She ran her eyes over the sharp blade of his nose, the strong set of his chin, the hewn lines of his jaw.

"I am not afraid of you," she whispered. "Do not ever think that I could be, Your Grace."

Jules could not explain why it was important for him to know this, only sensing that he must understand that she was not terrified to be here with him.

His gaze held hers inexorably, scorchingly. "You like being provocative and daring."

"Of course I do. If not, how else should I have attained such perfection in the art of standing unflinchingly before powerful men of your ilk?"

"It is your gentleman disguise that gives you the courage?"

Her chest gave a frightful squeeze. "I've never admitted that I am in any sort of disguise."

"I do not care what you admit or not. Your scent tells me everything I need to know."

There went that damnable trembling of her heart again, and instinct pushed her to touch her moustache to ensure it was in place.

His gaze tracked her movements. "It is rather brilliant."

"I admit I am quite clever," she whispered, aware that she was not at all scared that he knew her secret.

"Arrogant," he said softly.

"Confident," Jules murmured.

"I like it. I do wonder whether, if you are stripped of it, would you be the same…"

Jules hoped it was not evident how her heart raced. "Is that what you wish to do within our…alliance, strip away my layers?"

Something truly mysterious sparked in those beautiful eyes. "And what would you do, should I attempt to unravel you?"

"I fear you are unequal to the task, Your Grace."

"A challenge, Wildflower?"

Something primal hummed along her spine, warning Jules to retreat, for she played in unexplored waters. Yet she did not listen. "Would you accept it?"

Something savage flickered in his eyes. "No, I would not."

"Why not?"

"Because you are of no real, lasting interest to me."

Shocked, her eyes widened upon his face. He looked so indifferent his expression could be considered cruel. Those flat words stirred an unidentified emotion inside Jules. Befuddling, it felt like…disappointed hurt that nothing about her enchanted him enough where he believed she would stay in his thoughts long after they parted.

"I admit I wish to know you," he continued. "Why, I have yet to understand."

She tried to gather her scattered wit into a semblance of order. "Is there any point in wishing for it? After a few weeks we will be strangers passing in the streets of London. *If* we pass each other at all, Your Grace." *Three weeks. Not enough time.*

"You are correct. This mysterious allure will be fleeting and vanish before I can know why I was even mildly curious."

Once again, that peculiar sense of losing something without even having possessed it wafted through her. "I quite agree, Your Grace."

"James," he replied instantly.

"James," she slowly repeated.

Shockingly he gently tapped a finger along the bridge of her nose. "What do I smell like, Wildflower? Tell me."

*Who are you?* The sudden desperate need to know burned through her with alarming fierceness. He was truly outrageous…and she liked him like this.

"Like the cold night air," Jules said with candor. "Brisk and chilled yet refreshing."

"How does it move you?"

Her belly tightened at that odd question. Yet somehow she understood his meaning. "Move me?"

"Do not prevaricate with me," he ordered, his tone almost hard, yet his gaze…gentle.

*Trust. Honesty.* The building blocks of whatever connections flowered between them to hook inside her chest. "Your scent enters like a breath of air inside my body. One that does not want to leave. It moves through me with a power and feel of…wonder that I do not understand."

*There is my truth, Your Grace, and the earth has not*

*crumbled.*

The pleasure he took in her words made itself evident from the gleam in his gaze. "Good," he murmured.

Jules stood, desperately needing some space. This honest discourse between them might be harder than she'd anticipated. She did not like feeling exposed or vulnerable, and it startled her that being truthful with the duke was akin to such feelings.

The duchess wanted the *haut ton* to see a man of refined gentlemanly qualities, one who would smile easily, ask a lady to dance and flirt, perhaps seduce one or two. His mother was desperate for him to appear *normal.* The duke clearly understood this goal but did not believe in that role for himself. That he only wanted to know how to put on a veneer of gentility informed her of that much.

Jules had less than three weeks to perhaps help the duke reshape his perception of his former life so that he might desire to truly be a part of it, to truly hunger to transform himself into the Duke of Wulverton. Or perhaps only enough to satisfy the queen and those society carrions who would watch, eager to pick him apart with their wild speculations and gossipmongering. For a wild moment, Jules felt a profound sense of panic.

"Will you learn to dance?" she asked him once again, without turning around. "Reabsorb etiquette lessons?"

"If I must."

She did not jerk to hear his voice so close. "You must."

"I do not believe in bowing to any part of society's ridiculous expectations."

There was that rough humor beneath his tone, as if everything was ludicrous. There was something else there that she could not decipher.

"You *cannot* fail," Jules said, glancing over her shoulder to hold his stare.

An indecipherable expression flickered in his gaze. "Then I shall endeavor to do my best."

The duke did not yet understand his mother was hoping they could soften the hard dangerous edge that cloaked him like a second skin. The duke had been standing alone for so long, and against such insurmountable odds, his character had been sharpened and honed into its own blade that followed his own rule.

The duke...Jules closed her eyes and looked away from him. *Not the duke...James.* Removing that formal barrier suddenly made her feel frightened, less certain that she might be able to maintain only professionalism. Jules already felt this encounter with him had shaken the bounds of propriety.

"Are you fearful to face me?"

*Yes,* that internal warning cried, yet she said, "No, why would I be?"

Jules turned around. Their gazes collided and in the deep blue of his eyes, she spied an aloneness that nearly choked her breath. Something desperate inside of her reached for him, wanting to comfort...to understand and to heal. "Is there anything that you miss, Your Grace?"

That arrogant head lifted. "Miss?"

"What do you long for...in the nights when your sleep is restless and you peer around the darkness, a hole awakens inside of your chest. If you are indomitable enough, you will question what is needed to fill that space and you may sense something can fill it if only you should reach for that something. I already know you are indomitable, and you have peered into that abyss. *What* do you long for?"

It flashed then in his gaze, a hunger so raw and primal her heart jolted. *There is something.*

"Would you share with me, James? Or better, I invite you to make a list."

"A list," he repeated slowly, those eyes tracking her every

gesture.

Though his barely there smile was mocking, the gleam in his eyes was...cynically amused. She wondered if he knew he had the mannerism of a predator, one confident of its hunting skills. "Yes. A list of things that you would like to do. Things that you have thought of, even in fleeting moments since your return."

And it was in those needs she would understand him more. "James?" Those piercing eyes held hers. "Be honest with your desires...be honest with me."

He lifted his head to the sky, his side profile stark and almost forbidding. The duke was silent for several beats, and she patiently waited.

"These woodlands were one of the last places I saw my father."

Jules stilled.

"There was a time, in those first few months when all I had were memories. Of my family, my friends, the life I lived and loved. Those memories became dangerous."

"Why dangerous?"

"They were a taunt."

"Could you...elaborate?"

"Those memories were a painful thing I would never again enjoy, a reminder of all I had lost and might never regain. The hope...the endless hope that I might see my family again was the worst. It is such an ugly feeling—hope. I cannot fathom why anyone believes it a good thing. It is merely endless wishing. I learned to discard those useless emotions like hope," he said, his tone indifferent. "I did a good job. I can barely recall my father or what it felt like to love him."

Something cracked inside her chest. Jules recalled that his father had died seven years past, yet the duke would have only learned of it a few weeks ago. Had the duchess realized everyone had received the chance to grieve that loss, but her son had not? "You miss your father."

He said nothing, merely contemplated the night sky for long moments. "He died not knowing his son lived."

Jules lifted her face to the sky as well. She wanted to offer him comfort, even though she did not understand how to. Would he even accept it? Her father would have known the right words to say. She frowned. Would they have been honest words from her father? Or merely methodical science to allow the duke to open more to him?

"I miss the feeling of someone touching me," the duke said. "That is what I longed for the most when I lay awake in the dark."

"You have not been touched in years." The sense of loneliness and isolation would have been brutal to endure. Yet he had not been broken from the ordeal. A hunger to know everything about him curled through her, and she wondered if the need only resided in professional curiosity.

"Not by another person."

She thought about the careful way he kept others from coming close, even his mother.

"Though I crave it, I do not like being touched by others," he said, tone low and introspective. "It is an inexplicable feeling...this terrible want yet to also be repulsed by the notion."

"Do you worry about what it might be like to...woo a lady, to eventually marry her and the intimacy required in such a union?"

The duke went astonishingly still. For some odd reason, Jules's heartbeat had accelerated. "Pray do not distress yourself," she said, sensing the biting tension climbing within him. "An answer is not necessary. My question was more to encourage retrospection than anything else."

The duke turned to her, and to Jules's surprise he took

her chin in a firm clasp. Her pulse tapped briskly in her ears, and she affected a calm composure as their gazes collided. The sharp angles in his face were arranged flawlessly and so beautifully, she was tempted to touch her fingers to his jawline.

"By what strange process of reasoning do you derive that I might be distressed?"

*Such arrogance.* Jules lifted a brow. "An erroneous conjecture on my part, I surmise. Do you feel odd to be touching me now?"

"We are not skin to skin. This is different."

"Is it?"

His gray-blue eyes gleamed with harsh amusement. "Yes. There is a barrier, a distinct lack of sensation."

"Have you willingly touched another recently?"

"No."

Though he had given his word to be truthful, his honesty was painfully jarring. How far would he expose himself to her and she to him? Indefinable needs shifted in his gaze, burning the cobalt in his eyes to a brilliant hue. That peculiar ache tightened her throat. "What are you thinking now, James?"

"That I want my Wildflower to touch me and that perhaps I wish to touch her as well. Skin to skin, without any gloves on our hands."

Jules's heart stuttered inside her chest. *His wildflower?* Somewhere the professional wall between them had cracked, and Jules suspected it was from as early as the promise of an exchange of truth. Honesty revealed vulnerabilities and pain and hunger and fear. To be truthful revealed the part of oneself that is kept hidden and that they would give this caveat to each other surely exceeded any professional relationship she had been foolish to think they would have.

*A touch.*

Such a simple request yet so complicated. The duke's eyes gleamed with sudden humor, and it rendered him most charming.

"Would you be willing to, Wildflower?"

"Willing to what?" she asked, centering herself against the unfamiliar sensations washing over her senses, hoping for time to collect her wits and think.

"Touch me."

Against her better judgment, she shifted even closer to him, seeking something she did not fully understand.

"Are you afraid?"

"No."

"Liar," he said tenderly, the dark blue of his eyes firing with amusement. "You sounded like a little rat just now."

"It was more like a frog," she whispered shakily.

The duke smiled, the slow curve of his mouth languid and sensual. "You are a rather interesting character."

Jules knew she should step back and create a proper, respectful distance between them. She should not touch the duke in any regard, for surely that would irrevocably cross the boundaries of professionalism. Perhaps for now she only stood on the precipice and there was time to retreat.

No other sense comforted, assured, aroused the senses than touch conveyed, and he had not permitted touch or given one in decade. Jules wanted to gift him this...yet she was terrified to allow his exploration.

*Why must this be so complicated?* she cried silently.

Jules felt caught in a vortex of complex sensations she had no hope of ever controlling. The scientist inside Jules viscerally rejected the idea. Yet she was positively transfixed by the smallest of touch against her cheek. It was with a sense of shock she realized she had denied herself the familiarity of touch with those she called friends. It had been imperative that no one was allowed too close or else her lifetime's disguise might be discovered, and the consequences could not be imagined—the scandal for her entire family, losing the treasured freedom to live her life unfettered, losing her dreams of being a noted mind doctor, and then suffering the fracture of her family. To protect her secret and all she stood to lose, Jules did not know the hug of her father, a friend's arm tossed over her shoulder, or a *faux* lover's initial seduction.

Her mouth dried because with James, she felt a sense of belonging that was a dangerous delusion. He was a duke and a patient of her father. There was nothing about her that could ever belong in his world and life, not even as a friend.

Still, without removing her regard from his, she reached for him. A fine tension had wound itself through the duke's body, and his eyes were too intent as he watched her. That unsettling sensation, swirling and deep, landed once more inside Jules.

There was something about His Grace and her reaction to him that frightened Jules's heart, even while his mesmeric personality tugged her dangerously closer. Though her fingers reached out to him, he leaned away, the move instinctive and cautious, like a wounded animal uncertain of the toucher's intent.

He would have endured touch starvation, and he would have acutely wished for the touch of others only to be denied. What did he feel now that her fingers were scant inches from his mouth? "Are you afraid, James?"

"I fear nothing."

The words were like a feral hiss, the coldness leaping into his eyes raking against her skin and stuttering her heartbeat. Jules sensed then there had been a time when the duke had been so afraid, it had stripped him of everything he thought he knew about himself. Yet somehow, he had reforged himself by conquering the idea of fear.

A stunning recognition flowed through her. *He had*

*buried that fear in the stillness…and perhaps all emotions.*

Jules took a quick breath, lifted her hand to his face, and lightly touched his chin. He reared his head away as if she had planted him a facer. Cheeks burning, she started to lower her hand, only for him to catch it, holding that single digit in a too tight clasp. His chest lifted on a harsh breath, then a slow, controlled one. A tremor went through the hand that held her finger before he released her.

Jules stood there, her hand suspended in midair, as wings of indecision took flight in her belly. She wanted to tell him that everything he felt was normal. She wanted to inform him of all the psychological theories she had learned about sensory deprivation and the true power of touch to human beings. It was one of the first senses humans developed, and it would have been one of the most painful to lose. An awful ache crowded her throat, and Jules held his eyes as she lifted her finger once again and lightly touched his cheek.

His skin…it was cold yet hot. Silky yet hard and unyielding to the soft pressure of her finger. Those long, inky lashes lowered, and his eyes closed. He turned his face ever so slightly, brushing his nose against her finger.

"Not enough," he said gruffly, a flush of color staining the savage elegance of his jawline. "More."

The command burned through her, and those terrible sensations of fright and thrill clutched at her chest. That element of fear gave birth to a deeper sense of curiosity and hunger to understand this man before her, and with a small murmur, she leaned closer and explored.

• • •

The brush of Jules Southby's fingers was delicate, searching… shaking as they swept up James's shoulders and traced a path to his throat. Ah…what was this feeling wending through his chest? It was unfamiliar and...puzzling. This person—this *woman*, he was damn sure of it—was a mere speck in his life and would soon flit from it. *Unimportant.* A simple touch from this creature should not be so interesting. Her fingers caressed the hollow of his neck, and James saw the instant she felt the shakiness of his pulse. Those slender fingers tensed, pressed a little deeper into his skin, absorbing the erratic nature of his heartbeat.

Her gaze widened and those green eyes burned a little bit brighter. She held his regard as her finger stroked up his throat to his chin, an infinitesimal movement that echoed unendingly inside his body. This was the intimate gesture of a person struggling for a connection, and something inside of James reached for it...reached for *her.*

That cold place inside him yielded by the smallest increment and he leaned into her caresses, breathing deep of that scent that was wholly Jules Southby's, enjoying the feeling of being anchored to something this soft and precious. He almost laughed at his absurd thought. There was nothing precious about a single touch. Yet he felt starved for it, hungrier than those times when he had not eaten or drank water for days.

Brutally honed instincts which had kept him alive for a decade said he should not conquer this hunger but allow it to be a part of his life. This feeling she roused inside him should not be pushed aside as a speck. James wanted meticulously to explore it—to break it apart so it could be understood, then he would absorb it and let it fill him until he was satiated.

Nothing less would do.

For too long, he had been deprived, and here was a source before him that he wished to gorge and glut upon. The desire felt ruthless and implacable, uncaring of the will of others, yet he did not shun it. "I want you to touch me whenever I want, Wildflower."

She laughed, the sound quick and startled. "Spoken like a duke."

The words were chiding, teasing almost, but the curious hunger in her gaze surely mirrored what rose inside him. It felt unstoppable and unquenchable. "Do you agree?"

An unknown expression flickered in her gaze. "I am undecided."

*It is not a rejection. Good enough for now.*

He clenched his hands again, fighting against the nearly overwhelming need to just touch her. To run his hands down her arms, to feel her hands against his chest and back.

"May I touch you?" he asked when everything inside him urged him to ruthlessly take. He did not understand it and it felt like a concept he had long forgotten, but he gentled the primal cravings and asked again, "May I touch you, Wildflower?"

If she denied him, he would damn well walk away.

Her throat worked on a tight swallow. "Is the need imperative?"

"It feels like a desperate hunger. I do not like it."

A small smile touched her mouth. "Yet you chase the feeling?"

"Yes."

Her head canted slightly. "Why?"

James carefully thought about it. "It is new and different."

Her gaze searched his before she nodded. James was considerably surprised and pleased. What would it feel like to touch another's skin after so long?

"Go ahead," she whispered, as if she sensed the clash of needs rising within him.

James hardly cared that his hands shook as he lifted them to her face. Right before he touched her cheek, he clenched his fingers into a tight fist. He had not allowed the touch of another for a long time, nor had he reciprocated. This need felt alien to him, and he briefly wondered at the ease of doing so with this creature. Was it because in touching her or allowing her to touch him, there was no expectation of normalcy?

James did not have the answer, but he had not been able to allow any touches from his family or give any in return since stepping back into civilization. He unclenched his fingers with a force of will he'd not expected to need to exert, not when he wanted to feel this connection with such visceral intensity.

A shaky breath escaped Southby, and though her eyes urged him on, her lips did not move. James gently cupped her cheeks. Softness and heat. Those impressions crowded his awareness, and an unfamiliar sensation prickled beneath his fingertips.

It felt like pleasure...

He teased a too-rough thumb over the elegant softness of her cheek, and her eyes went so wide that James thought she might faint. It occurred to him that Jules Southby might have never been caressed by another in such an intimate fashion. A possessive satisfaction hummed deep inside, briefly shocking James.

"You are soft, like the petal on a flower."

A quick scowl marred her loveliness. "I am tough like rawhide."

He did his best to hide his amusement. "Perhaps you are both. Beautiful yet filled with unbreakable resilience. Wildflowers depend only on the rain and the sun from heaven. They can be invincible and very independent." *Wildflower.* "A wildflower lived with me in a cave."

She peered up at him from beneath incredibly long lashes. "How long did you live in a cave?"

"Months, hiding from the relentless fury of the winter wind. That wildflower was alone, too. It was the only splash of vibrancy in the unrelenting cold and darkness."

He drifted his fingers down to the supple hollowness of her throat. *You remind me of it.*

"There are some psychologists who believe living without the touch of others is an impossible feat," she said, lifting her fingers back to his face.

James leaned into that soft, almost hesitant caress. The muscle tensed beneath the tip of her fingers and reacting with instinct, he darted his hand to loosely capture that single digit. "Do not remove your hands."

"I won't," she whispered, those tips feathering over to his brow.

James pressed his thumb against the hollow of her throat. That inexplicable craving clawed up inside him, and instead of constricting it, he gave it free rein. The need spilled through him to just feel her, so he did. He coasted his fingertips over her collarbone, daringly unknotting that neckcloth so he could fully feel the soft hollow of her breastbone. A deep, thumping pleasure pulsed through James's body. It was indeed a foreign sensation that wrenched violently inside his chest.

*All from touching her?*

A spicier touch of apricot flavored the air. Her eyes snapped to his and he noted the fractured beauty in the depth of her eyes, made even more lovely by the flickering fire. Her regard felt invasive…intimate. James wanted more.

That impatience bit at him and he tugged the neckcloth fully away, even the slide of it against his palm a sensual rasp. He dropped it to the ground and flicked open the few top buttons of her shirt. He wanted an expanse of skin against his hand. A single gliding touch with his fingers was inadequate.

The softest of skin bared to his gaze. James ran his hand across her clavicle, feeling the warmth of life and energy beneath his palm. His wildflower's scent changed, became sultry and dark…yet had the light tinge of frosted wind and apricot blossoms...and also sun-ripened peach. James's mouth watered. And something inexplicable tightened low in his gut. As if she somehow sensed his reaction, she laughed. Light and tinkling. Eyes mysterious as the ice-capped mountains of the Northern Sound itself.

James needed to find the sultry lushness beneath the lightness, to understand its source. He ran his nose down across her chest and lower still, ignoring the squeak of dismay sounding above his head. Clearly, he was acting the beast, a man without any manners or refinement. He would find the withal to tender an apology later.

"James!"

"My name at last," he murmured, dipping his nose in line with her waistband. Ah...there it was, that lush fragrance that evoked naked limbs tangled in primal rhythm right here in the wood. Fingers thrust through his hair and yanked his head up.

James rose. Her cheeks were red, her eyes bright, and the pulse at her throat visibly tapped. "I am not sure if I am appalled or filled with humor. You *must* control your nose, my good duke."

That smile could have been a bullet given the force with which it tore through James's chest and lodged itself. A damn smile and he was destroyed. Something in her eyes said she knew it very well and was intrigued by his reaction to her. The absurdity of it unsettled him, yet it also tugged at an unknown place deep inside.

"You smell like apricot blossoms...it makes me want to lick you, everywhere. I have never given any thought to licking another before. I can tell this desire will follow me to bed and tease and torment my sleep. I look forward to the experience of...licking and tasting you."

Her eyes widened to an astonishing degree. "I...*Your Grace!*"

"Ah, should I have not said that?"

"You *devil*, you very well know it," she gasped.

"Why not? It is the truth."

"Not all truths are meant to be spoken."

"Between us, they will. Did we not agree on this exchange of honesty, Wildflower? Surely you have not forgotten so soon, hmm?"

She made a hopeless gesture with her hand, a sound, a curious croak emitting from her. "We do not speak the dangerous ones."

"Why not?"

"Because they are dangerous," she said with a touch of sardonic mirth. "I do not want to think about you wanting to lick me."

He saw it then, lush golden skin splayed on the verdant grass, a feast for him to inhale and glide his fingers over. The contrasting roughness on the tips of his fingers would rouse her sweet, soft body…

A spark lit in his veins, and he found himself reaching for that pulse of need, wanting to inter that sensation deep inside him. The nature of it felt unknown; though he was certain to have felt desire before, this felt new and necessary. "I also want to touch you. *Everywhere.*"

Her lips parted but no sound emerged. Finally, Southby delicately cleared her throat and said, "Well, I…I…" Her lips closed on whatever she meant to say and then to his delight, a beautiful smile bloomed on her mouth. "You have a bit of a devil inside you."

"You've met him, have you?"

"Is he not the master of temptation?"

All at once, life seemed to consist of sweet and definitely wicked possibilities. Ah…she was tempted. "So you do want me to touch you everywhere, Wildflower."

"I admit that I am infinitely curious."

He stroked a finger over her quaint little brow. "Then I shall satisfy you."

Her lids fluttered and veiled the glorious depths of her eyes. "I daresay ladies on the marriage mart will appreciate this mysterious yet devilish charm you are exuding."

"Will they?"

"Yes," she said with a wistful sigh. "You'll be charming…a bit rakish perhaps, and in no time you'll find yourself the perfect duchess."

*The perfect duchess.* The warmth invading his chest leeched away, and the cold returned. James stepped away from the maddening temptation of Jules Southby and lowered his hand. Suddenly he needed to put an end to this. "Thank you for the privilege of touching you. You may leave, Southby."

Her eyes widened but she did not protest, merely dipped her head in acknowledgement. "I…I will return to the main house."

"Your company has been lovely. Thank you."

"I enjoyed being out here with you, Your Grace. Thank you for trusting me enough to share it."

"Do not betray that trust."

She lowered her lashes, hiding her expression from him. "I ask the same of you with my…my disguise, Your Grace."

"Of course."

They stood there with that tiny space between them, only needing one to reach for the other to…to what? James raked his fingers through his hair, biting back the hiss rising inside his throat.

"I bid you good night, Your Grace."

"Sleep well, Southby."

She executed a sharp yet graceful bow, snatched her neckcloth, then darted past him, hurrying from the woods and away from him, taking all the warmth with her.

# Chapter Seven

"It is a dance that communicates passion…it is the language of love for many. It is imperative you allow me closer, Your Grace."

At James's silence, Monsieur Gillespie's eyelid twitched.

"Once more," the dance tutor said stiffly. "Recall the Viennese waltz is full of grace and elegance but also vigor! It is a dance where you and your partner are constantly turning either in a clockwise or counterclockwise direction interspersed with steps to switch between the direction of rotation."

The short, rotund gentleman who was rather graceful and swift despite his corpulence lifted a hand, and his lady assistant who sat on a stool some distance away raised the bow of the violin and started to play. The sound of the waltz floated on the air, and James swallowed down the ire slamming at the cage of his equanimity. They had been at it for an hour, and the idea of another five minutes was intolerable.

Masking his emotions, he lifted his hands to an invisible partner and started to move with the sound of the music, spinning and rotating, trying to imagine this phantom lady he would do this with in a few weeks.

"No, no," the tutor said, "You must hold your arms up like this—"

The snarl that ripped from James's throat at the man's touch sent Gillespie stumbling back, fear settling on his face. Without thinking, James struck, clamping his hand around the man's throat. "Never touch me!"

"*Aahhhh!*"

A piercing shriek ripped through the air, the sound too close for his liking. James glanced over his shoulder to see the lady hiking up the hem of her dress and running from the room.

"He means to murder Monsieur Gillespie!" she cried out, dashing through the door as if the devil chased her. "*Help!*"

*For bloody sakes*! Biting down the hiss rising in his throat, James shoved the man from him and whirled away, stalking to the windows. The tutor had approached him from behind and grabbed his hand. James's reaction had been dangerous and instinctive, mildly surprising him at the visceral distaste which had burned inside his veins. Pushing out a breath, he raked his fingers through his hair. He did not need the scrutiny this incident would bring from his family. Not for the first time, he was tempted to banish them all from his home, only to invite them when he was damn ready to socialize, if ever.

The sounds of many feet running toward the ballroom echoed.

"What happened?" the duchess cried.

"He tried to *murder* Monsieur Gillespie," the overwrought assistant sobbed. "It was such a shocking sight. His Grace's hand was around Monsieur's throat!"

If James had not felt as if the walls were closing in on him, he would have been impressed with her dramatic rendition.

"Your Grace?" Dr. Southby said. "Would you permit me

to ask what happened?"

James turned around, composing his expression. The dance tutor stood there, pale and rigid. His mother, Uncle Hubert, and Dr. Southby stared at James as if they actually thought he would give them some explanation. He'd already told the tutor there would be no touching during these lessons. James's wishes had been ignored and he was not of the mind to be forgiving.

The walls of the room seemed to shrink even more, and his gut churned. "There will be no more dancing lessons," he clipped icily. "You are dismissed Monsieur Gillespie. You'll depart Longbourn Park tomorrow."

His mother's eyes widened. "James! Monsieur Gillespie is in high demand; you must not—"

"There will be no more!" he hissed, for once not reining in the raw emotion that surged through his chest.

He stilled when his mother lurched back and even his uncle shuffled away. A cold pricked at his skin and buried deep in his bones. Did they fear him? "Everyone out."

"James!"

Her voice was a mere whisper, but it resounded with anguish.

"Out," he snarled. "Monsieur Gillespie will leave Longbourn Park, and if I am disobeyed in this, madam, everyone will leave."

The duchess made a gesture of frustration before whirling away, her motions stiff. Dr. Southby and his uncle retreated on the heels of the duchess, leaving James alone. He stood there feeling the space shrinking, the air stifling. This was all damnable nonsense. Why the hell should he belong to a world with people who would dare judge him if he did not dance well? His aunts fluttered around if he attended dinner without a cravat. Only this morning, Cousin Eloise affected a mock swoon to see him walking along the hallways without shoes.

How silly and self-pampered they were, buried in their world of artifice. Did they know starvation, or screaming until one's voice cracked, or weeping in the endless void because everything that they cared about was gone? Did they even know what it was like to be bereft or alone for even a moment, or starved and filled with such despair that their bones ached?

He was bloody tired of hearing about balls and dancing and what centerpiece would complement the dinner table. James hissed out a breath. *This is not life!* He ripped the neckcloth from his throat and stared at his fingers clenched around the fabric. It was a piece of cloth. This was not a challenge, it was not a bear to fight or a jagged cliff edge to scale. Yet he stared at the scrap of linen, unable to bear it to be around his throat for even a minute longer.

*I am not weak.*

Needing to be outdoors, he went to the large doors that opened onto a terrace. James took off his shoes and stockings, removed his jacket, shirt, and waistcoat, uncaring that he was bare chested, and stepped outside. He inhaled deeply, letting the brisk air into his lungs, accepting the peace seeping under his skin from simply taking in the myriad scent of the outdoors into his being. The grass prickled beneath his feet as he walked across the lawn, feeling the stares of his family and servants on his shoulder blades like ants.

Thunder rumbled overhead, and a soft, misting rain fell. James raked his fingers through his rain-dampened hair. He lifted his face to the sky, accepting the icy sting of the drops pelting his forehead. He missed the emptiness of the mountains. The awareness shocked a rough, low laugh from him.

How could he, even for a second, long for the abyss?

Once at the edge of the woods, he started to run. He

moved in sharp bursts of sprints and then long, looping strides. James sprinted over the grass until his muscles strained and filled with a burning pain. The wolves were no longer before him, urging him on with growls and howls, and he felt a surge of such loss, he stumbled. He caught himself and continued his run, wishing that his wolf brethren were with him. Or perhaps Jules Southby. She was strong and self-reliant, perhaps she would manage a hard run.

A vision of her naked, splayed on the wet grass and surrounded by nature, rushed to his thoughts. He held the image; fire filled his veins and the whisper of arousal ghosted over his cock. The hairs along the back of his neck prickled, warning him that he wasn't alone. James lifted his head, drawing in the scents surrounding him.

*Wildflower.*

His entire body suddenly felt alive and as if it belonged to someone else. James shifted, watching her approach. She did so boldly, as if there was nothing to fear. In the distance, he could see several members of his family had ventured outside under parasols and umbrellas as if they were watching a play. Southby stopped and stared at him, her gaze lingering on his naked chest for long moments. James was almost amused by the slight color dusting along those elegantly slanted cheekbones. Her eyes widened when she saw the blade in his waistband.

Those lovely green eyes met his. "What is it made from?"

"Bone."

"Is it sharp?"

"Yes."

She looked from his weapon and off into the woods for a moment. "Are you not joining the family for dinner?"

"No."

An emotion he could not read flashed in Southby's eyes. James merely waited.

They stared at each other, and he raised a brow, curious as to when she would mention the reason the duchess bid her to follow him. His skin prickled once again and the need to run with the wind roiled through him. James turned away from her and started walking. A feeling he did not understand hooked into him, and he paused. "Run with me, Wildflower?"

"Yes," she said softly.

Her lack of hesitation humbled something inside of James. Jules Southby was an unusual creature of strength and kindness and such patience. She darted ahead of him in a mad dash across the western lawns. James smiled and gave chase, easily overtaking her. He slowed his pace to keep even with her, and they ran until she was breathless. She surprised a smile from him when she tipped her face to the heavens and shouted before stumbling to a breathless halt.

Southby collapsed onto the verdant grass, taking ragged gulps of breath. She peered up at him smiling, the moustache twitching. "If the duchess is still watching I daresay I will be fired."

James sat beside her. "I'll rehire you."

That lush mouth hitched in an imperceptible smile, but she made no reply to that assertion. An undeniable curiosity rose within him as he watched her. She looked around them, noting they were on the edges of the woods and the main house was some distance away.

"Monsieur Gillespie touched you without your permission," she murmured.

Their gazes collided.

"Are you so certain I did not try to murder him because I am a beast?"

"If that had been your intention, I daresay you would have succeeded. You do not strike me as a man who does anything with half measure."

"Is that a sort of delicately placed rebuke?" he drawled.

"Am I to now feel encouraged to continue lessons, hmm?"

"Only honesty between us, Your Grace. I would not try to manipulate you."

"There will be no more lessons."

A small frown flickered on her face. "These lessons are important. Please consider—"

He felt the indifference wind itself around his heart. "There will be no more lessons."

Frustration flashed in her eyes, but she did not offer any further protestation. Silence lingered between them for several moments before she softly said, "Touching reaffirms safety and security. That you were deprived for so long was incredibly painful, James. You no longer believe in many things…and it is quite normal that you would only allow those whom you perhaps…trust with that privilege. I understand why you have dismissed Monsieur Gillespie and I want you to know the rage you possibly felt, the disgust…is also normal, because he violated your boundaries."

James stiffened. That understanding he'd not anticipated, and though something raw and primal inside him rejected the compassion in her eyes, something else far more insistent lurched toward this creature. Driven by an imperative need that overwhelmed his good senses, James leaned forward and reverently inhaled her—the forgotten fragrance of summer and peach blossoms. The tight tension he'd not been fully cognizant of eased, and he carefully guarded her scent within his chest.

"You are too close," she whispered shakily, her scent changing, becoming more sultry and sweet.

*Thud. Thud. Thud. Thud.*

The rush of her heartbeat filled that scant space between their bodies. Suddenly hunger fell against his heart like a hammer. James wanted Jules Southby.

He had to hold his body very, very still to fight the primal urges beating through his blood, the one urging him to drag her beneath him and ruthlessly seduce. The pounding waves slowly subsided, and he leaned away. Only then did Jules roll away from him, coming up to her knees before standing. Southby brushed the wet grass from her trousers, careful to keep her eyes from James. But he did not need to see her expression—her ever-shifting scent told him everything yet not enough. Without bidding him farewell, she rushed away from him, heading toward the main house.

• • •

A couple hours after Southby had hurried away, James entered the main house of his estate, enjoying the peace found in the emptiness of the prodigious hallway. He usually stayed deep within the woods for hours each night, retreating inside on the cusp of dawn. Tonight…he wanted to be inside, and he idly wondered if his extraordinary encounter with Jules Southby had influenced his decision.

As he turned to step onto the first stair, a sound arrested his attention. James frowned, glancing down the hallway toward the music room where the lonely ping of the piano keys lingered in the air. He ignored it, only to pause halfway up the curving staircase as a haunting melody sounded. It was usual for the house to be quiet, everyone exhausted by the mind games of the day, tiptoeing around him, or the mental energy they inputted dissecting his every gesture and action, or pretend they were not keenly watching and whispering about his supposed feral nature. Later on today, he just might bare his teeth to his aunt, to see if she swooned.

James turned around and quietly went back down the stairs toward the music that plucked a most peculiar chord within his chest. The person who played was…unhappy, or perhaps adrift and unable to find an anchor against whatever they felt or endured. The door stood ajar, bright light seeping into the hallway. He eased the door open and faltered.

It was Felicity. The fireplace roared, staving off the chill coming inside from the open windows. The two gas lamps provided ample illumination for her to read the music sheet, though James did not think she followed it. His sister was garbed in a flowing light blue nightgown, her feet were bare, and her dark raven locks tumbled down to her hips. He noted the open decanter of brandy on the rosewood table by the fireplace and the empty glass beside it.

Felicity stirred restlessly, running her fingers over the keyboard, her expression a tight grimace of emotions he did not understand. James considered her, thinking of the last time he had laughed and romped with his sister. Ten years separated them, and he vaguely recalled how happy he had been at her birth. As she grew, he had been a proud older brother who found every opportunity to dote on his sister. She had been a small thing, always under foot. And he…he had adored her. He pressed a hand over his chest, wanting to rekindle those old feelings of warmth and affection. He felt… nothing. The shock that covered his senses felt cold and dark.

Her shoulders stiffened, and he gathered she sensed his presence. James noted that those elegant fingers hovering over the piano keys trembled before she formed them into fists. She took a deep breath and shifted fully on the bench to face him. They stared at each other across the expanse of the room, her eyes wide with apprehension, and James was uncertain as to what he should be feeling. Since his return, they had never been alone. She had not sought his presence, and he had treated hers with mild indifference, for the loving bond they'd formed had been stagnated by necessity.

"You startled me. I did not anticipate your return," she said, tucking a wisp of hair behind her ears. Her gaze lowered to his bare toes and damp hair. "You normally stay in the woods."

The soft, hesitant sound of her voice jolted him. He recalled her to own an unflinching spirit, daring to do so many things as a child even when the duchess tried to restrain or scold her. Who was this young lady who looked upon him as if he were a creature she did not know, or perhaps one she feared knowing? James shoved his hands inside his trouser pockets, feeling an unknown sensation writhing around inside his chest. He did not like it. "Do you wish to be alone?"

She hesitated, tucking a wisp of hair behind her ears. At her continued silence, James chose for her, releasing the latch and turning around.

"Please do not go!"

He glanced over his shoulder, noting how she now stood with her hands fisted at her sides.

"I think that is the most you have said to me since your return," she said with a shaky little smile. "Please do not go."

Surely, they had conversed. Yet he could not recall it. She had always hovered in the background of everyone's chatter, watching him with wounded eyes and an emotion akin to fear. A tight feeling wrenched through his chest, and James turned around, closing the door behind him with a small *snick*. He went to the rosewood table, lifted the decanter, and poured a healthy serving into two glasses. "Will you join me for a drink, Felicity?"

Her mouth formed a small moue of astonishment.

"A drink of *brandy*?"

"You've already started."

A flush rose on her cheeks. "That was done in secret. This is entirely different. You must absolutely tell no one of this, especially Mama."

"I can be the soul of discretion."

She walked over, eyeing him warily. Still, she took the glass, closing her fingers firmly over it as if afraid it might slip through her fingers. Felicity took a small sip, and her lack of grimace or coughing at the strong liquor informed James she had pilfered many times before from his stock. Unexpectedly, he felt a spurt of humor at her daring.

"Why do you look at me so, Your Grace?" she asked with a small, nervous smile.

*Your Grace.*

"There was a time you called me James...or Jamesy."

Her fingers tightened on her glass. "You remember?"

"I have not lost my memories of the past."

Her expression crumbled, and he saw that she struggled not to cry.

"So you've remembered me all this time, Your Grace?"

The hurt in her tone scraped against his senses and tugged at something deep inside James that he had long forgotten. Or merely buried. He followed the pathway of the sensation instead of pushing it even further into the recess of where it lingered. Still, he had no wish to share anything with her. How she looked at him, with fearful expectations and a sturdiness that braced for rejection, reminded him of the time she had followed him about as a child. She had done so bravely, and when he had caught her, she had looked this very way, and he'd not had the heart to turn her away even though his friends had laughed at having her underfoot.

He'd chosen her then, leaving their presence to trample through the woods with Felicity and even take her fishing. Since then, his friends had understood that he loved his sister and had gotten used to her following three young gentlemen on several larks.

"In the first couple of years...I thought about you every day." James couldn't say why he chose to inform her of this... except it felt right.

The tears that had gathered in her eyes spilled over, and she swiped at them almost angrily.

"Only in those couple of years you thought of me?" she demanded harshly, her light blue eyes flashing with indefinable emotions.

Despite her wounded countenance, he could only provide the unvarnished truth. "Yes."

She flinched. "Well, I did not stop thinking about you, brother. Not one day I did not pray before I slept, asking God to keep you alive and bring you home."

A taut silence lingered, and he emptied the content of his glass in a long swallow. Felicity followed, coughing slightly. He refilled their glasses, and though her eyes flared in surprise, she made no protest.

"Why did you stop thinking about me?"

James held her stare, knowing he had no answer to give her.

"You will not answer, will you?" she said with faint accusation ringing in her tone. "You do not care enough to answer."

She emptied her second drink and walked away. The tight feeling inside his chest worsened, and a hiss slipped from him as he fought against the tearing feel. He owed her nothing... yet he felt like he owed her everything. She was his sister...a person he should love and want to protect with every breath inside of him.

"When I thought of you, it hurt," he said gruffly.

Felicity stopped and whirled around, pressing a palm over her chest. "What did you say?"

He swallowed down another drink. "If I stopped thinking about you...longing for you and everything that I lost, then I could remain sane...then I could survive being torn from my family and everything I know. I could not hope as you did, for I found hope to be a cruel, endless torment as the days, then months, then years dragged on endlessly. So I stopped hoping to be with you...and here. In that way, Felicity, I lived."

Silent tears trekked down her cheeks, and she nodded slowly. She did not press him for more but took halting steps closer. "I need to hug you...*please*."

Every instinct recoiled.

"James?"

"Not now," he said gruffly. "Maybe one day...but not now, Felicity."

James saw that she wanted to question why but held her tongue, and a soft admiration rose in his chest. She had grown into a beautiful young lady, and he had missed it. She had suffered not being connected with him and had done so with remarkable grace. James canted his head and studied her, realizing she was one of the only people in his family who did not speak about him in veiled whispers or watch him with dubious frowns.

"I like to watch the stars," James said.

There was a pulse of silence in which he felt the lingering surprise and curiosity. Finally, she asked, "Are you inviting me to watch the stars with you, Your Grace?"

James met her stare. "Instead of a hug."

A smile bloomed on her mouth, and her eyes sparkled with a delight he'd not anticipated. "Thank you, brother, I would very much like to watch the night sky with you."

He walked over to the large bay windows and pushed the heavy drape aside, revealing the rolling lawns and the beauty of the dark sky speckled with stars. His sister came up beside him, standing as close as she could without touching him. He did not crave her to be any closer, nor long to hug her, but her presence was...tolerable. More than tolerable, pleasant even.

"Is there anyone you've allowed to touch you?" she whispered, her face lifted to the view. "I've noticed even that you keep Mama at a distance."

"Jules Southby."

His sister jolted slightly. "Mr. Southby?"

"Hmm."

"Should I ask how that happened?"

"No."

Her soft laughter curled around him, and James found himself smiling. "So, you think a God is up there?"

She shifted, and he felt her stare upon his profile. "Yes."

"Whimsical."

"Perhaps," she said softly, "but you are home, aren't you? If not God, then how? *Chance*? That notion that our lives are directed by chance is what is fanciful. Mama hopes society will welcome you with open arms when you return to London in a few weeks."

"Jules Southby will help me accomplish that."

He felt his sister's curiosity but did not elaborate.

"A gentleman is thought to be of top quality and very marriable because of his lofty education, *very* polished manners, considerable charm, and the productive management of his inheritance. A duke is that and even *more*," Felicity said. "Will Mr. Southby prepare you enough for the *haut ton*?"

"I was already assured I have a bit of devilish charm," James said, trying not to think of the wildflower at this moment. She was too distracting and thought consuming. He had yet to decide if that was indeed a good thing. "At the very least, I will ensure society does not get a snarling wolf."

Her eyes widened and then she giggled. James liked hearing it.

"I...I hope your acceptance goes smoothly." Felicity sighed, a sound which echoed with pained hope.

"Why does it matter?"

"You are my brother, of course it matters."

"There is more." *Your heart is beating impossibly fast.* Yet he did not say that, for James did not wish to speak about his sharpened senses. "If you have no wish to speak about it, do not."

Her fingers tightened once again over the glass, and he felt the tension rise in her.

"I had a season last year and I met someone…"

She cast him a quick sideway glance, but he kept his regard directed at the distant woodlands.

"We…I…we have exchanged several letters for the last few months, and I was certain that upon my return to town this season, he would make an offer."

"You no longer believe this offer will be forthcoming."

"Since the news of your return and possible malady of the mind, he has only written once to ask if the rumors held any truth. Even my friends who frequently wrote have not sent a letter in weeks, and my correspondence has not been replied to in kind. I am uncertain if I wish to return to town with Mama in a few weeks, but she is insistent that we must show a unified front to the *haut ton*."

James looked at his sister. Felicity bravely smiled, but her lips trembled and the vulnerability in her eyes deepened.

"Who is this gentleman?"

"I…" She glanced away for a brief moment. "He is the Earl of Somerton."

The duchess had been so certain, despite the power of James's name, many would still be hesitant to associate with him. The idea was…simply incredulous, yet the pain in his sister's eyes brought some of the consequences of the scandal surrounding his return into sharp relief.

It was everyone in his family who needed him to be more. James very much doubted he could speak around the emotions clawing up his throat. "He is not worthy of you if he stays away because of rumors."

A small hiccup came from her. "Mama threatened everyone today that if she should hear any rumors about you…running naked in the woods about town or in the village, they will feel her wrath."

"I am not insane or addled." Yet the world would think it because he no longer fit the perfect mold of a duke.

"I know it. I am glad you are home, James," Felicity said in a choked voice. "I am most happy that you asked me to watch these stars with you. Thank you, brother."

James made no reply, and his sister appeared contented with his reticence. They stood silently for several minutes, drinking brandy and watching the stars.

# Chapter Eight

*You smell like apricot blossoms…it makes me want to lick you everywhere.*

As Jules lay in the dark, the duke's words whispered through her heart in an intimate caress. She thumped her pillow for the tenth time, groaning her frustration in its soft depths.

"He is the devil!" she cried with considerable bewilderment.

Why were his words haunting her sleep for a second bloody night? Last night they had kept her awake for long hours and had even stayed with her throughout the day. She had left him in the rain more than three hours ago, and she believed he was still out there…perhaps running still. Jules had met with her father and the anxious duchess, carefully answering their queries. When the duchess asked what was in the woods that drew the duke there, Jules had merely replied "peace" and had not spoken about the cottage in the tree the duke had built deep in the woodland interiors. He would invite his family there when he was ready. She had not told her father of the tree cottage, either, feeling she would betray the duke's trust by revealing something he had not invited her father to be a part of.

The duchess wanted to know if he would resume his lessons, and Jules had not known what answer to provide. He needed space and time to acclimate, and that was being denied.

Jules had only spent a few minutes with her father before retiring to her chamber to take a bath. She had not lingered in the bath and had scrambled into the bed, hoping for a well-rested sleep tonight. It would not do to have another restless night without slumber.

Jules had never before been tossed into such disorder because of mere words.

*It makes me want to lick you, everywhere.*

There was a wanton ripple of response between her thighs, and a wicked heat rolled through her body, and she kicked the coverlet repeatedly until it tangled at her feet. If only she could blame her sleepless state on his words alone. The whisper of his fingertips over her chin and throat had felt sublime…wicked…decadent. The heated way he had stared at her through the mist of rain, as if he meant to consume every part of her… Jules huffed. A simple touch or a damn stare should not have such power over her slumber.

"You wretched devil," she cursed at the ceiling and then laughed. "This is *ridiculous*."

Pushing from the bed, Jules started to pace. The heat from the fireplace filled her with warmth yet it did little to dispel the cold knot of doubt tightening low inside her belly. This attraction she felt for the duke was absurd…and dangerous. It was indecent to think so avidly of his mouth touching her in places no one had ever seen or felt. And why in God's name was the desire even there, eating at her every sensible thought?

A plan needed to be formed to manage her encounters with the duke. It would be ideal if they met daily. There were so many things they could unlock through conversations, and while she desperately wanted to know about his ten years of isolation, she would not probe for more than he would allow. Instead, she would try to direct their conversations on how to make him presentable for the *haut ton*.

*And his future duchess.*

Jules stiffened at the faint sound of footsteps in the hallway. Had he returned inside tonight? She hurried over to the massive oak door and pressed her ear to it. The footsteps echoed closer, and she held her breath when they stopped. The sound of a door opening and closing did not reach her ears, and Jules hovered her hand on the door knob, wondering if she should peek into the hallway. The duke had been sleeping in the woods and had no notion she occupied his wing of the house. Jules lowered her hand with a sigh. What would she say to him should she encounter him now? Lament on her sleeplessness? Blame it on his incendiary words?

"I can smell you through the door, Wildflower."

She lurched back at the unexpectedness of his voice. Jules slammed her eyes shut at her silliness. Why was she even jittery? Since he had not asked her a question, she remained silent, not wanting to confirm she was really behind this door.

"I can tell you are standing right there," he murmured.

Her knees weakened, and she rested her forehead against the wood. Could he really?

The duke made an odd sound, almost like a groan. Was he hurt?

Her damnable curiosity pushed her to ask, "What is it, Your Grace?"

"There is another scent coming from you...it was there in the woods, except now it is...richer."

Jules closed her eyes, heat flushing over her face. What

smell was that? She thought of the agitation that had kept her tossing about on the palatial bed. "Is it a bad thing...that scent?" *Oh, why am I asking?*

Into the silence, his words fell quite softly. "No. I like it."

Was it possible James could smell her burgeoning want for things she hardly understood? *Oh God.* It was too mortifying to contemplate.

"Open the door."

She stared at the door, wondering how he stood...and where. "Why?"

"I do not like speaking to you through a block of wood. I like seeing your expressions. They are very telling."

"In what way?"

"The corner of your eyes crinkle when you are amused, even if your mouth does not curve. Your eyes darken...to the green of the forest, and you place your fist beneath your chin when you are deep in thought. It is endearingly quixotic."

"You are observant," she said huskily, her heart racing.

"I've learned to be. Open the door, Wildflower."

Jules took a slow breath and released it. "I confess opening the door feels perilous."

"Oh?"

Was that amusement she heard in his tone? She clenched her hand on the door, barely noticing the ache in her fingers. "Perhaps I am overthinking the matter."

"Perhaps."

Rolling her eyes at her absurdity, Jules stepped back and opened the door. Everything about him washed over her in a dangerous wave of heat. There was a wildness about him that might never be contained. The duke remained dressed in a state of dishabille without a jacket, missing neckcloth, the opening of his shirt revealing the strong column of his throat. The clasp holding his raven hair in a queue had been removed and his locks flowed over his shoulders in a curtain of midnight silk.

The glitter of his eyes appeared stark and far too dangerous in the dim light of the hallway. The shock of it almost pushed her back into the room. Pushing aside the instinctive flight response, Jules stepped more into the hallway, closed the door behind her, and leaned against its solidness.

The duke inhaled; it was subtle yet unmistakable. A slight color tinged along the savage elegance of his cheekbones, and his lashes fluttered closed as if he needed to shut away that sense to savor whatever fragrance he detected from her. What was this hot, aching sensation throbbing at the very core of her body?

Jules jutted her chin and met his stare. "You must really learn to control your nose, Your Grace."

His lashes lifted, the gray blue of his eyes sparkling with an unfathomable gleam. "Impossible around you, I'm afraid."

She felt too breathlessly aware of him and could only glare at his pithy reply.

He reached out and pinched her chin caressingly. "Why are you here in this part of the house?"

*Oh God, why is his touch so provocative?*

"I asked to reside here and have been since Monday. You were simply unaware of it because, well…you sleep in the woods."

"Hmm, the night you stole into my chamber."

*Blast.* He really knew of it. Jules held his stare. "Your fingers are holding my chin, James."

"It is the first I am seeing you without your curled moustache…and stage face paint." His gaze caressed over her face, down to her throat, and over her body.

Jules curled her bare toes into the lush carpet, feeling as if he peered through her nightshirt to the bare flesh beneath.

"You are incredibly…lovely, Wildflower," he murmured,

meeting her regard once again. "Without the stage makeup and moustache, your skin is soft, creamy, and glows beautifully. Your lips are lush, generous, so pink and soft. There is a stubborn pride in the set of your chin, and your eyes are the finest I've ever seen."

Her heart tripped and butterflies wreaked havoc within her stomach. Jules had forgotten she no longer wore her full disguise. He thought her lovely. She wasn't certain how to feel that he looked upon her femaleness and seemed appreciative. Jules certainly did not fit the image of ladies she saw in society. How sweet, delicate, and even ethereal they sometimes appeared, at odd times filling her with bemused wonder.

"You are still holding my chin," she said softly, painfully aware they were alone in the west wing, with only a few wall sconces providing light in the long hallway. They felt intimately sheltered.

The duke lowered his hand. "You should return to the east wing," he said gruffly.

"Do you really wish me to?" The duke did not respond, and some tension eased from Jules. "Are you sleeping here tonight?"

"Yes."

They stared at each other, and she nervously wondered why everything felt so...*heightened*. "I—"

"I spoke with my sister. We watched the stars."

Jules leaned more against the door. "How was the experience?"

A small frown split his forehead before his expression smoothed. "It was pleasant. I might watch more with her in the future."

Gladness surged inside her chest, and she smiled. "I am sure Lady Felicity will be happy to know it."

He stared at Jules for several beats. The air became

heavy with a promise she did not understand. She curled her toes more into the carpet, releasing a soft breath when he said, "Goodnight, Wildflower."

"Goodnight…James."

Yet neither moved. She laughed, the unexpectedness of it even surprising her. He lifted a brow in inquiry.

"Share," he commanded.

"You need to work on your manners," she said pertly. "Society will not care for your bluntness."

"I have no need to pretend with you, surely you are aware of this."

That warmed her more than it should. "I know," she said softly.

"Why did you laugh, Wildflower?"

"I merely thought it very strange that we were standing here…alone…just simply existing. A week ago, this was not my plan to be here at Longbourn Park. It is rather extraordinary how one decision can change so many things."

The eyes that stared at her so unflinchingly were deep and unfathomable.

"The Northern Sound is a vast land of ice-capped mountains and trees. Sunlight barely pierces its denseness, and its beauty intimidates even the most stalwart of hearts. I hunted deep in the forest for years and merely turned left one day toward where it always felt dangerous. The ice fell away beneath me, and the rapids dragged me for miles. That one decision led me here. It is indeed extraordinary."

*It is you who is extraordinary.*

The duke bowed, turned around, and went to his room. She watched as he gripped the doorknob but did not open his door. A tension invaded his limbs, and something warned Jules she should hurry inside her room.

"Do you know that list you told me to make?"

"Yes."

"I have been thinking about it."

Inexplicably her heart started to pound. "Good."

"What are your expectations of what I should do with the things I have on it?"

Jules swallowed. "Find them...experience them. They are the ordinary things in life that will help you reclaim the part of yourself you had to leave behind to survive. You craved touch because you were deprived for so long, James. Do not be alarmed if the other things coming to you speak to your basic heart or baser self. Trust in those wants and needs and see them fulfilled. Some measure of normalcy might return then."

He dropped his hand from the latch. "I want to taste a woman...I want to take her mouth against mine, savor the feel of her lips, enjoy the glide of her tongue against mine, feel the vibration of her moan against my mouth."

"I am sure there are many ladies who will eagerly oblige," she whispered, shocked that she hated the image of him kissing another.

"You?"

Jules's heart thumped. "No, of course not!"

"And if I want it to be you?"

"Once again spoken like a true duke," she said, feeling a measure of amusement. "Be aware that while many ladies will be eager to fulfill all your wants, there are some who will also deny you, Your Grace."

He turned around, and in two steps, he was right there, touching her. Her heart started to pound its harshest beat as he reverently cupped her jaw, sliding his thumb to the fluttering pulse at her throat.

"James?" she gasped, her pulse tapping even faster at his intensity.

"I do not wish it to be you because you are convenient, Jules Southby. The desire cuts its way deep into me simply because of you."

The words shouldn't have sent a thrill racing through her chest, but they did.

"Do you understand what I am saying, Wildflower?"

She was silent, still, for long seconds. "Yes."

The duke tugged her into his arms and pressed his mouth against hers. They stilled against each other, the awareness of his actions seemingly washing over them at the same instance.

*He is kissing me*, she thought dazedly. "I want more," she whispered.

James groaned, flicked his tongue along her lips, and she gasped. *Oh God*. From his mouth Jules tasted something dark and dangerous, something frightening yet also exhilarating.

The kisses against her mouth were small, provocative nips that should have felt questioning, but it was clear he coaxed her with arousing knowledge. Raw pleasure rushed through Jules like a petal unfurling inside her chest. She moaned, rising onto her toes to slip her arms around his neck. He caged her against the door and kissed her deeply, fisting the short strands of her hair, sliding his tongue against hers. Jules felt consumed. There was a terrible hunger in his embrace, but there was also a reverence in the way his mouth moved atop hers, a slow savoring of her taste as if he wanted to greedily suck her in but instead tenderly held her close.

A crackling liveliness surged inside Jules's veins, energizing Jules from the inside. She fisted her fingers through the thick strands of his hair, responding with helpless greed. It felt as if he surrounded her, stealing the air and all the logical reasoning that had guided her for years. Want and fear wrenched through her, tugging her in different directions. The duality of the needs clashing terrified Jules.

*Do I run to you or away from you? Do I chase this feeling or hide from it?*

She felt his heartbeat as if it was hers, and she didn't want to ever lose that feeling.

Their kiss grew wild and desperate. Their tongues tangled hotly, then slowed to a more provocative dance and glide. It felt as if he ravished and also savored her. It was an impossible heat, a delight that singed her from the inside and sent her into a swirling quagmire of want and lust. That invisible yet potent power went even lower, tugging at that secret place between her thighs.

Her want for him was exposed in the soft breathy whimpers from her mouth to his and how she trembled against him. Jules felt vulnerable...yet powerful, for the duke also trembled against her.

James pulled his mouth from hers, breathing raggedly. Her chest rose and fell, her breathing a bit fractured. James dragged her into his lungs, dipping and sensually running his nose over the curve of her neck and down...

Jules squeaked, her shock visceral when he went down to her navel and lower still to her quim. He pressed his nose to the space between her legs and inhaled. A fiery blush covered her entire body. "James!"

"You are wet, Wildflower. And your scent...*fuck*!"

His voice was a rumble of sensual want, and her belly grew hot and tight. Jules knew what he wanted, and she wanted to give it to him so badly, her body shook. *This is madness.*

Gripping the strands of his hair, she tugged, knowing he obliged when he rose, for she had not the strength to move him.

"This must never happen again," she whispered, shaken by what she had allowed.

Those dark eyes held hers for an unending minute. "Have you ever felt this before?"

"Never," she said, granting him the honesty he demanded with his steady regard.

James was silent for long moments before he spoke. "Neither have I, Wildflower. Why must it be denied?"

She felt light-headed, off balance. "Denial and restraint are a part of…living."

"What is the purpose of this restraint?"

"To protect oneself from consequences that might be too hard to bear," Jules said hoarsely.

He faltered into stillness before stepping back. "Perhaps in this, you are correct. I bid you goodnight, Wildflower."

This time he whirled and went inside his room without hesitation. She wilted at the closing of his door and tipped her head to the ceiling. *What just happened?* Surely it could not—

The opening of his door careened her thoughts.

"Given the primal urges and temptation beating at me, it is best I do not smell you behind that door again, Wildflower."

She swallowed. "I will remove myself from it."

He closed the door without replying. Jules smiled, at a loss as to why she did. Wrenching open her door, she spilled inside the bedchamber, hurried to the bed and under the covers, and promptly fell asleep.

# Chapter Nine

James closed the book he'd been reading for the past few hours, an annoyed grunt leaving him and echoing in his bedchamber. Leaning over, he set aside his copy of *Progress and Poverty* by Henry George, an American author whose work had even reached England's shore, on the desk beside his bed. It was just one more book added to the stack he read this week.

James had always been an avid reader, and he'd devoured many books upon his return, keen to understand the societal and political changes he had missed. He could not show himself to be ignorant of the laws and state of society when he entered Parliament at the next sitting. Some might challenge his stance and any motions he would support simply because of the fact he had been missing and had not received any formal education by attending Cambridge like his father, grandfather, and great-grandfather.

Concentrating was proving to be difficult, and James knew the source of his current distraction—Jules Southby. That inexplicable sensation rattled inside his chest, and he closed his eyes against the memory that had been his constant companion. The feel of the wildflower's mouth was still imprinted upon his, the sweet taste of her still an indescribable wonder on James's tongue. Three days had passed since he took her mouth in that carnal kiss. Three damnable days of a hunger unlike anything he had ever known. Nothing replaced that taste, not even eating or drinking several glasses of brandy each night before retiring. James drank the bitterest coffee, the harshest liquor, and even sweetened his tea deplorably. Her taste had become a part of him and would not leave.

Yet this damnable craving did not stop at her flavor. There had been a time James felt such intense need for physical contact it had petrified him, for there had been no one he could touch or receive it from in return. His survival instinct had killed the desire for that contact, and even though somewhere inside of him he wanted to be touched, there was another part that preferred the exile of the desire which he had forced upon himself from necessity. Yet now he wanted Jules to touch him…and he wanted to touch her in return.

James hissed at the needs pummeling his body and with an irritated grunt, he pushed the covers from himself and tugged on his trousers. James padded barefoot from his chambers, down the winding hallway of the west wing, and outside into the bracing cold. The chill of the night wrapped around him like a soothing blanket. The feel of the grass brushed the soles of his bare feet as he walked across the lawns toward the edge of the wood. He would sleep in his house in the forest tonight.

But first…

James plucked a few leaves from a bush and tossed them into his mouth. He would eradicate her taste so he could damn well concentrate on what was necessary.

"Good heavens. You are eating *grass*," a choked voice

said from behind him.

He closed his eyes and slapped a hand over his forehead, as if that small sting would spare him from the need crackling through his veins. She drifted closer, her scent floating before her like a siren's call.

"Why are you here, Wildflower?"

"Well...I could hear you pacing in your room like a caged animal...and when you left, I followed," she said with an unapologetic air. "I was concerned. Why are you eating grass?"

James turned slowly to face her. He raked his eyes over the gentleman's suit of clothes she was wearing. She had discarded her cravat and her white linen shirt was undone at the throat, although only the top button had been opened. Her coat and trousers were dark gray with a faint pinstripe and her waistcoat almost black in a stiffer cloth than most men wore. James suspected it helped prevent any shadows in the cloth revealing her form beneath, noting that the curves he had felt against his body were not distinguishable in any way. Southby truly had the appearance of a slim, refined gentleman. "You *heard* me pacing?"

Those lovely green eyes widened, and a sheepish smile touched her mouth. "My room is connected to yours, Your Grace."

For a moment he heard nothing but the sound of his own heartbeat like a war drum within his ears. "You are beyond the connecting door in my chambers."

"Yes."

"A few nights ago, you were across the hallway." And a mouthwatering temptation he'd wanted to ruthlessly devour.

She lifted a shoulder in a shrug, but a slight pink dusted her cheekbones. "I thought it best to be closer."

"I did not smell you." Impossible, given how much she had occupied his thoughts.

Her eyes gleamed with laughter. "I thought I was rather clever to put several vases of flowers in the room, and also sprinkle the chamber with lavender oil. I believe it worked."

James would allow her to think that. He had still smelled her; however, he had simply believed it to be a remnant of her haunting after he had checked the room across the hallway and found it empty.

Her eyes caressed over his bare chest, before flicking back to meet his regard. "Are you not cold, Your Grace?"

"No."

She stared at him for a beat, unrattled by his curtness. "Do you wish me to return inside?"

And deny himself her presence? He let those feelings of want and hunger and primal possession wash over him, for they were sensations that no longer lingered in a dark, empty space. They seemed to take up every corner and crevice of his body, and suddenly it felt damnably foolish to deny its existence. "No. Stay."

Her shoulders relaxed. "I gathered you have been avoiding me."

"I have been busy, Wildflower, nothing more."

James turned and walked away into the wood, heading for his sanctuary high in those trees. An irritated sound left her, no doubt at his presumed rudeness, but she followed him, alerting the forest she approached with her trampling footsteps. The darkness covered them, and she reached out and gripped his hand. James stopped as if he had slammed into a wall. Jules snatched her hand away as if she'd been stung.

"I am sorry."

"Do not be," he said gruffly. "I like when you touch me."

James felt her smile more than saw it, then she slipped her hand over his once more and he led her along the darkened path until they reached the clearing leading to his tree cottage. The paths were barely lit tonight, and the moonlight struggled to shine through the towering trees. Still, moonbeams painted her face in soft light, and he spied the curious hunger there.

"Would you like to come up with me?"

Her fingers tightened on his arm, before Jules released him. "I suspect it was not easy for you to welcome me into your sanctuary. Thank you, Your Grace."

Wasn't that the problem? It was remarkably easy.

. . .

The duke hauled himself up the tree with extraordinary grace. He had no use for the ladder, and Jules suspected he'd perhaps installed it for his young valet.

"Follow me, Wildflower. Be careful and watch where you step."

Excitement thrumming through her veins, she grabbed onto the rope ladder and started to climb. They were several steps up when she slipped, sliding down the rough bark. Moving with shocking speed and agility, he caught her only using one arm and swung her so that she found purchase against a limb.

"Goodness," she said shakily, glancing down at her palm which stung something fiercely. It would have been a nasty fall if he had not caught her. "You were rather remarkable just now…" Jules's words tapered off at the expression on his face. "What is it, Your Grace?"

"You are breakable. I did not consider your fragility."

Jules peered down at her skinned palm for long moments, unable to look up at him. There was a throb of awareness in his voice, as if he thought she did not match his strength. "I grew up as a boy. I've lived as a gentleman…I *am* living as a man. This is a mere scratch." She kept her tone light, though her heart pounded. "I have several of them."

"Why are you afraid?"

She met his gaze. "I am not."

"Your heart is racing."

She jolted. "Surely you do not expect me to believe all your senses are so heightened you can hear my heartbeat?"

Humor deepened the blue of his eyes. "I lived with wolves in a den in a cave for years."

Shock tore through her. "*Wolves*?"

"Yes."

His affirmation was simply too incredible. "And they did not attack you?"

"No."

"Will you like to tell me about it?"

"Which part of you is asking?" he asked, a curious lilt in his tone.

"What do you mean?"

"Is it the mind doctor who wants to know, the one who will report her findings and conclusions to Dr. Southby for dissection? Or my Wildflower?"

*My Wildflower.* Jules dismissed the intimate and possessive way he said her moniker and thought about his question. It was both. Yet she was also aware deep down it was more than a desire to explore his experiences for scientific reasons. She wanted to know who he was...simply for herself. And what she learned she did not want to write down for others to read and speculate upon, to analyze, dissect, and form theories.

She wanted to hold it close and unpack it in the night when she lay in her bed alone. She wanted his words only for herself. The awareness shattered her, and as she stared at him, a large lump grew in her throat. "I believe it is best I return inside, Your Grace."

"Stay with me." He hauled her up onto a large branch that

easily held their weight, lifting his hand to cup her cheek. He hissed, pleasure sparking in his gaze. All from touching her. The awareness was a painful ache that spread to encompass her body.

In a tender glide, he rubbed his calloused thumb over her cheek. She loved the way he touched her, how he allowed her to touch him.

"I believe a part of your job is to ask about my day, hmm?"

The gentle request hooked low in her belly and tugged. Why is it that she couldn't look at him and not feel that irregular skip of her heartbeat? Jules had been around many gentlemen throughout her lifetime, and not one had ever made her breath catch or her breasts ache beneath their linen bindings.

It was a damnable curiosity. Suddenly she wished to have had a female friend she could sit and speak with, a person she could ask about all these feelings and questions bubbling inside. When she'd decided to leave England, her mother had tried to speak with her about being wary of the opposite sex and their wily ways. Jules had been so astonished she had laughingly brushed her aside. Her entire life had been lived as a gentleman, and she wanted to maintain that life. How would there ever be an encounter where she had to worry about the flattering attentions of a gentleman? Now a part of her wished she had listened, perhaps there would have been something in her mama's gentle advice that would help her in this moment.

Bafflingly, the duke seemed to have aroused her sensuality and she could not understand these complex feelings. Jules had always known it was there, but it had been more of a mild irritation and not this insistent urge to...to do what she did not know, and frustration surged through her veins in a fiery wave. She felt intrigued, unsettled, heated, and flushed. The weight of his stare, and the soft press of his thumb to her cheek filled her with aching want.

"Somehow going into your tree house feels...also dangerous."

He smiled. "I believe one must challenge dangerous things to feel truly alive."

It was instinct that prompted Jules to turn her head and nip the pad of his thumb before kissing the skin that she bruised with a tender brush of her mouth. She felt driven by something far more complex than mere desire. This wanting went beyond a physical need, and it scared Jules, for she had never dreamed it was possible to feel this way about anyone. What would it be like when they inevitably walked away from each other because they simply did not belong in each other's world? Would she even miss his presence? Would dreams of kissing him still visit her sleep and rob her of proper rest?

He held out his hand and she took it, allowing him to take her up several more branches to the tree house. There was a large opening, and Jules stepped through it, her breath catching in wonder. The tree house smelt of pine trees which Jules assumed were what the unstripped logs it was made of had been. There were two large windows which were simple bare openings into the fresh air of the woods, and hinged to the openings were two pairs of shutters which were half closed against the night air. Through them Jules could see a few stars in the dark indigo of the night sky.

There was little in the way of furnishings, although there was a bed of sorts, covered by some shaggy dark fur. On the floor another cream-colored fur was spread over the bare boards. From its irregular shape Jules assumed it had once belonged to a bear of some kind.

One rustic wall had a built-in bookshelf filled with dozens of books. The only other furnishings were a small card table and a battered armchair. On the table was a small pile of books, a newspaper, some sheets of paper with a stone resting on top of them, an oil lamp and tinder box. There was no fireplace, but beside one corner was a small oil burner which would provide some warmth on a cold night. There was also a leather bag leaning against another wall, which Jules thought might contain wine or water.

She went and sat on one of the window ledges, peering out above several trees. They were a long distance from the ground and the view was simply breathtaking.

"So, wolves?" she murmured.

"Yes, wolves."

"Would you tell me about it, James?"

James sat on the ledge of the other window, and they stared out into the lush beauty of the night for several minutes.

"Within a few days of being lost, I stumbled upon a small pup hanging from a high ledge on the side of a mountain. It was my first sign of life, and my desperate hunger led me to believe I only needed to get that pup and eat it. Raw if I had to."

Arrested, Jules shifted, staring at his stark profile.

"Somehow I went down that mountain face, breaking my fingernails until they bled."

James leaned against the window, lifting his face to the sky. "How I had survived to this point is a mystery. I was bitterly cold and had walked for days. The white around me was endless with no discernable direction in which to go, the wind's brutal pounding against my skin cut into me like a poison-tipped knife. Wanting to lie down and sleep was a lure, but somehow, I knew it meant death, and I wanted to live."

Jules closed her eyes, letting the smooth cadence of his voice take her to another place...to those ice-capped mountains and the stark, cruel beauty of them.

"I rescued the pup, but I could not eat it. Instead I bound its broken limb and continued walking with it. I passed out and when I came to, I was in a cave. The alpha had bit into my jacket, even breaking through to my flesh to drag me there."

"That…my God, James, that is most incredible."

"It was. The pack even shared their meal with me, and I fell onto it like a ravenous animal."

"What was it?"

His gaze snagged hers. "Raw meat. From which animal I did not know. I cast up my accounts minutes later, but to live I had to continue eating and make it stay down."

The shock of those words settled over her. Jules knew there was so much more to his experiences and acknowledged the unyielding will it must have taken to survive such odds.

"The wolves…did they accept you in their pack?"

A small smile tugged at his mouth. "I was always on the edge of their family. I was different than they were, but somehow, they understood I saved their cub, and that I was alone. I hunted with them…and when they traveled, I moved with them. I adapted to the wilds, learned to feel the hint of danger at the back of my neck. If I hunted alone, I carried back my kill to share with the pack, always. I learned to run at a pace to keep up with the pack and at times when I fell behind, they waited."

Wild wolves had been his family. She glanced at the bearskin rug on the small cot, recalling the rumors that he had killed a bear. At the time she had dismissed it as a ludicrous gossip on a rabidly curious society, clearly borne from the evidence of the things with which he returned home. "Did you kill a bear?"

"Luna and I did."

"Luna?"

"The pup I rescued," he said, an echo of something indefinable in his tone. "I believe she was truly the only one in the pack who thought of me as a friend. Often we slept beside each other and shared our warmth. Out hunting one day we came upon a bear. It was ferocious and went after Luna."

"You didn't leave her," she said softly.

"Of course not. We fought and we took it down."

Jules smiled. "I am glad you had her. There are other..." She cleared her throat. "There are others in history who have survived such insurmountable odds when pitted against nature. Many lost their sense of self and even emerged feral. You are very resilient, Your Grace."

"Luna allowed me to tell her stories of my family," he said drily. "There were times she replied in yips and howls, but she listened most avidly."

Jules imagined man and wolf together, by a fire in a cave, one talking and the other paying attention and keeping each other company. That unknown emotion squeezed her chest. "How long were you with Luna and the pack?"

"Years," he said softly, looking out into the night sky.

"How many were there?"

"Seven." He shifted, his gaze landing on her like an anvil. "Tell me about yourself, Wildflower. What do you enjoy?"

The question startled her, and she hesitated.

"We exchange our truths, remember? Are you unwilling?"

The duke was utterly still as he awaited her answer. They stared at each other in silence for several moments. Jules did not understand why her heart started its slow and almost painful drumbeat. "I enjoy psychology. It was my area of specialty at university."

"Which you had the privilege to study because to the world you are a gentleman."

His expression was difficult to interpret. "Yes."

"It is rather interesting you were not discovered. Did you not take lodgings at the university?"

She gripped her fingers together. "I took it nearby from

an elderly couple who provided a room and dinner. They were very kind."

He studied her for a moment. "Why did you choose psychology?"

"Growing up, my father used to sit me on his lap and read his books to me. They were rather complex, and I hardly understood the theories, but I held on to his words, basking in the sound of his voice, loving that he wanted to share his love and passion with me. Somehow my interest sparked and grew, and I found myself combing his library to read the different thoughts and concepts of our time. By the time I was twelve I had read books like *A Description of the Retreat* and found it enlightening."

"Those readings helped you decide you wanted to be a mind doctor?"

She shifted on the ledge, folding her body so that she could rest her chin atop her knee. "Books like *Principles of Physiological Psychology* by Wilhelm Wundt. It was published only a little over a decade ago. It is a most brilliant read, James. I could tell my father wanted me to follow in his footsteps and I was happy for I enjoyed all the knowledge I consumed. I also had an experience with a young girl in our village that helped shaped my desire for the pursuit."

"Would you tell me of that experience?"

Jules frowned, pulling up on her recollection of the matter. "Her parents considered her wild and difficult, unmanageable was the phrase the townspeople used. They even thought she might be afflicted, given her behavior was so wildly different from what they or society expected. Louise was only twelve years of age…at the time only two years younger than myself. My father took her into our home and tried to help her. He would spend so many hours trying to speak with her…to study and understand her reasoning so he could alter, or I should say positively influence her behavior through understanding and guidance. She resisted Father at every instance, and he concluded she might need to be institutionalized. My heart broke for Louise, and I wanted to understand the pain in her eyes. I wanted to help her. I started speaking to her...without any expectations of reciprocity."

Jules leaned her head against the wooden slat behind her. "It took days, but I did not mind that she remained indifferent to my overtures. I hungered to understand her because I wanted to help her. Slowly Louise opened to me, revealing the wound that haunted her."

"What was it?"

Jules smiled. "Love."

He arched a brow and made a low, rough sound of disbelief in his throat. "*Love*?"

"Louise lacked love from both her parents. She had never known what it was like to have their arms around her, to feel the comfort of their touch, or to bask in their praises and acceptance."

"Such a simple thing would see her altered?"

"Yes, because it is not really that simple, is it?" Jules held his gaze. "Love is the compelling reason behind life."

The duke went remarkably still. "Do expound."

"How does one live without love when it is so intrinsic. How do we not desperately long for it," she said, aware of a hidden part of her opening within his presence. "Love can be affectionate, kind, tender, forgiving, and passionate, but it should never hurt or deliberately inflict wounds. Love *is* healing...enchanting...even bewitching. That Louise had lacked the foundation of such essential needs from her parents, it was logical that she would then be denied it also in adulthood because she did not know how to recognize love and might be led down dangerous paths to seek that which she did not understand she longed for."

"Did Louise heal?"

"It took months but yes. She learned to understand her actions and what it was she lacked and the healthy, sustainable way to achieve it. Louise is also recently married and is quite happy. I loved that there were theories that could teach me about someone's wound and how to help them overcome those wounds to enjoy a better life. How could I not study it more?"

There was a curious glint in his gaze as he stared at her. "Is that why you are here now, to help me heal a perceived wound?"

Jules said tenderly, "You are not addled. You are lonely, perhaps feeling a hollowness that you do not understand. That empty feeling inside was born from being alone for so long without human touch or interaction…and because you had to use your will to conquer your fear of death and loss, you have exiled yourself from feeling. The more you share with me and your family the less alone you will feel, James. The more you allow touch…life will once again feel normal. I am here at Longbourn park to help you realize this, but I am here tonight in this tree cottage because I want to be with you."

Something intense flared through his eyes, and she suddenly felt out of sorts. They stared at each other for several long moments. Finally he asked, in a gruff tone, "What do you long for, Wildflower?"

"I am quite content with my lot in life," she said, aware of the sudden racing in her heart, and the desperate ache of an unfulfilled longing she did not understand. The duke could tell her heartbeat had increased. Dropping her foot from the ledge, she stood. "I should return inside."

She did not wait for his answer but surged toward the door. Jules felt as if she were running away, and a part of her hated that she did, for she did not shy away from complex situations but yearned to understand them. Also, why did being here with the duke suddenly feel so damnable complicated? Her steps faltered at the wide-open entrance, and she whirled around only to gasp.

"I did not hear you move," she said, peering up at him, aware of how close he was to her.

His lips quirked slowly. "It is a skill I've mastered over the years. Your scent changed when I asked what you longed for...so tell me."

Her gaze dropped to the cruel yet sensual curve of his mouth. A delicate thread of intimacy interlaced itself around them.

"Ah...now I see," the duke murmured.

She wrenched her gaze to his, noting the dangerous glitter lurking in the depths of his eyes. "What do you see, Your Grace?" she demanded caustically.

"You want the same thing that I want. Only you are afraid of it."

Those words snapped taut from him, as if he deplored the very idea of weakness or fear. It caused all of her senses to feel raw and painfully aware of him—her heart was beating absurdly fast and erratic. Jules hated that she felt as if she would crumple if she did not kiss him. The want clawing through her was a terrible thing indeed.

*I am afraid of nothing*, she wanted to snarl, yet she made no reply, only lurched toward him as if some inexorable force shoved her.

Perhaps the duke moved as well, for suddenly he was there, cupping her cheek and lifting her face upward. His fingers speared into her hair, clenching into the short, silky strands as his lips covered hers. His tongue claimed hers with possessive hunger, and she sighed helplessly into his kiss, the wicked sensation of wanting to crawl inside his skin claiming Jules.

His kiss did things. To her, to her body. She felt an ache

low in her belly...and even lower. The feeling made her hot and restless, and she made that little sound in the back of her throat again and pressed closer to him. It felt as if the duke sucked her inside of himself and consumed her.

He spun with her, pressing her back into the rough wood of the tree house. There was a desperate air to their kisses, and she craved it, moulding her body to his, all but climbing his leg to get closer. James touched her everywhere, the curve of her throat, the press of his thumb against her pulse, a drag of his palm over the slimness of her back, and down to the lush curves of her backside.

He nudged her legs apart with his powerful thighs and settled in the space he'd created. She arched to James, her own thighs widening, her body straining against him. He broke their kiss, his fingers inching down her stomach, slowly, so slowly until he was at the opening of her trousers.

Jules couldn't look away from the savage beauty of his gaze. His gray-blue eyes were drowsy, dark with sensual heat. He tugged the shirt loose, opened her trousers, and shoved them down. There was something savage and arousing about his intensity. Jules felt faint, yet she did not stop him. She couldn't, not when she wanted his touch so much. His fingers delved between her folds, and she opened her legs as far as the trousers would allow in instinctive want.

The rasp of calloused fingertips against her soft folds sent shivers of heat cascading through her limbs. He stroked his fingers between the aching flesh of her sex, rubbing over her nub. The one she had touched a few times in soft curiosity before she had snatched back her fingers.

Jules jerked to her toes as a long, desperate moan left her lips when his palm pressed against her swollen clitoris, two fingers sliding deep inside her sex. Jules cried out with the burning pleasure-pain of the impalement.

"The fit is tight," he murmured, his voice low and rough.

"You'll feel incredible on my cock, Wildflower."

Heat blushed across her entire body and the tension that had mounted the instant he touched her snapped, and wetness flooded his fingers, and a twisted knot of need thumping in her belly loosened.

Jules dropped her forehead forward, bit into his shoulder and she swore he growled. A thumb and forefinger gently pinched her chin, lifted her face, and then he was kissing her again. The stroke of his tongue against her was deep and carnal, a perfect mimicry of the way his fingers moved inside her sex.

*Oh God.*

Each wicked stroke brought an awful burst of pleasure and pain, sweet delight, and utter madness. James dragged his mouth from hers, moving his lips over her jaw, leaving fire in their wake, coaxing and seducing. "I want inside, Wildflower."

His fingers flexed so that she would not be in doubt of exactly where he wanted to be. She had been in enough pubs, acting as a gentleman to know he spoke of swivving... or tupping...or even as some of her mates had crudely said, fucking. Hearing those words and phrases then had not even filled her with mild curiosity. Now her knees weakened, and she clung to James, her heart a pounding drum in her ears.

Temptation and want beat at her senses and everything inside her screamed to say yes. His thumb glided over her nub once again...the move soft and insistent. Jules moaned. She couldn't help clenching her muscles, holding his palm in place. His fingers retreated, then in one slow, delicious movement slid inside her again, going provocatively deeper. Brilliant flares of pleasure tore through her entire body, and she cried out.

Alarmed by her visceral response, Jules pushed away from the duke and stumbled back. He was a male wonderfully aroused, his cock surely too large of a bulge against the front of his trousers. The intensity emanating from him frightened her, and before she could do something reckless, she tugged up her trousers, closing the flap with shaking fingers, and then ran from the tree house.

Jules went down the roped steps so fast she stumbled. When his hand caught her waist to steady her, she slapped at it, and James released her. Jules descended the rope ladder, and once she was on the ground, she tried to run but her legs simply gave way and she dropped into the grass.

"I am the one that has lost all sense of self and am an addlepate!" she gasped, her breath leaving her on a harsh gust. *Oh, what am I thinking?*

Jules pressed her forehead between her knees and took huge gulping breaths. She had almost given herself to the duke. *Bloody hell!* She dug her fingers into the grass and plucked out thick clumps and tossed them aside with her frustration.

Jules wanted to be with him so desperately. She wanted to make love with him, to allow him to sweep her away into a world of pleasure she might never get to experience again. Jules pushed to her feet, whirled around, and looked up. He was standing there on the ledge, peering down at her. She could feel his hunger deep inside her body. A trickle of perspiration ran between the small hollow of her breasts and heat flushed over her.

A little whimper broke in her throat. Jules lurched forward and clambered back up that roped ladder until she was standing in front of him.

"I cannot leave," she said hoarsely, fisting her hands at her side.

His eyes gleamed with a carnal savagery that should have frightened her, but she only felt assured that he wanted her just as badly.

"Then do not leave, Wildflower. Stay with me."

A tense silence ensued. A dangerous charge emanated from him, lighting every nerve in her body.

"It is not so simple." Her words were whispered but steady.

Denial flashed in his eyes. "Why must it be complicated?"

The words fell unbidden from her lips. "Should we become lovers, what then, James?"

Those dissecting eyes settled on her once more. "We are lovers with no expectations of each other. I will promise you nothing more than pleasure, nor do I expect any more from you."

Here was a chance to experience pleasures of the flesh without compromising anything. When it ended, she could move on and live her dream of being a noted doctor of the mind, living the life she dictated for herself and not society or anyone else. The sweetest longing beat at her senses, even as a sense of fright filled her chest. Could she tangle herself with a man like the duke and escape intact? Jules sensed he had the power to break her, even if she as yet did not understand how he would do it. Logic and instinct screamed at her to run away from the madness he was proposing. "I want..."

He took a step closer. "Yes?"

It felt imperative to be honest with him even if the vulnerable sensation almost cleaved her in two. "I want to experience pleasure with you, James. I've never felt this... desire before. It is baffling, thrilling, and I want it, not only because I may never feel this again but because it is...with *you*."

He closed his eyes briefly. "I can smell your fear, Wildflower...and also your need." His hand darted out, gripped her hip, and hauled her against his chest. His fingertip stroked along her chin lightly. "What do you fear? Tell me."

"I do not know because it is instinctive."

The duke leaned down and rubbed his cheek against hers, like a sensual jungle predator.

"James?"

"I might be rough and no longer refined but you'll be safe and treasured in my arms. I vow it, Wildflower."

The shock of those words wrenched her heart in several directions.

"Treasured for how long, Your Grace?" she whispered, sensing she was on the cusp of falling into something she did not understand.

"For as long as I am able."

Only another promise that there will be an end before they even started. He arched her and licked along the curve of her throat. "My mouth is aching to taste you…"

"You are tasting me," she whispered, surrendering to the madness surging between them.

"Did you forget I want to lick you everywhere, Wildflower?"

Twisting dark knots of sensation rose between her legs. His head lowered as though he couldn't stop the action, until he was right at the hollow between her legs. He inhaled deeply. "I want to lick you here."

His voice was rough, filled with hunger, tugging at the lonely, empty place that lingered within her, stroking over her body with shocking heat. The taste of the duke was running through her veins. Her belly knotted, and the breath inside her chest stilled.

"Then taste me there," she invited, softly gasping when he swung her into his arms, took a few steps toward the small cot, and bore her down onto its softness.

He sucked at the flesh of her throat, and she knew it would leave one of those violent, strawberry marks. James seemed to inhale her into his lungs as he went down the length of her body. She reached between them and undid her flap, pushing her trousers down. He grabbed the edges and pulled them lower.

His breathing was harsh, his forehead pressed against her quivering belly. Her trousers were still hooked at her knees, her thighs barely widened, yet he dipped his head even lower, opening her sex to his gaze and licked her.

*Oh hell!*

It felt as if lightning struck her clitoris. Jules's cry choked off as she twisted under the sensation. He slid his hands beneath her buttocks and lifted her quim to his mouth. This time Jules cried out, uncaring that her voice echoed in the stillness of the forest. He scraped his teeth over her nub of pleasure before sucking it into his mouth.

"James," she gasped.

Her fingers slid slowly into his hair, tangling into the strands until they pulled at his scalp. It was a pleasure she didn't know if she could endure. Her body was sheened with sweat, her breathing harsh, her cries desperate as he tongued her sex, stroked her hotly with his mouth. With each wicked kiss against her cunny Jules felt another part of her surrender to James. He worshipped with his tongue and teeth until she was a writhing, sobbing mess. Pressure built in sharp, wicked spikes, until ecstasy burst over her senses, sucking her under until she felt as if she couldn't breathe. Then it expanded throughout her body, and Jules felt as if she floated in clouds of bliss and satiation.

Dimly, she was aware of James carefully arching her hips and pulling her trousers up. He arranged her clothes, scooped her into his arms and took her out onto the ledge. Somehow, he sat with her in the hammock and draped her so that she lay on top of him, her back pressed against his naked chest. She could feel the pounding of his heart, and the hardness beneath her back.

James was still painfully aroused. She tried to turn in the

cage of his arms and the hammock dipped.

"Watch the stars with me," he murmured roughly by her ear.

"You are tense and unfulfilled."

"I can still smell your fear, Wildflower."

Her heart stuttered. "I..."

James held her close, resting his chin atop her head, and her body softened against his as if it had a will of its own. "I'll wait until I only smell desire from you."

Jules wondered at the fear James scented from her, as she had felt only passion in his arms. Frowning, she stared through the towering leaves of the trees into the star-studded night. Jules hadn't even known she was cold until his wonderful heat enfolded and surrounded her. This was where she wanted to be, inside the cage of his arms, feeling this inexplicable sense of comfort and belonging.

*You make me feel so much, James, and with such little effort.*

Was it that awareness that made her feel uncertain still? The weight of how she felt about the duke was unbearable. Yet Jules squared her shoulders, took a deep breath, and resolved to carry it, for it felt infinitely precious and rare, and she would not keep it for long knowing one day she would let it go.

# Chapter Ten

A couple days later, several ladies from elite families of society descended on Longbourn Park, with their parents or chaperones. Clearly the duchess had started planning a long time ago, or people were simply eager to catch a glimpse of the much talked about duke. The duchess's week-long house party was avidly written about in the newssheets back in town, with the greatest fanfare and speculation. Jules's mother sent her the announcement in the sheets which ranged from simply ridiculousness to the profane.

There had been no doubt in her mind all would accept the duchess's invitation, even if it was unusual to host a house party right before spring. Everyone was damnably curious about the Duke of Wulverton. Some would attend purely to gain information for gossip, many wanted his wealth, and some were just fascinated and secretly horrified by his experience. And even if he were insane, according to the *Morning Chronicle*, the duke was still the season's most eligible and sought-after bachelor.

Jules watched him stroll across the floor, interacting with

his family, displaying that touch of insolence, arrogance, and boredom that seemed to characterize his every action. Since their wicked encounter in the tree house, they'd not spent any time alone together. She was thankful for that, for while Jules knew an affair with the duke was inevitable, she wanted to savor falling into his arms and bed, and not recklessly tumble into it. Everything with the duke felt fast and impossible to stop. She did not like that feeling of not being in control, and at least in this way, she would walk into whatever they had together with her eyes and heart open to the full experience.

Since that night she had begun to look forward to his appearance each day with mingled excitement and apprehension. What she had done was observe the duke's interactions and made a few notes. The discussions she had with her father each night only revealed that he, too, believed the duke was in possession of all his faculties. Jules agreed, even though it was evident that his experiences over the last decade had shaped a gentleman that was incapable of being altered.

Even with that supposition there existed a shift between the duke and his sister, for it was evident in Lady Felicity's smiles and her interactions with the duke. He appeared more indulgent with her, whereas he stood aloof and watchful with the rest of his family. His mother was delighted by this progress even as sadness still shadowed her eyes. Uncle Hubert watched this change with more suspicion, and the cousin who had been ousted from any possible inheritance of the dukedom had departed for town only this morning.

"My nephew seems to have taken to you, Mr. Southby," a crisp voice said at her elbow. "I wonder why is that?"

Jules turned and almost groaned at the sight of his Aunt Cecily holding a lorgnette over her eyes as she stared at Jules. His aunt, Lady Shrewsbury, a countess, was a rather eccentric lady who had too much fondness for elaborate hats and coiffures. Today her gown was a deep shade of purple that harked back to earlier days. Although it was styled similar to current fashions, the ornate cloth and ornamentation suggested the lady would prefer to dress in a crinoline and her stiff posture was used to more rigid corsetry. Her face was long but unwrinkled and so it was hard to guess at her age. His aunt's hair was snowy white and piled high in an elaborate confection of curls and jewels which would not have been considered excessive by the late, no-longer-lamented Queen Marie-Antoinette.

"It is perhaps because we are close in age, my lady," Jules politely murmured.

The countess pursed her lips, lowered the lorgnette, and skewered Jules with her direct glare.

"Your father revealed you are three and twenty young man, you are hardly close in age to the duke, and it would not benefit you to presume any friendship."

It was amusing, but she understood there was some hurt underneath that pique. "His Grace only needs time to reacclimate with his family," Jules said gently. "I suspect you were once close?"

The countess's eyes widened, and her fingers tightened over the lorgnette. "Has he...has he mentioned me to you, Mr. Southby?"

"I am sorry, my lady, he has not. The duke hardly speaks of his past or his family, however, his reticence is expected. He is learning to trust others again when for so long he has only trusted in his own instincts, which is the most primal part of us and has little to do with learned, civilized behavior."

The countess sniffed, narrowing her gaze on him. "He allows you to touch him. I wonder why is that."

Jules jolted. She had not been aware the family observed them so attentively. Keeping her expression carefully composed, she murmured, "Only fleetingly, my lady."

The countess *harrumphed* but continued staring at her nephew.

"Do you truly believe there will be a time that James… that he will return to the lad we all knew and love?"

Jules folded her hands behind her back. "No."

The countess snapped her regard to Jules, her eyes widening. "I beg your pardon?"

"Harsh experiences have shaped your nephew, my lady. How can he be the same? Are you the same lady as you were ten years ago? I doubt it. Perhaps the family can learn to accept the changes presented and love him still for it," she said gently.

The countess considered her with a measured stare. "I suppose that is what your studies of those newfangled ideas taught?"

"Some," she replied, careful to suppress her amusement.

The countess carried on, and Jules went outdoors and headed over to her father who sat underneath a gazebo. He was furiously writing in a notepad, barely sparing her a glance when she sat on the bench opposite him. Earlier she had answered his questions about the duke's behavior, careful to only share observations that did not violate the duke's trust.

Jules waited for her father to complete his observations, staring at the ladies who peppered the lawns like the prettiest and most delicate of butterflies. They preened and walked with lovely grace, their smiles beautiful and flirtatious, their laughter tinkling and airy. They all stared at the duke like he was a great prize to be won, a few expressions were wary, but most seemed challenged.

Did they secretly wish for his Grace to fall in love with them?

*Who are you, James, and why do you still seem like an enigma?*

As if he heard her silent question, the duke shifted his

regard, and their gazes collided across the expanse of the lawns. The corners of his eyes crinkled, and there was a slight tug at the sides of his mouth, yet a full smile did not form. More by habit than anything else, Jules checked to ensure her moustache was firmly in place, before dipping her head in a respectful manner.

The memory of his mouth against her most intimate flesh brought a rush of heat to her face, and Jules looked away from him. Instead, she directed her regard to a young lady who sauntered over to the duke, dipped into a most elegant curtsy, and started to engage him in conversation. Jules directed her regard to the duke, searching his expression. She could not read what he thought but he seemed to be politely responding to the young lady. The duchess who observed from a short distance away gave the pleased appearance of the cat who stole the cream.

The duchess waited a few beats before joining her son and the young lady with two of the duke's aunts. He courteously held out his arm to the young lady, who fluttered her lashes up at him, her mouth curving into a rather beautiful smile.

What was it like to be courted? Jules wondered if all ladies felt the same twisting sensation of want and deep yearning she felt whenever she encountered the duke. Was such a feeling common, or was it singularly unique?

"What is that look of longing on your face?"

Startled, she dropped her regard from the lady and shifted to meet her father's gaze.

"I was thinking about courtship."

The shrewd gaze of her father lingered on Jules's face.

"It is human to think about companionship. I fully expect that you will start thinking about taking a wife yourself, Jules. However, those ladies are not for you. We do not have the connections or wealth for you to hang your hat for an earl or a marquess's daughter."

Shocked, she laughed. "Papa, I assure you I am not thinking about any of the ladies in that manner. I would not dare to be so presumptuous in my interactions, however little they are with the duchess's guests."

Her father studied her, brows furrowed. He twirled the pencil between his thumb and forefinger. "Have you developed feelings for someone that you wish to speak about?"

Oh God, this was beyond uncomfortable. "No, Father. And if I should, I would not discuss it with you. That would be a private matter I must see to myself."

A smile hovered about his mouth and his eyes gleamed with sudden humor. Her heart lightened to see it there, and Jules shared a smile with her father, that ache surfacing in her heart once more.

"Well, whichever young lady you take to be your wife will be very lucky indeed. You are a fine fellow, son."

Jules stared at him, the heaviness returning to her shoulders. "What if I should live the life of a bachelor?"

Her father pushed his spectacles atop his nose. "I thought that of myself once; the only thing that mattered to me was scholarly pursuit. You are very much like me, and I am proud you have followed in my footsteps with your studies. Very proud. I also know that, like me, when you meet the right person, your perspective will change on many things."

She closed her fingers on the edge of the gazebo railing. Was it possible the sensations of want were the same for men and women? "What did it feel like, Papa, when you met Mama?"

A faraway look entered her father's eyes, and he sighed. "It felt like life suddenly made sense. That bit of life that always seemed empty even if one did not understand the reason for that emptiness was filled, and I knew your mother was the lady for me."

Unexpected anger wrenched through her chest, and she took a deep breath. "If Mama was so very precious to you, Papa, why was it so very important for you to have a male heir?"

Papa jerked, before faltering into stillness.

"What do you speak of?" he demanded gruffly, lowering the pencil and closing his notebook. "Why would your mother speak of this to you?"

Jules curled her nails so tightly into her palms that they dented her skin. She had not yet confided to her mother that she wanted to reveal everything to her father. The only time Jules had suggested it, she had been twelve when she had finally understood her femininity, with the arrival of her menses, and her mother had dissolved into hysterical tears and fainted. Jules had felt then she had to protect her at all cost, even though she had not understood the depth of her mother's anxiety. If father loved her as he claimed, should her mother fear revealing the truth this much?

"Mother and I speak about many things, Father," she said drily. "Your need for a male heir was simply one of them."

For a moment her father appeared angry and uncertain before his expression smoothed. "I was a much younger man then, less learned, and less tolerant. I wanted a son very badly, and your mother understood her duty."

Jules narrowed her gaze on him. "What if I had been born a girl, Papa?"

He blinked. "I cannot understand this line of questioning; it is rather nonsensical, as you are my son."

Jules's heart beat so fast, her chest ached. "I gather Mama would have been forced to the marriage bed once again if I had been born a girl...despite the risk to her health. A very odd way to show your love and devotion to the lady that filled that emptiness in your heart."

His eyes flashed and he surged to his feet. "You dare to

speak to me in this manner about a situation you have little understanding about, or better, a situation that is not your business?"

Jules released a deep breath and stood. "I should tender an apology, but I am not sorry, Papa. I merely wanted to understand…"

"The past between your mother and myself is our private business," he snapped.

Her father stepped forward, before stiffening and closing his eyes. He seemed to master whatever emotion tore at him for when his lashes flickered up, he was contained. "We shall not have this discussion again. The duchess approaches; I shall go and speak with her."

Her father went down the steps and strolled toward the duchess, an air of geniality settling on him. Jules stared after him, that awful ache rising inside her chest. She would say nothing more to her father until she spoke with her mother. That would be a distressing discussion and she knew she'd need to be very delicate in how she approached the matter, but while she did not wish to shed the advantages of being believed the male sex, the feminine side of herself was struggling with wanting to be fully a woman—at least with James.

• • •

Lady Emelia Johnson was the daughter of a duke. It was expected for her to marry another duke and give birth to a duke. She peered at James with bright blue eyes filled with gentle humor and compassion. Lady Emelia was rather beautiful, if one appreciated delicate English beauties. Her long blond hair was worn in a shower of ringlets and bounced as she moved. Her tightly bustled ivory gown was festooned with ruffles of coffee-colored lace and although he thought it was a bit too much, it suited her. And from how his mother acted, this was the young lady she would select as his future duchess.

"My mother is very much anticipating meeting you, Your Grace," Lady Emelia said, smiling at him prettily. "She hopes you will be able to attend her yearly ball, which will be held in a few weeks. It is a most coveted invitation, and you will be Mama's honored guest."

"I shall look forward to it," he said smoothly, tasting the lie and not liking that he had sprouted such nonsense.

Her expression brightened. "Longbourn Park is beautiful, Your Grace. You must have missed home very much."

James leveled his gaze on her, only seeing warm compassion in her blue gaze. "I did."

Her eyes widened at his succinct reply, but she did not probe for more; instead, she spoke to his mother of the loveliness of their gardens, admiring the azaleas.

Then the lady seemed to stumble on the air itself and took a most graceful fall to the ground, crying for her ankle and staring up at him with wide, imploring eyes that impressively held a glisten of tears. James stared down at her, suspecting this was somehow part of the courtship games. He was supposed to gallantly recuse her by lifting her into his arms and carting her away. Everyone on the lawns seemed arrested by the scene, and clearly waited for his reaction. Lady Emelia anticipated with an air of satisfaction and a smug glance over her shoulders at a few other ladies.

James canted his head. "What are you waiting for to stand up?"

The shock approbation that widened her eyes would be comical if he was not so irritated. And empty.

"Will you at least offer your hand, Your Grace," she gasped, stricken.

His belly tightened. "No."

Her blush of mortification stained her cheeks and she inelegantly pushed herself to standing and dipped into a curtsy. "I must return to my friends," she said with another forced bright smile, "I can see they are very eager to hear about our meeting, and I might indulge them."

He stooped and collected the parasol that had fallen with her. James offered it, and when her grasp closed over the handle he said, "I do not like touching others...or when I am touched."

*Except for Jules Southby.*

He ruthlessly masked his reaction, for surely the hunger that sparked in his veins would be interpreted by anyone.

"Oh," Lady Emelia murmured, and her expression softened. "I...I am sorry to have fallen at your feet then. It was badly done of me."

"It was a beautiful fall."

Her eyes widened and she laughed, fascination shifting in her gaze. "Would you perhaps one day tell me about your experience in the mountains, Your Grace?"

"No."

She jolted at the flat indifference in his tone, but he would not offer her such ridiculous expectations, nor did he care if he was perceived as rude. James struggled to recall his sister's pain and took a deep breath, releasing the emptiness. "Perhaps one day, Lady Emelia."

It was not a promise he would keep, but it would be enough to convince this young lady he was not a beast without any polite manners or gentlemanlike graces.

Pleasure glowed in her eyes and Lady Emelia dipped into a curtsy. He watched the lady stroll away, nimbly twirling her parasol, laughing as she joined a few other ladies on the lawn. Footmen and servants were busy milling around, setting up lawn blankets and chairs with a covering. A picnic feast was to be had, and he was to walk through the midst of the fine offerings to vet his potential bride.

"Is she not beautiful?" his mother asked by his side, she, too, staring after the duke's daughter.

"She is."

That agreement seemed to please the duchess.

"She is nineteen, and this will be her second season. Lady Emelia did not lack for suitors last year and received no less than five offers, which she rejected."

"Her father is indulgent."

"Very," his mother said with a small smile. "He has four sons, and Lady Emelia is his only daughter. That her parents allowed her to attend my impromptu garden party informs me that they are very open to an alliance with our family. Viscountess Beecham, who accompanied Lady Emelia as her chaperon, is a cousin of the family and has the ear of the duchess."

"I presume you are advising me to impress Lady Beecham."

His mother laughed, and the warmth of it seemed to seep inside his bones.

"Are you of a mind to impress her?"

"No."

At first his mother seemed flustered, then she rallied and said, "Good. You are a duke...it is *you* whom the viscountess should try and impress. The ball will be held in a few days. Do you believe you will be able to dance with her?"

James glanced down at his mother and lifted a brow in query.

"I am aware you do not like the touch of others. Not even your dance instructor. It is the reason he fled Longbourn Park with mutters that he feared being murdered. "

"I will try to tolerate it, but I make no promises," he said.

Her expression brightened. "Thank you, James, that is more than I expected. As for your hair—"

"No."

"It is rather unfashionable that way," she said tartly.

"Dukes can set their own fashion."

His mother blinked. "I suppose they can."

She shifted closer to him, and he held himself still. It was not that the idea of her touch repulsed him, yet he could not find it in himself to seek that touch as he did with his Wildflower. Heat curled through him at the mere thought of her, and James ruthlessly willed himself to not look in her direction.

"Do you believe you will be able to select a duchess from these ladies," his mother softly asked, staring after their guests. "They are all from the finest families of the *haut ton*."

"I am certain of it."

She jolted. "It was my oversight for not querying before, but do you have any preference for your duchess?"

"No."

His mother met his gaze, and he spied a sadness he did not understand in her eyes.

"I am sorry, James, I did not mean for you to see marriage as only a duty. I…" Frustration flashed in her eyes as if she struggled with what she wanted to say.

"There is nothing to worry about, Mother," James said. "I understand my duty. "

"I know," she said in a rush of desperate air. "My heart is gladdened by your willingness, but I also want you to…long for affection and love within your union."

He drew back, putting space between them. *Love and affection?* He canted his head and stared at his mother. She returned his regard, that sadness deepening inside her gaze. James swallowed back the hiss of annoyance scraping inside his throat. He did not like it when he lacked understanding of what she needed of him.

"Marriage need not be complicated," he said flatly. "I

will marry a lady of quality, one with all the requirements suited to be a duchess. Now, if you will excuse me, I've received several letters requesting sponsorship for charities. I will attend to them and also do some reading."

He walked away, feeling the cravat at his throat tightening but he ruthlessly suppressed the desire to rip it away. Instead of going into the main house, James headed for the woods. The air carried a delicate thread of scent his way, and he slowed his step. Jules Southby. James held her unique flavor trapped within his lungs, hungry to keep it there, almost desperate to fully understand its wicked lure. The feeling of desperation allowed him to part his lips, relax his shoulders, and slowly ease the scent from his being. He shifted slightly, watching her approach, taking in the long, confident stride.

Their gazes met, and the memory of their heated encounter seemed to spark life in the space between them. *Why her?* The question weaved itself through him. James had never known a reaction so intense, so immediate to any woman. He had been introduced to at least a dozen lovely ladies today, and none had set off these dark, forceful needs that seemed as if nothing could truly assuage them.

*I am not at all certain what you are to me, Wildflower.*

Jules Southby was neither friend nor foe, yet her presence was necessary. *A lover...she is my lover...the woman I feel I need to kiss and consume.*

Jules carried herself with easy grace, smiling at a few ladies playing croquet on the lawns. She tipped her hat and bowed to a couple of ladies as a gentleman of manners would. He could not look away from the beauty of her eyes and that smile. He ought to, for it revealed his want and hunger, which should be kept private. A great longing assailed James. He wanted that smile directed at him and no one else. When that wild possessiveness roared inside him, he did not shy away from it but canted his head thoughtfully, allowing it to grow as she drifted closer.

"Your Grace," she murmured, coming to a stand before him. "The duchess informed me this morning that a ball is to be held in three days."

"You are angry."

She jerked, and her eyes widened. "I…"

He reached out for her, then pulled his hands back, clenching them. "If you have no wish to speak of it, do not."

Perhaps when they exchanged truths, it was just as difficult for her as for him.

"I will always be fascinated that you can sense my mood when I so carefully hide it."

"Perhaps in time, it will go away."

"Another theory to explore. Can senses honed by brutal experience dull after years of a tamer existence?"

They smiled at that, and the tension he'd not realized had invaded his chest eased. Being with her felt…easy.

"My father is not a part of my disguise."

Words momentarily eluded him. "You have been pretending to be a man your whole life, and your father is unaware of it?"

"Yes."

"Accept my compliments. I believed it to be a deception by both of you so that you could freely study."

A tremulous smile curved her lips. "It was a deception by my mother only. I learned of it when…when…" A flush rose on her cheeks, and she looked away from him across the lawns.

Ah, she learned of it when changes began within her body. James imagined how confused and wretched she must have been. Even frightened. "What motivated your mother?"

"My father's desperate need for a son," she said flatly.

"It is not only wealth and land men wish to pass on," James said. "Legacies are also of the mind, and the need to leave those legacies behind can be imperative. I gather your mother had a good reason for keeping your sex a secret."

"She did," Jules said softly.

"And you want to break down these reasons and reveal yourself to your father?"

"I am not certain what it is I want. I do not like that this deception exists, yet it feels so necessary. How would my life change should I reveal it to my father?"

"Do you wish the world to know?"

She recoiled. "Never! I would lose *everything*."

"Then you want Dr. Southby to become a part of the deception and to share the burden of fooling the world."

She raked slim, graceful fingers through her short curls. "I confess I do not fully understand what I want, James. My parents admit their love for each other so very often, yet this lie exists between them, a taint I loathe, yet to reveal my knowledge to my father might irreparably harm their relationship. My father still does not know of my mother's lie. Some days I cannot fathom that he looks at me and does not see it."

She made an incredulous sound loud in her throat.

"Your disguise is brilliant."

"It did not fool you."

"If I was an ordinary man, it might have."

She laughed. "I find your arrogance charming."

"I find your laugh beautiful."

A flush rising on her cheeks, she tilted her head in question at his silent scrutiny, but she didn't look away. In the depths of her eyes, he spied a wariness he somehow understood.

"Speaking to you about this is...soothing. The knots inside my chest have eased." Her eyes twinkled, and she tugged at her cravat. "I watched you today interact with a few ladies. The duchess seems pleased."

"I try."

A taut silence fell.

"You are staring, Your Grace." As she said this, she surreptitiously looked about the lawns. "And we are being watched most keenly."

Perhaps this was not the time to mention he found her unspeakably lovely. That longing once again awakened inside him. She sensed something from him or saw it in his gaze, for hers widened, that hint of wariness deepening, along with a burn of want. That evident want hooked itself into his belly and tugged him toward her.

"James," she gasped softly, her green eyes widening. "You are standing too close."

He stepped back. "Follow me, Southby."

James turned around and walked toward the main house. She walked beside him, holding her curiosity in check. Once inside the house, he went down the hallway to the library. He opened the door, stepped back, and allowed her to precede him inside. He closed the door with a *snick*, and she faced him.

"What is it that you...*oh*!"

He snagged his hand around her waist and drew her against his body. He didn't need to tell her of the need pummeling him. His Wildflower seemed to understand because she flowed against his body, wrapping her arms around his nape. Their mouths came together in a burning kiss. James became lost in her taste, scent, and the sounds of startled pleasure she made, as if with each kiss she uncovered something wonderful.

He broke their embrace, breathing raggedly.

"Kissing you is rather incredible," she said with a shaky laugh, her eyes gleaming with delight.

"It is rather interesting kissing someone with a moustache," he murmured, pressing another hard kiss against her lips.

James swallowed her muffled laugh and soft moan of pleasure. He couldn't stop touching her, caressing her throat, tugging at the neckcloth, and loosening it to feel the frantic pulse at the hollow of her throat. She sucked at his tongue, and he groaned his pleasure. His Wildflower was stealing something he had not planned to hand over, and he did not understand what alchemy she used to do it. Was it by her smiles, the intent way she listened without pressure? Her lush scents, the hot wicked sounds she had made when he'd licked her into orgasm?

Or was it this…that long moan made against his mouth, the way she shivered in his embrace and slid her tongue against his? James spun, pressing her against the door, coasting his hands over her body, wishing to rip the jacket off and consume her. His Wildflower smelled hot and sweet and arousing. James could tell that she was wet and aching for him. That lush scent of sun-ripened peach wafting from her made his mouth water and his cock throb beneath his trousers. He kissed her over and over, short, fierce kisses that would possibly bruise her mouth.

Dragging his lips down, he touched his tongue to the base of her throat and groaned, for she tasted like honey. Closing his eyes, he breathed her in. Then he bit into her flesh tenderly. She sighed against his chest, a soft little sound that wrenched complex sensations through his heart.

"We must stop," she whispered shakily. "We should never be here where we might be discovered and unable to bear the consequences of being thought of as two men caught in intimacy."

James released her. "I can shoulder any consequences, Wildflower."

Her expression was one of bemused wonder and need mirrored in the gaze that looked back at him. "*I* cannot."

A knock sounded on the door and she jolted, instinctively

patting her hair.

"Wulverton!" a gruff voice called. "Open the door!"

James canted his head and stepped forward.

"Do not open it, James!"

He glanced at his Wildflower. Her cheeks were flushed, her lips red and swollen. Anyone with a keen sense of observation would conclude they had been kissing.

"Am I presentable?" she asked, smoothing over her moustache, and retying her cravat.

"You are lovely."

Her eyes lit with humor; she took a steady breath and went over to the windows, giving the room her back. He opened the door and stilled at the familiar face peering at him in disbelief.

"Wolfe," Stephen Foxley, the Marquess of Linfield, said, shaking his head, his light brown eyes gleaming with disbelief. "I just got the news upon my return from abroad, but I did not believe it. You are really alive."

The man who had been his closest friend during his years at Eton stepped inside the library. The last time James had seen Linfield was the week before his departure to Canada. They had raced their carriages recklessly through the streets of London, some sort of rite as their fathers, who were also close friends, had done some twenty years before them.

The marquess was still staring at James as if he were a creature from the marshlands.

"My God, man, *how* did you survive it? Are there any truths to those damn newssheet articles?"

"Some," he said, knowing it sounded more mysterious than he intended. James held out his hands, and his friend slapped him against his palm in a handshake. Something inside him recoiled but he ruthlessly pushed through it.

"I am damn glad you're alive, my friend," Linfield said with a grin, his eyes crinkling at the corner. "Marsden and

Sutton will be damn glad to know the news is true."

He'd hardly taken the time to recall distant friendships during those cold, bitter years of survival. Yet now, the memories of himself, Linfield, the Earl of Marsden, and the Earl of Sutton's revelry as young men on the cusp of starting Cambridge roared through his thoughts. They had gone wild through London drinking and carousing, bemoaning that they would one day have to take wives and could not be as free and rakish as they should. A warmth kindled inside his chest, and James found himself smiling. "Allow me to introduce you to Jules Southby."

It was then the marquess realized they were not alone in the room. Jules turned around and, to her credit, was composed and appeared a slim and thoughtful gentleman, even if wet behind the ears.

"Jules, this is the Marquess of Linfield. A friend."

Jules bowed to the marquess. "Lord Linfield. A pleasure to make your acquaintance. I have read your arguments on the Third Reform Act. Impressive."

Linfield smiled. "Flattery shall get you everything, my boy."

Jules smiled and dipped her head again in a quick bow. "I shall leave you to your reunion, Your Grace."

James slid his gaze over her face, noting the slightly heightened color. "I am pleased for you to stay, Southby."

She blinked and quickly glanced at the marquess, who gave an affable nod. The tension eased from his Wildflower's shoulders, and James went over to the mantle and poured brandy into three glasses. Linfield took his glass and lifted it.

"To whatever the hell saved you, Wolfe. I am damn glad you are here."

"Here," Jules said, taking a sip, eyeing the marquess with considerable curiosity and admiration.

James dipped his head close to her ear. "Do not admire

his handsomeness."

She choked on a sip and shot him an aghast glare. Linfield arched a brow at the exchange, and James merely smiled. Jules drank with them for several minutes before excusing herself on the pretext she needed to meet with her father. Once the door closed behind her, the marquess leveled him a stare.

"He is the son of the mind doctor? What are they called, alienists?" Linfield asked with a grimace. "The duchess informed me of it."

James took a drink, knowing his mother had been the one to invite the marquess down, no doubt to garner his support. "Hmm."

"I do not understand it, man, an alienist treats and studies mental maladies. What in God's name are they doing here?"

"I have not departed from my senses if that is what you are asking. Dr. Southby and his son are guests."

Relief lit in Linfield's eyes. "I did not doubt it. What I remember of you was your dogged stubbornness. No damn ice wilderness was ever going to defeat you." The marquess raked his fingers through his dark blond hair. "You seem close to the lad."

James considered the subtle query. "Southby is one of my important persons."

The marquess nodded solemnly as if he understood that Jules Southby had crawled underneath James's skin. There were parts of himself James did not know or understand, parts shadowed by dark obscurity and pain and loss, a place where dreams and hope once resided. Somehow this creature had the power to prick at that hidden place, and he did not like it even as he accepted its existence. Jules Southby had dropped into his life like a giant from the heavens, shaking the foundation of things he had yet to comprehend.

# Chapter Eleven

The next four days passed in a blur of activities for the guests—croquet on the lawn, boat rides on the lake, charades in the grand parlor, lavish dinners in the evening, and picnics on the lawns and outside games which allowed the ladies to mill about in their beautiful finery, all coveting the title of Duchess of Wulverton. The duke at times would join the ladies on the estate grounds, keeping a careful distance but making a reasonable effort to engage them in conversation, though he allowed no accidental brush or touches.

Jules would observe from the gazebo, careful to keep the longing from her gaze. At times she wondered what it would be like to stroll across the lawns with him, boldly flirting like the ravishing Lady Emelia and Lady Mariah. What would it be like to drive in a phaeton with the duke in Hyde Park, or be held in his arms for a dance? Those whimsical wants at times befuddled and amused Jules, even as she acknowledged the ache it left in her heart to want to freely enjoy such outings with the duke.

*Whomever he chooses to be his duchess will be a most*

*pleased lady.*

Jules frowned, wondering at the peculiar prick deep inside her heart. It felt like the beginning of a wound she most certainly did not understand or appreciate. It was not as if she had any wishes or longing to be with the duke beyond the promised pleasure.

*And when will that be, my good duke?*

In the nights she waited in the west wing, hoping he would come inside from the woods, wondering if this was the night they would become lovers. The hallways remained empty, and she would lie in the bed, staring at the ceiling, wondering if she should invade his sanctuary without an invitation. The bustle of the days left little room for private meetings and interactions. All of their conversations were done within the presence of others, and even then, Jules was treated to his cool reticence.

She hungered to be alone with him…to speak and know everything about him. The door to the drawing room opened, tugging Jules from her musing. Stiffening her shoulders, she rose as the duchess entered and lowered her head in a bow of greeting. Her father entered on the heels of the duchess, his notebook clutched in his grip. He smiled at her over the duchess's head, and Jules returned it, grateful that the tension between them had eased a couple of days ago. Though he had not brought up the matter again, she caught her father at times staring at her with deep contemplation.

"My son is doing remarkably well," the duchess said as she stared at Jules and her father. "I wanted to meet this morning to express my gratitude, Dr. Southby. This is more progress than I had anticipated."

Her father smiled. "I assure you I have done very little, Your Grace, for the duke will not speak with me through all fault of my own. We owe his remarkable recovery to my son's efforts."

Annoyance shafted through Jules, though she tried her best to present an unruffled composure. "His Grace only needed time to assimilate with his new situation, he did not suffer from a malady of the mind."

"But he *suffered*," the duchess said quietly. "For he still does not allow me to touch him."

"Yes, he did suffer," Jules admitted softly, merely loathing when it was implied the duke was afflicted because he did things differently. "Please let me assure you, Your Grace: how one's behavior becomes altered due to sensory deprivation and social contact with others is still something we are understanding as psychologists and mind doctors, but we do know enough to say with confidence that with time, the duke will once again allow certain privileges."

"I wish he would cut his hair for the ball," the duchess said with a grimace. "Though he speaks more to his sister and dined with us last evening, there are some things he is simply being stubborn on! I fear he will never change and what are we to do then? His manner is not gentlemanlike at all! I suggested an etiquette teacher and my son *growled* at me."

Jules hid her smile and made no reply.

The duchess leveled them with a stare. "I do hope you understand my reasons for not extending an invitation to the ball to you, Dr. Southby and Mr. Southby. There are already whispers about your role here, and I do not want anyone to see you at the ball and believe you are there to observe the duke and make a report on his state of mind. I am perhaps being overcautious in this matter, but I want no gossip."

"You are not being over cautious, Your Grace," her father said with a smile of reassurance. "Your care is understandable. My son and I will stay within our rooms and ensure we encounter no guests on the night of the ball."

The duchess nodded regally, then swished from the

drawing room, her steps lighter than they had been a couple weeks ago.

"Walk with me," her father murmured.

They headed outside to escape the bustle of the house as a multitude of servants prepared for the ball to be held tomorrow. Jules was fascinated as three footmen brought down a large chandelier and cleaned the crystals and removed the burned-out candles. Meanwhile a group of workmen were hanging green damask drapes to some of the walls of the ballroom, while others were winding gauze in a paler shade of green twisted with gold braid around the room's marble columns. More workers were carrying in boxes and carefully constructed displays of flowers.

Jules was certain that around the manor, other servants were striving to bring the house to a perfection of cleaning and that it would be difficult to keep out of the staff's way.

Once outside, shrieks of laughter drew Jules's attention, and she noted that Lady Mariah strolled beside the duke, smiling up at him. He walked with his hands clasped behind his back, listening attentively to whatever she said. As if he sensed Jules's stare...or perhaps smelled her across the distance, he looked in her direction. That volatile surge of awareness crackled through her body, and her heart thrummed. Jules looked away from the duke, giving her attention to her father.

"You must find a way to get the duke to cut his hair in the fashion of a man of his rank and stature. The duchess once again noted His Grace spends an inordinate amount of time in the woods. We need to devise a strategy to urge him to stay within the main grounds. Uncle Hubert also reported to me about seeing the duke running in trousers alone in the night across these lawns. These behaviors are very unsettling to his family."

An incredulous laugh pulsed from her, and her father

frowned.

"I was not aware I said something humorous," he said stiffly.

"Papa...the duke will not cut his hair. He stays in the woods because he finds it peaceful, and if he chooses to run across the lawn barely clothed...I daresay there are far more eccentric personalities within society. There is little to be unsettled about."

He opened his notebook. "Are you now suggesting his behavior is unalterable?"

"I am suggesting the duke's reason for not cutting his hair is his own, and he protects his peace and privacy. That he does so, quite ruthlessly, and might be unforgiving of those who violate his boundaries, does not suggest an unhealthy behavior."

He took a breath. "I've observed the duke watches you often, especially when he thinks no one is aware of it."

Her heart kicked painfully inside her chest. "Does he?" she asked, striving for a casual tone.

Her father merely arched a brow at her tone, and Jules felt as if he peered behind the veil of her insouciance.

"You do the same," he said. "Watch the duke. It is curious behavior on both parts. I am not certain what to make of it, son."

"We are friends," she said simply, careful to fight the need to blush. "Such conduct between friends is quite normal and does not need any scrutiny or analysis."

"Even if you are the relative of a viscount we do not own the station where you can bear the consequences of being friends with a duke, especially one as powerful as Wulverton," he said sharply. "We are only here in a professional capacity, try to remember it."

"Yes, Father." The words felt as if they had been scraped from Jules's throat.

Her father remained silent, and she walked beside him, casting him sidelong glances. "Did you wish to speak with me about something else, Papa?"

He cleared his throat. "Did I mention I was very proud to receive letters from your professors of how well you did in your studies?"

Her chest warmed. "Yes, Papa, you did. Thank you."

"Have you considered what you will do after we leave Longbourn Park?"

An odd sensation hooked itself inside her chest, and she ruthlessly prevented herself from looking back at the duke. "Even before returning to England, I had considered further studies at The University of Padua."

"First Germany and now Italy," he murmured, fiddling with his spectacles on his nose. "Are you running from home, my boy? Are we to live wishing you were closer to us but not having you near?"

A knot tightened in her belly. "You know I am hungry to learn, Father. England offers very little in psychology and advancement in the field."

He stopped, and she slowed as well, turning to face him.

A hopeful expression settled on his face. "Would you consider working alongside me for a few years before you hie off to Padua?"

Excitement leaped in her veins. "In what capacity, Papa?"

His eyes crinkled at the corner. "The compensation is not very impressive, but the work will be very rewarding, and I believe your dedication, intelligence, and empathic nature would be a great asset. I was invited to become a part of the team at Our Lady of Bethlehem in London. You know many of our vulnerable citizens with mental malaise or distemper of the brain are cared for almost entirely by their families. This is not the proper care when our skills and compassion can assist in curing or even alleviating their pain. New funding has been made available by the Queen for specialized care."

Jules took a deep breath. "I would love to be a part of your team, Father, and I would be happy to stay on for a couple of years before I leave for Italy. I have also missed you and Mama, very much, in my time abroad."

"Good." Pleasure sparked in his gaze, and he rested a hand across her shoulders, gently patting her. "Your mother will be happy that I convinced you to stay."

"That hardly took convincing," she said with a smile. "I am very pleased with this opportunity." Jules had always wanted the practical experience of working beside her father in the field and that he would offer it now showed her how much he believed in her. That wistful ache to share everything rose within her and she forcefully suppressed it.

They spoke for a few more minutes before they returned to the main house. As Jules strolled past the duke's private study, she noted the door was slightly ajar. He'd not invited her into his space and she knew she should continue walking by. But her feet slowed as if commanded by an external force, and Jules paused at the door, noiselessly easing it open.

He stood by the mantle, resting his elbow on the mantelpiece, his other hand thrust deep into his hip pocket, his side profile stark in his aloneness. His hair was unbound, its raven locks flowing over his shoulders in a curtain of silk. His cravat had been removed along with his jacket. Her fingers itched to brush back one errant lock from his forehead, to stand beside him and help him shoulder whatever he seemed to brace against. A quick glance around the room revealed it was the same as when she had first met him. He'd added nothing to the space except a few more books which were strewn across the carpet.

Jules's belly tightened. He still found comfort in emptiness. Something dark and unfamiliar moved through her body. His lashes fluttered closed, pleasure flushed along his savagely elegant cheekbones, and it was in that moment she knew he smelled her. His regard shifted to her, and that aloneness that had cloaked his body gleamed in his eyes. Jules then realized all the chatter and activity surrounding the duke had not touched him. His assimilation was a mere pretense for his mother...perhaps his family. She felt the weight of his solitary existence and wanted to wrench it from him, carry its weight if only for a moment's reprieve.

Jules couldn't say why she did it, but she went over to him, cupped his jaw between her hands, tipped onto her booted toes, and pressed her mouth to his.

*Give me your emptiness*, she silently whispered, kissing him with all the stirring passion she held in her heart for him. An inarticulate sound thrummed from somewhere within the duke, but he did not haul her into his arms, merely allowed her to coax and to seduce. She bit his lower lip, then licked that spot to remove the sting.

Oh God, he tasted good. *So good.*

Their tongues glided against each other, their mouths greedy as they consumed each other. Lust pulsed between their bodies and the flesh between Jules's legs heated. He groaned and she sighed, sucking on his tongue until he growled against her lips. That primal, provocative sound hooked low in her belly and pulled, twisting dark sensations of lust to throb inside her sex.

He kissed her as though he were starved for her, he brushed his fingers over her face, through her hair, because he had clearly needed to touch her. Jules allowed his touch, holding herself still and giving James whatever he needed. Instinctively she coasted her fingers over his brows, his jawline and throat, granting him also the privilege of her touch.

He cupped her cheeks, dipped slightly, and kissed her with violent tenderness.

"I do not understand the why of it, but I needed this," he

said against her mouth, before kissing her deeply.

When they parted, her breath came in shuddering gasps, and it took a few seconds before she regained her composure. Fingers trembling, she lowered them from his jaw, pulled back, and without speaking, turned and walked away. The duke did not bid her to stop or to keep his company, so Jules kept walking, shocked to see the door had been left ajar, and she had almost recklessly compromised them. Her heart shaking, she took a deep breath to steady herself.

*We must be more careful.*

She went over to the west wing, entered her chamber, and closed the door. Jules carefully removed the moustache, then went over to the wash basin and cleaned the stage paint from her face. Next she removed all her clothes, and the bindings over her breasts.

Walking over to the bed, she lay down on the sheets, moaning at the cool feel under her naked skin. Dampness lingered between her thighs, the ache in her nub throbbed, and her nipples were hard. Desire was such a curious and fascinating sensation. A sound in the hallway had her gripping the sheets into a fist.

Would he come into her room?

She listened to the sound of his door opening and closing. Jules waited, aware she was naked on the sheets, and that the door connecting their chambers was not locked with a key. She stared at that connecting door until her eyes smarted, then she took long, deep breaths. Jules wanted James until she was burning for it. She wanted to feel the heavy heat of his powerful body atop hers, she wanted to feel that hardness beneath his trousers sliding over her sex. She wanted to lick his flesh, taste him all over. She understood the anatomy of lovemaking and craved to experience it in full—but only with the duke.

Jules tipped her head to the ceiling, releasing the sheets

to trail her fingers over the smooth hollow of her belly, down to hover above her mons, breathing out a small, strangled groan at the sensation sparking under the tip of her fingers.

What would it be like to feel him there…

A distant corner of her mind was warning Jules to beware, that she was sliding too deep, but she ignored it. What would it feel like when he entered her with his cock? Would it hurt or would she only feel the wicked pleasure his tongue had bestowed?

Closing her eyes, she allowed her fingers to fall away from the temptation of exploring her folds. Jules turned onto her stomach, relishing the cool feel of the sheets on her heated flesh. She thought of the ball tomorrow, and imagined James dancing with the ladies, one of whom would inevitably become his duchess.

A pinprick of discomfort lanced at her chest, and she shied away from examining the nature of such feelings. Instead, she closed her eyes and imagined what it would be like to be held in James's arms, dressed as a lady, dancing under glittering chandeliers holding a hundred candles.

A most improper notion unfurled inside her heart, and she gasped, snapping her eyes open. Here was an opportunity to bask in another thing she might never experience with anyone but the duke. What if she should attend the ball? The idea felt far too wicked, scandalous, and improbable. She would only have a day to prepare. Where would she even procure a ballgown that would make her worthy to walk in a duchess's grand ballroom?

"Do not be silly," she whispered in the silence of her bedchamber, "this is a foolhardy idea."

Jules groaned at her recklessly daring heart and closed her eyes once more.

*What if I am recognized? My father and I would have to leave at once and in disgrace. How will Papa react if he discovers my duplicity so suddenly, and on the heels of being sent away?*

The consequences were too great for her to risk it, yet the longing that scythed through Jules ripped the breath from her.

*I am going to do it...aren't I?*

She pressed a hand over her belly, feeling that yearning opening there and sinuously twisting through her. Jules pushed from the bed and stood before the mirror, naked. Her heart pounded and her body flushed pink. Even her eyes glowed with a luminosity that was unknown.

Tipping her face to the ceiling, she closed her eyes. Her father would not attend the ball. Her stage makeup and moustache would be removed, and she would wear a wig. How could anyone recognize her?

• • •

Jules took a steady breath and allowed her feet to whisper across the hallway as she walked ahead, hoping she would not be stopped before she entered the grand ballroom of the duchess. As she drifted closer, the merry noises of conversation and laughter spilled from the drawing room and the hallways. The sound of an orchestra playing wafted closer, and her heart thrummed as she entered. The ballroom was already full of a crowd in a blaze of riotous colors.

Several local gentry and aristocrats were present, and while the ball was smaller than a London one, Jules was certain there would be at least two hundred guests. It had taken a pretty penny to procure a suitable gown from the village modiste. Jules had implied it was for her sister, who desperately needed a gown to attend the duchess's ball. The dark red gown was simple in its design, with its small, puffed sleeves and lace-trimmed neckline. It clung to her upper body in a way that felt far too revealing and sensual.

The gloves clasping her arms to her elbows felt supple and comfortable, the shoes on her feet soft and delicate. Her face had been stripped of all stage paint, the moustache removed, and her hair styled in short curls around her cheeks and ears. She had discarded the idea of a wig and used a scarf made from an offcut of the dress wrapped around her hair to disguise the short length. The style was hardly up to current fashion as she had done it herself. When she'd seen her reflection in the cheval mirror just now, Jules had been startled by her prettiness and soft femininity. There had been no jewels to adorn her throat, and no diamond earbobs winked at her ears. Still, she had taken a deep breath and walked down the lonely hallway and stairs of the west wing to the grand ballroom of Longbourn Park, a feeling of pleasure and sensuality washing through her in anticipatory waves.

Jules ventured farther into the ballroom, aware of the racing of her heart and the breathless sensation sweeping through her. It felt odd to be walking around in a ballgown, her strides felt clumsy, yet she also felt...*free.* It was a perplexing awareness. Several ladies nodded their heads in greeting, though she saw in their eyes a question to her identity and which family she'd arrived with at the manor.

A few gentlemen's gazes lingered on her decolletage and tightly corseted waist, made even more sensuous by the small wire bustle flaring over her derriere, but their attention soon flitted away. Jules surmised she was not interesting or radiant enough...except possibly for one gentleman.

*You are beautiful.*

The echoes of his words rippled over her skin, pushing a small smile from her. It was the duke she searched for, and Jules found him on the terrace, partially hidden in the shadows, observing the merriment around him. She drifted closer, staring at James, aware of the whispers about him from several ladies.

"*I am determined to dance with him tonight. He is so handsome!*"

"*And very wealthy!*"

"*He has not asked anyone to the floor as yet.*"

"*I am certain he is to ask Lady Emelia, she has already declared herself to be his future duchess!*"

A bout of giggles followed that, and Jules ignored the hitch inside her chest, keeping her attention on the duke and not those gossipers. She noted the way his lashes fluttered closed, how his nostrils flared as he took in the new scent which wafted from the ballroom. He faltered into absolute stillness and canted his head, his lips curling in sensual pleasure. She knew it then...that he smelled her, even as impossible as it might have seemed given the mass of bodies and perfumes in the room.

Her throat went tight. For the first time in her existence Jules felt her sensual power and allure with a thrill of delight. Something inside of her unfurled like a flower in bloom, desperately reaching toward sunlight. Except the man hovering in the shadows of the terrace did not feel warm, his beauty was dark and mesmerizing like the night, his allure oddly dangerous in ways she did not comprehend and might never do.

He came toward her, his steps languid and confident, his gaze never leaving hers. The harsh sensuality of his cheekbones and the hard lines of his jaw were richly accentuated by the tight way his hair was pulled back into a single clasp at his nape. The duke was disturbingly intriguing in his formal black-and-white evening wear, which fitted to his frame so perfectly that it left no doubt as to his elegant masculinity.

He radiated an aura of savage elegance that made her intensely conscious of her own burgeoning sensuality. Jules's heart and body responded in a very physical, extremely disturbing way. She inhaled, then exhaled, long and slow.

The crowd watched him, and a small frown touched the duchess's face when she saw the direction her son traversed. The duchess stared at Jules with a very decided frown, clearly trying to discern her identity. She had been foolish tonight. Donning a dress. For him. Pretending to be someone she was not. The usual standard of propriety constricting females had never applied to Jules, so it felt silly to feel so uncertain now.

*This was a mistake.*

The thought whispered through her, urging her to slip from the crowd and disappear before the duke reached her side. If Jules possessed any wisp of rationality at the moment, she would have acted on the warning. Instead, she waited for him to reach her, held fast by the hunger crawling through her veins for him. The duke stopped before her and she lifted her face to his, almost defiantly.

"Wildflower."

He said her name like a benediction, and because she was out of sorts, she teasingly replied with, "Wolfe."

"You are beautiful."

Fire throbbed low in her stomach, hot and wicked.

"You also appear exceedingly uncomfortable," he said gently. "Why did you come as you are?"

"For you," the words escaped before she truly thought about it. "I…I wanted to dance with you."

He said nothing to that, merely stared at her in that still way of his. Jules almost fidgeted.

"It is the *only* reason I am here," she admitted softly, even as it revealed too much of her yearning. "I wanted to feel your arms around me like that."

His eyes flashed, darkening as if they held a storm caged within. For a second, they blazed with breathtaking heat.

"Dance with me," he said.

Something she couldn't understand began beating in her heart, and she placed her hands within his, allowing him to lead her inside. A ripple went through the crowd, and Jules became aware that everyone seemed arrested by their walk to the dance floor.

"Everyone is staring," she said, annoyed at the nervousness coursing through her body. Jules could feel her breathing deepening and quickening.

"I have not taken to the floor since the ball started."

Despite hearing the earlier whispers, Jules was startled. "The duchess is disappointed."

"I find the crowd…discomfiting."

For a man who loathed the idea of fearing anything because such emotions were a weakness, she knew it was not easy for him to admit that.

As if reading her mind, he said, "I am not afraid to share any truth with you."

They took their position on the floor, and she placed her hand on his shoulder. The strains of the waltz leaped to life and filled the space with its elegant melody. "I am not afraid to share any of my truths with you, either, James."

A small smile touched his mouth and a warm feeling suffused her entire body. "You will need to dance with someone else. Otherwise everyone will wonder who I am, especially your mother."

His eyes caressed over her face, searching every nuance of her expression. "No."

"James…"

"No."

There was that unbending resolve in his tone. Her mouth closed on further protests as he took her into his arms. Jules had learned dancing as a gentleman, and she had been taught to lead. Yet that did not matter, for the duke was so commanding in his movements that she had no choice but to surrender all control to him as he twirled them to the elegant and sensuous Viennese waltz.

"No one else is dancing," she gasped, closing her fingers reflexively on his shoulders.

"I know."

Oh God, this would indeed be a disaster. Why were they all watching instead of coming on the dance floor?

"Your eyes on me, Wildflower," he softly commanded.

Jules lifted her regard to his and became lost. There was a look in his eyes that was as unfathomable as the terrifying depths of the ocean. That sense of smallness he had alluded to that one felt when staring at the power of nature, Jules felt it now. He sucked her under, and her heart ached at the cruel beauty of the need she felt burrowing under her skin. An unexpected dart of fear went through her.

"Do not fear what is between us," he said, spinning her into a twirl. James commanded her steps with graceful and powerful movements, and with each glide and twist and turn it felt like the eyes of the *haut ton* dissected their every move.

"Are you not at all uncertain about it?"

"No."

Her mind groped for something, anything else, yet nothing came to Jules. The ache of want in her chest became a physical thing, and there was no ease in its tightening grip. James tugged her a little closer than what was considered proper, and a breath trembled from her lips. They glided across the expanse of the ballroom, staring into each other's eyes. Jules felt dangerously alive, her heart and body exquisitely tormented by the intense feelings burning through her for this man.

"I am not afraid, James." *Liar*, a small voice inside taunted.

He spun her away from him, and she twirled in two rotations before she was back in his arms, this time even scandalously closer.

"Good."

The waltz ended, and he escorted her to the refreshment table where he bowed before making his way from the ballroom. Another ripple of shock went through the room, and she could feel the duchess's eyes burning into her. Jules snagged a glass of champagne and emptied the contents, somehow knowing that James was out there waiting for her.

# Chapter Twelve

Jules sauntered from the ballroom, uncaring of the multiple eyes piercing into her shoulders, especially the duchess's own. She could feel the intention in the stares, dissecting and digging deep, trying to uncover her identity and the reason their duke had danced only with her. As if a mere glare would allow them to see the thread of connection that had inexplicably tethered them together, or the nerves cascading through Jules.

Once outside, Jules looked around, yet he was not there. An empty feeling swirled up inside her chest, but, taking a steady breath, she swallowed down the nerves erupting through her. She had no difficulty in guessing his current whereabouts. James had gone into the woods, leaving the choice entirely up to Jules to follow him. Gripping the edges of the ballgown, Jules made her way across the lawn, her delicate shoes whispering over the grass as she moved away from the laughter and revelry, the darkness of the night obscuring her venture across the lawns from inquisitive eyes.

On the edge of the woodlands, her steps hesitated for

a moment. The night was black and intimidating. The tree limbs towering and gnarled. She entered the path leading to his tree house and faltered. There were lanterns lit along the path. Her heart started to pound a wild rhythm.

Had he been so certain she would come? She felt as if she made an irrevocable step, and even though she'd always known being with the duke in an intimate fashion had been long decided, now it felt unalterable. Jules hastened along the path, the breath easing from her chest when she saw him waiting below the ladder leading up to the tree house.

A wild emotion leaped in his eyes when he saw her. Jules went to him. He touched her cheek with the tips of his fingers, and for a moment, she savored the wonderful caress. James stooped and removed her shoes, placing them neatly at the trunk. She sucked in a harsh breath when he slipped his hand underneath her gown, untying the tapes to her stockings, and gently rolled them off. She turned around at his urging, finally smiling when he unhooked the full skirts and assisted her to step out of her gown and the bustle.

Jules climbed the tree half naked but much more secure that she would not accidentally topple from the ladder. She entered the cottage and slowed her steps, peering at the dozens of candles that lit up the space.

"I made it a bit…softer for you," he said gruffly.

A well-padded and sweetly scented pallet had been added. And at least a dozen cushions, all made from dark gold, blue, and green brocade. A table was pushed against a corner, and there rested a decanter of amber liquid—whisky perhaps—two glasses, and a plate of cakes. The night was alive with the sounds of the owls, birds, and other creatures as they made their music and the whispering of the wind between the trees. Everything felt enchanting.

"Thank you," Jules said, hiding her smile and the warmth spreading through her entire body.

She closed her eyes and leaned back against James when he hugged her from behind, pushing his nose against the curve of her throat, and inhaled.

"I like when you smell me."

She felt the curve of his mouth against her flesh.

"I knew you would come to find my nose charming."

Jules turned in the cage of his arms, peering up at him.

"Give me your honesty. What are you feeling?"

"I long for your touch, James."

"Good, because I ache to consume you and fear I might fall on you like a savage beast."

A sharp ache stabbed downward through her womb and along her inner thighs. "Fall on me," she whispered. "I want that…I want you."

Their mouths came together in a burning kiss. He kissed her with a fierce, consuming hunger that turned her nerves to fire. She wanted to crawl inside him. No, she wanted him inside her. There was a tightening within Jules's chest and also a loosening. James couldn't stop touching her, caressing her throat, over her collar and down to her breasts. He undressed her, his fingers nimble and swift, then rough when the garment resisted his advancement. Soon it fell away, and she was caught up in lust and hardly aware that she was perfectly naked before another person.

James swiped his thumb over her nipple before capturing the hard pebble between his thumb and forefinger. She gasped at the pleasure throbbing through the tip and leaned more into his wicked caress. Jules pulled away from him, and a little laugh that was remarkably breathless left her. "I have taken leave of my senses."

"Do you want to leave?" he muttered roughly against her mouth.

He used the back of his fingers to brush against her throat before trailing down to her collarbone.

"No," she gasped.

The hand that wasn't holding her against him came up and gripped her hair in his fist, tugging her head back. Jules's nipples became so hard, so tight, they were a near violent ache.

"Good, because I was not damn sure I would have been able to let you go," he groaned, hauling her against his chest, lifting her into his arms, and bearing her down on the cushions. His head lowered, his lips covered hers, and she was lost for endless moments. He launched from her, ripping at his clothes with impatient hands. She came upon her elbows, staring at him in awe. His body was delineated with brutally honed muscles...*everywhere*. James was simply breathtakingly stunning in a savage, beautiful way.

"You are so amazing," she whispered.

He prowled over to her, dropping to his knees on the blanket. He dipped his head and kissed the top of her knee, the soft brush of his mouth reverent. James's fingers trailed a path over her quivering belly, down to her thighs, and placed a cushion under her, as the heat in his gaze seared her sex.

Jules flushed to be so wantonly exposed to her lover.

"You are so damn lovely, Wildflower."

James lowered his head, and without any hesitation licked over her sex with a wicked curl of his tongue. She gasped, gripping the cushions to her sides.

"You taste sweet, so sweet and soft," he murmured and then he did it again.

Jules arched, biting her lips against the raw sounds that wanted to rush from her throat. The callous tips of his fingers stroked up her inner thigh until he reached the aching heart of her sex, where he sank two fingers deep, sucking her clitoris into his mouth. Jules moaned at the shock of terrible pleasure. Her upper body came off the bed, only to have his hand flatten against her stomach, pressing her back as his lips covered her wet sex.

"James," she cried out, instinctively threading her fingers through his hair to hold him even closer to her.

Her body tensed, drawn tight as the pleasure built inside her until it broke, cascading heat through her. The kisses and licks as he moved down her body to her inner thighs and the back of her knee she hadn't expected, and every touch felt like a sensual assault on her senses, leaving her disoriented but wanting more. James kissed her all over, inhaling and licking as he roused her body to feverish heights.

Her heartbeat throbbed against her ears as he explored the lines of her hips, belly, and breasts. Her nipples firmed instantly under his touch. And the way he inhaled her...oh God. The strength in his hands as he flipped Jules onto her belly was intimidating and arousing. His teeth sank into the globes of her buttocks, and she arched her hips, trembling. He licked along her spine, nipping at the curve of her hips and up to her shoulder blades.

He ran his fingers through her wetness, his touch edgy, and she cried out as he thrust two fingers inside her once again. His answering groan of pleasure reverberated through her entire body. The heat of him pressed along her back as he parted her thighs and slowly invaded her quivering sex. The pleasure-pain of his inexorable invasion was a fiery cascade of sensations that swamped Jules. It was too much...yet not enough for she still felt cold...and empty.

He curved his tall, muscular frame over hers. She turned her head and met his gaze, her heart trembling at the lust and the tenderness in his eyes.

"Hurt?"

"Yes."

He snaked a hand underneath her belly and rubbed her clitoris, filling the sensitive bundle of nerves with pained bliss. Jules grew so wet it was almost mortifying.

"Do not close your eyes, Wildflower."

She snapped her gaze open, gasping when his cock grew even harder insider her, though he did not move.

"I am cold, James," she whispered, wondering at the inexplicable emotions sweeping over her senses.

He kissed her with rough passion until heat pounded the blood through her heart, chest, and entire body. The cold fled and only the taste and scent of James surrounded her. He started to move within her, she cried out into his kiss, and he sucked the noise inside of him and returned it in a soft growl of pleasure.

His cock dragged from her, her sex clinging to it so tightly, she felt every inch of him as he retreated and then sank back inside her to the hilt. Their lips parted and he licked across her mouth, the curl of his tongue hot and evocative.

"Ease slightly onto your knees," he hissed, licking at a corner of her mouth.

A small sob of want and hunger clawed from Jules, and she pushed to her knees when he lifted some of his weight from her back. She panted when he bit into the curve of her throat, then kissed the sting away. Sweat slicked her body as his skin slid against hers, her fingers tightening in the cushions, and her breath trembled from her lips to his. He rolled his hips, plunging into her, over and over. He kept his rhythm slow but hard and heavy, and her arousal grew so intense her thighs shook.

The reactions filling her were like nothing she could have imagined. Sensations gathered within, drawing her closer to rapture. His hips snapped harder, and the pressure built inside, and pleasure rolled over her in hot, devastating waves. Jules forgot to scream, to even think, lost in the bone-jarring pleasure that consumed her.

*I like you too much,* she whispered silently, feeling as if her soul cried for his.

His fingers glided over hers, and their hands clenched together in the cushions as he rode her through her release, chasing his own pleasure until he groaned in the crook of her neck, withdrawing to release outside of her body.

He held her to his chest for unending minutes, before moving from her. She instantly missed his heat but was too tired to protest. Their pleasure had been pure and explosive; startlingly she felt drained and wanted to sleep. Jules did not resist the temptation, closing her eyes and allowing the darkness to claim her.

Sometime later, when Jules stirred awake, she was snuggled atop James's chest, stifling a yawn as she listened to the jerk of his heartbeat. It was slow and steady and soothing.

"You smell of the fragrance of spring and the crispness of winter. I will never tire of this scent, and I shall miss you when you are gone," he murmured.

*Gone.* She buried down the raw flare of emotion his words elicited. "How did you know I awakened?"

"I heard the increase in your heartbeat."

Jules trailed her fingers over his chest, turning her nose against him to inhale.

She loved his scent, and she nipped his flesh, kissing his body because he was just so beautifully formed with corded smooth muscle, full of power and elegance. This man drew at an instinct within her that had not been apparent before during her entire existence, and Jules was helpless against its awakening. "I shall miss you, too, James, very much so."

She worshipped the terrains of his body, whispering kisses over the brutal cut of muscles shaped by the wildness of surviving those ice-capped mountains. She glided the tip of a single finger over the deep furrows that ran from his lower back, across to his hips, and down the muscular trunk of his thighs.

Jules shimmered down his body and laved the brutal

scars with her tongue, smiling when his body stirred. "What caused these?"

"The bear Luna and I fought."

She rested her chin on his thigh. "How did you survive it, James?"

"I was lost for a time to fever and delirium. I have no notion of how many days passed, but when I came to, the pack was there, holding a vigil in a tight circle."

Her chest tightened at the impossibility of what he suggested. "They saw you as a pack mate," she whispered, awed.

A sound rumbled from his chest, a hiss of pain she wondered if he knew he made.

"You miss them...and you hurt."

A taut silence fell.

"I cannot fathom why," he said.

Jules turned over on the cushions to lay on her belly, peering out into the night and the towering skyline of majestic trees. "They were more than wild wolves. They adopted you into their pack. They were your family...your friends...and you might never see them again."

"I suppose they were," he said gruffly. "Luna is not alone. She found a mate only a few days before I fell down the mountain. A wolf only has one partner in a lifetime. They are only separated by death."

A hitch darted through her heart. "That feels beautiful."

"It is."

A small silence fell, and within it Jules felt the echo of his peace. She pushed to her feet, quite aware of her nakedness and his hungry stare upon her buttocks. Jules peeked over her shoulder and when their gazes collided, she winked. He laughed, the sound low and husky. She went to the small table, poured whisky into two glasses, and handed him one, before collapsing against a mound of cushions, comfortable in her nakedness with the duke. Jules hid a smile in her glass, thinking it surreal that she was here in this perfect moment with him.

Her belly tightened with unexpected grief. *How long will it last?*

"Do you hunger to live as a lady, Wildflower?"

The soft, unexpected question jolted Jules, but her answer was immediate. "Never. If I did wonder about it, it was fleeting at best and not a true yearning."

"How certain you are," he mused, taking a sip of his whisky, looking very much like a powerful pasha sprawled against the cushions, his curtain of hair falling about his shoulders like midnight silk. "You've never thought of children...a husband?"

"Why should I?" she asked, knocking back the drink in a long, pleasurable swallow. "Because underneath the disguise I am a woman I must therefore think of babies?"

An indefinable emotion gleamed in his gaze. "Of course not. But even I find myself, when I stand on the ledge and peer at the night sky, thinking of the children I might have someday. A son...a daughter...I think of the world they might be born to and the courage they might need to face it. I think of how I will prepare the next duke...my son, to understand this world when I have been absent from it so long and no longer hunger to know it. What thoughts do you have of the future?"

Her heart ached at his words. "All thoughts I own are to continue as Jules Southby. To be anything else may lead to scandal, ruin, and most certainly I would live an unfulfilled life. That notion is rather unbearable."

"Unfulfilled?"

She almost felt lost in his intriguing stare. "Is it not only gentlemen who have all the freedom? Women are always confined to one corner of the earth, under the rule of the men in their lives. They leave one cage and go to another once they are married. I have a sister, Sarah, and I wish we were closer. If I should suggest to her that we race across the fields of our homes, she must first consider what our father might say, and then her husband. For something as simple as a race on our horses. Can you imagine it? Why would I want to live as a woman? A lady must see the man she loves as the great vast sky while she remains a speck on the fields below."

Jules opened her mouth to say more, but her voice caught in her throat, and she could not utter a single word. The only thing she felt was the harsh beat of her heart. *It is so damn silly that I want you to be my sky, James.*

As if he knew what she thought, he said, "You would be the stars within any sky, Wildflower. Nothing less."

Jules remained as silent and motionless as a statue. What were they admitting to? Afraid of the answer, she whispered, "A husband's ambitions and aspirations must be his wife's own. To live as a woman, I would relinquish all I have gained in my life. I would never be able to practice as a doctor of the mind or help others. Instead, my worth would be relegated to what my husband allows. I've lived as a male my whole life. I have no wish to change it."

He reached for her, and she set her glass down, curving her body against his. He trailed the back of his fingers over her cheek and down to her throat. "Have you no desires from the female persuasion?"

Jules touched his lips with fingers that trembled. "I've allowed myself this moment with you."

A lingering silence fell, then her duke said, "Tell me your story in full. How did you come to be this chameleon?"

"As my mother tells it, my father ardently desired a son. My mother found child birth extremely difficult so she cast this deception to give her that reprieve. She pretended I was a boy child with the intention to only pretend for a few years. We are still pretending," Jules said softly, "and we may forever pretend."

"How old were you when you discovered that you were not a lad?"

"I was a little over twelve," she said, resting her head against his chest. "My belly cramped...I bled, and I thought I was dying. No one had ever explained to me the changes my body would go through. My mother and I were close, so I ran to her with my fears. She forbid me to ever reveal this to my father and then she told me everything."

"It must have been a shock."

"I was more confused, but I then realized why my mother did not agree for me to attend Eton but have home tutors," Jules said, lost in the memory. "I was also afraid because my mother was afraid. I loved her and I understood it was very important for me to keep this secret. As my body changed I learned to disguise my features, bind my breasts. My voice started to change...and I had to learn to maintain a low pitch. I watched as my sister prepared for a season, I observed how life was different for her...more proper and rigid and then keeping the secret was more than about protecting my mother, it was also so I did not lose the freedom with which I lived."

She brushed a lock of dark hair out of his eyes, tracing a fingertip across his forehead and over a silky eyebrow, before tugging his head low to meld her mouth to his. James made a noise deep in his throat. A primal, masculine sound of desire that sent shivers straight through Jules. This was the only thing she would allow...and Jules refused to permit irrational wishes into her heart. Their moment was now...this wicked and terrible pleasure between them, and nothing more.

# Chapter Thirteen

After a night of untamed loving with James in his tree house, the very next day, carriages and several other equipages from those that had stayed over after the ball had lined up in front of the house, then set off, rumbling and crunching down the gravel-lined driveway until they reached the church in the village. It was all a part of the duchess and her father's masterful plan of allowing society to see that their duke was adjusting well.

There was a shrewd, no-nonsense air about the duke as he scanned the occupants of the village church.

"I vaguely remember attending this small church as a child and being bored. It does not seem to have changed much."

Jules glanced around, aware of the sense of waiting as they were observed. The church smelled strange and musty with the scents of mold slightly covered by paint, incense, and a few flowers. It was not a particularly old church, but it seemed to not have been very well built. The walls were mostly white-washed and largely undecorated, but the stained-glass windows were nice.

The vicar effusively greeted the duke, bowing so much that Jules had wondered why he creaked when he bent low. Then she realized that the portly vicar was wearing a Cumberland corset under his vestments. Vicar Henderson's odor was of sweet wine, possibly fortified with brandy. He wore some kind of hair dressing which was perfumed with a hint of peppermint.

She covertly peeked at James, knowing the varied odors must be an acrid assault on his senses. He appeared unruffled and did not appear impressed by the new vicar who had been far too gratified that the *duke* was attending his church.

The townspeople were not very circumspect in their ogling. Everyone looked to be collectively holding their breath. The duke they'd all been speculating about had come to attend the morning service. Jules wondered if those looking on could tell that everything had changed between them, that his taste and scent lingered on her body, and that beneath her clothes strawberry marks covered her breasts, belly, and inner thighs. Could they tell that only a couple of hours ago she had stared at her body in the mirror in wonder, her fingers ghosting over everywhere he had touched and kissed?

"You are blushing, Southby," he murmured. "I wonder what is it that you think of?"

She arranged her features into what she hoped communicated boredom. When she took another quick peek at him, it was to see James smiling, his eyes gleaming with something far too provoking. The duchess and several members of his family sauntered before them, taking their seats among their places of honor in the front pews.

James stepped forward. "If I cross that threshold and do not burst into flames it was God who kept me for the years I've been in the wild. If I even fart and my expression changes, the devil kept me and I am a devil," he said with caustic drollness.

Jules swallowed the laugh bubbling in her throat. "You are outrageous," she said from the corner of her mouth.

"I have a very inappropriate sense of humor, I have discovered," he murmured. "My sister says she is in despair of it."

"Please do not ever change," Jules whispered.

They ventured forward and sat in the second row behind most of his family. This outing was just the first in many performances to reassure society. Except Jules truly believed James was becoming more tolerant of people, and earlier she had even seen him speaking with his aunt who had seemed delighted, even as she prodded him about the mysterious lady he danced with last night. His reserve on the matter only seemed to inflame his family's ire and curiosity.

Jules attended to the vicar's impassioned sermon, which spoke in length about the prodigal son and God's faithful mercies. His speech might have been a bit inappropriate and there were some murmurings amongst those who sat farther back. However, those chattering were soon silenced by the announcement of a rousing hymn. The rest of the service dragged on, but after a final blessing, it was over.

Jules wondered how James was coping with it all, the people, being closed in and the strong scents that must overstimulate his senses. Then the vicar and choir traipsed out and shortly afterward the vicar appeared at the now open doors, dressed in a dark suit with a clerical collar. The congregation appeared to be waiting for the duke to leave first as no one moved. Eventually James stood and led his party down the aisle to say their farewells to the vicar. His eyes were politely indifferent, and Jules could not read what he felt. Her father and the duchess cast him glances of concern, but he did not attend to them.

"I will walk back to the estate," he said to his mother.

The duchess's eyes widened in dismay. "It will take hours, Wulverton!"

"Then it will," he said mildly, his gray-blue eyes unfathomable.

Jules suspected he did not wish to be confined in the carriage. "If it is not an inconvenience Your Grace, perhaps I might accompany you."

"The pleasure of your company would be appreciated, Southby."

He bowed courteously to his mother, and Jules followed, and as they strolled away she could feel the duchess's probing stare upon their shoulders. James took them along a path deep into the woods and away from the main road. They walked toward a grassy bank above a small stream. With each step she felt the tension leak from his shoulders, and he tipped his head to the sky, inhaling the brisk air into his lungs.

"Today we attended church, tomorrow night we will sin."

Thrill shot through her chest and Jules arched a brow in question. "Of what do you speak, duke?"

"Linfield has invited me for a night about town. Will you come with me?"

Her heart skipped a few beats. "To London?"

"Yes."

"Tomorrow?"

"We leave tonight. I have sent word to open the town house."

She stared at him in astonishment. "Is the duchess aware?"

It was the duke's turn to lift an imperious brow. "Am I to ask my mother permission to open my town house?"

Jules hid her smile. "Of course not, but the duchess may have other plans."

There was a dangerous gleam in the gaze that glanced at her. "Is it not fortunate I have my own mind, Wildflower?"

"And you wish for me to accompany you about town?"

"Yes."

The way he drawled his answer pitched sensations low in her belly. "Then I shall accompany you, my good duke."

James reached for her, and she flowed into his arms with a sigh of pleasure, tipping her face upward.

He paused, his lips almost touching hers. "I wanted to do this the moment I saw you this morning."

Jules trembled slightly, anticipating his embrace. James touched his mouth to hers. Somehow she thought he would have been ravishing, bruising her lips with his passion. Yet he was…tender, and something fierce yet sweet hitched through her heart as their tongues glided sensually and sinuously.

Jules moaned into his kiss. Oh, he was so very good at it. He sucked at her tongue, and she threaded her fingers through his hair, gripping him to her. She didn't want to ever lose this feeling, the taste and feel of him. A hungry little whimper broke from Jules when he pushed her against the rough bark of a tree and shoved his hand between their tightly fitted bodies.

He went straight for the front flap of her trousers, undoing the opening with impatient tugs, pushing his hands down to slide his fingers deep inside her sex. Jules gasped into his mouth, and he took the sound within him, returning a purr of pleasure that vibrated deep inside her body, landing hotly inside her quim.

She was sore from last night, but none of that mattered, because every prudent consideration had been tossed to the winds. Jules felt seared…consumed…and far too daring. Knowing they could be discovered by anyone wandering through the woods heightened something inexplicable inside her. James pulled from her, dropped to his knees, leaned forward, and licked her exposed sex. She cried out at the lash of exquisite pleasure.

The sound of the babbling brook, its swollen waters rippling over boulders and rocks, and the scent of the forest drowned away under a haze of arousal. It was only the duke and her in this moment.

James's fingers stroked even deeper inside her cunny, and Jules almost wailed when he added a third finger, stretching and devastating her senses when he sucked her clitoris into his mouth. Her thighs trembled and she sagged against the tree, slapping a hand over her mouth to contain her hoarse sounds of pleasure. Her other hand held his head to her as he licked and tormented her with his tongue.

James released her, whirling her to face the tree, his thighs shoving between her from behind. His cock pressed against her sex and Jules leaned her head back against his shoulder as he forged into her until she felt filled to bursting with the overwhelming pressure.

His teeth grazed her arched neck. "You are tight and wet...and smell so damn sweet."

The rough whisper had her clenching her belly to fight against the hot surge of arousal. Nothing should feel this intense, and Jules hated to admit these feelings scared her.

"Open the shirt. I want to see your nipples."

She licked her lips and breathed in raggedly, but Jules obeyed, her fingers shaking as she unbuttoned her waistcoat and then untied her cravat before unbuttoning her shirt. He reached inside and tugged the bindings until the cool air washed over her breasts.

"How pretty," he breathed, reaching around to cup them in his large hands.

He began a slow, deliberate massage of her breasts, fingers tugging and rolling her nipples. The feeling of his rough calloused thumbs pinching and plucking her sensitive tips pulled a whimper from Jules.

"I smell your lush sultriness before your response

soaks my cock, and these tight little ripples are killing me, Wildflower."

His lips moved to her shoulder, and he kissed right at the hollow of her throat, over her fiercely beating pulse.

"James?"

"Hmm?"

"Move," she choked out, "move now!"

His chuckle was low and filled with heated carnality. His fingers tightening on her nipples, he reconciled his hips and shoved his cock deep inside her, ripping a wild cry from Jules. Each penetrating stroke filled her with pressure and such pleasure that Jules sobbed. Ecstasy built in delicious, wicked spikes until she shattered, and with a ragged groan he chased his own pleasure, pulling from her body to release.

They stood there, breathing harshly for several moments. She laughed, the sound shaky when he reached down and pulled up her trousers, helping her to fix herself. Jules felt so weakened by their passionate encounter that she lowered herself to the thick grass, staring up at the foliage and the towering trees. James reposed beside her, and she shifted until her head was touching his shoulder. Somehow she knew when their affair ended, a place inside her would be devastated. A tight feeling entered her chest, and she took a deep breath to steady herself against it.

"The death anniversary of my father approaches," he said.

Jules shifted, slanting so she could peer at his expression. James was carefully composed, and that informed her that he perhaps felt much. Sensing her probing regard, he gave a grim, humorless tug of his mouth. That small smile was more of a warning, and she laced her fingers through his. "How long has it been since he died?"

The duke was silent for a long time, and despite their intimacy and friendship, Jules knew he was not a man given to easy sharing of his past and thoughts.

"Six years," he said gruffly. "I overheard the duchess speaking to him in the gardens...as if he lived still. She told him of her joy to have me back and how much I resembled him."

"How did you feel hearing her?"

"Empty."

Her fingers tightened on his and a quiet fell between them.

"She had not known of my presence, and I left before she discovered me there. The duchess tried speaking about my father this morning and I...I had nothing to offer."

"Do you think of him often?"

"He is gone," he said, an echo of an indefinable emotion in his tone. "There are other times I feel something wanting to delve through this crack in me, but I close it down, not liking it. Though in the quiet of the night I do find myself sometimes wondering what it is."

Jules thought about the will it must have taken to survive his ordeal. "Isolating oneself from emotions, from feeling anything too deeply is a defense mechanism to protect yourself from pain and torment. You severed that link, James, and it is natural for you to lack pain and guilt or even grief. Remember, I told you that feelings will come back as you allow yourself to open up again."

There was a contemplative beat.

"I feel, Wildflower."

The way he said this rumbled through her.

"Do you?" Her heart started to pound as she awaited his answer.

He rolled his body over hers, the power and strength in him equally comforting and intimidating. James threaded his fingers into the side of her hair, his hand cupping her head, holding her in place.

"All of it seems centered on you."

Jules's heart pounded. James held her gaze for long, silent moments. His gaze moved over her slowly, his expression shifting, his eyes darkening.

"Stay with me tonight in the woods."

"Yes."

He kissed the corner of her mouth. "Good."

It felt perfectly wonderful to simply lie there on the thick, verdant grass, the sun peeking from behind bloated clouds down at them, and talk about their shared experiences, even as Jules realized they deliberately made no mention of the hopes for their future or any friendship beyond her stay at Longbourn Park.

· · ·

James found his mother on the eastern lawns, sitting on a swing hanging from a large, majestic oak. He remembered being on this swing with her and his father as a lad, and even recalled teaching Felicity how to dig her toes into the earth to propel herself forward.

The duchess's lovely face held a faraway expression, and he suspected she was lost in the memories of his father. James allowed his bare feet to crunch over the leaves on the ground and she snapped her regard to him.

"James!"

A frown creased her forehead when she noted his casual mode of dress and his feet bare of shoes and stockings. Her sigh was filled with censure. He sat on the second swing, glancing up to the half-moon painting the sky.

"I leave for town in a couple of hours."

"I beg your pardon!"

A humorless smile touched his mouth. "I leave for town soon."

"I cannot credit that you would—"

"Jules Southby will be with me."

"Is that supposed to reassure me, Wulverton?" she said frostily. "You are not ready—"

He leveled a curious gaze at her. "It is not up to you to decide what I am ready for. I'll not be running around town like a lunatic if that is your worry."

His mother's lips flattened, and she made a sound of frustration. James had only meant to inform her he was leaving for a few days. Now that he had done so he would retreat back into the woods and to his lover whom he had left sleeping deeply after another bout of lovemaking. He stood, frowning as he recalled the words his lover had said to him as they held a long, intense discourse.

*Eventually it will be perfectly well to allow those cracks to widen, especially for your family.*

He lowered himself back to the swing and met her regard.

"I keep with me always that I am the Duke of Wulverton. The family's name will be safe from scrutiny, Duchess. I assure you, there will be no need to worry I will shame the family."

Emotions flared her eyes wide. "Then why have you not answered anyone's query as to who the mystery woman was you danced with last night? Everyone was in an uproar when you left!"

"Her identity is not important."

The duchess narrowed her gaze. "Is this person someone you might make your duchess?"

An intense, primal sensation hooked itself through his chest. "She is…a friend, nothing more."

"You did not look at each other as if it were only friendship. I was mortified by your…intensity, and Uncle Hubert speculated this lady might be your *mistress*. You *cannot* marry somehow who does not have the social connection and reputation to make our family. I do not wish for you to be mortified by anything, and our society can be vicious."

A dark humor washed through him. "Nothing can embarrass me, Mother."

"You have no humility," she said tartly. "Or concern for my nerves which have not been settled since last night."

"Is that lack of humility not the mark of a good duke?"

She blinked. "You are smiling."

He lifted a brow. "I have been known to do it from time to time."

"Never with me or the rest of your family," she said, smiling in return. "Only with Mr. Southby. The connection observed between you both is rather...interesting."

There was an inquisitive, almost hesitant nature to her probing. James glanced toward the path leading to his woodland cottage and his sleeping lover. He had nothing to say to his mother's assertion and chose to remain silent.

"Your Uncle Hubert, Aunt Margaret, and your cousins will also withdraw to town in a few days in preparation for the start of the season. All the preparations are underway for the ball. It is to be held at a new town house I'd purchased in Mayfair. That is where it has been held for the last three years."

James assessed the pointed way his mother stared off in the distance. "I have sent word for the town house in Grosvenor Square to be opened."

Her throat worked on a swallow. "Very well."

"Why did you make a new purchase?"

His mother met his gaze, and a sharp feeling lanced into his chest at the flash of pain.

"It was where your father went on to his rewards." Her gloved hands tightened on the rope of the swing. "It has been most difficult to return to Grosvenor Square."

"Some of my last memories of him is that year I turned eighteen and he took me with him to Westminster."

Her face softened. "He spoke of it often as well, James. Your father never believed you had died and that you would return home one day. Every day we spoke of you."

James's heart started to pound. "The anniversary of his death looms."

"Yes," she said gently. "I no longer spend it weeping but in conversation with him. You might think it silly, but I feel as if your father is here with me. Even when I sleep, I feel his arms wrapped around me and I am comforted."

"There is nothing about you I find silly. You are a woman of strength, Mother."

Her lips parted in surprise, and she stared at him as if she did not know what to make of him in that moment.

"And your strength amazes me, my son," she said with another smile, reaching over to touch him.

He froze, and as she snatched her hand back, James reached for it and held it between his. It was not an unpleasant feeling. His mother stared at where they touched. When she looked up at him, unshed tears brimmed in her gaze. Unable to hold that connection for too long, James slowly released her. She did not seem to mind it, for she beamed at him, her happiness naked on her face.

"Do you believe you will be ready to dance with Lady Emelia at the ball in town?"

That coldness whispered through him. "With some contrivance it might be bearable."

Though the duchess nodded, worry burned in her eyes, reminding him how much she still needed for him to present the perfect facade to the world.

James stood, leaned forward, and brushed his lips over her cheek. "I shall return to Hertfordshire in a few days."

As he walked toward the woods, the tension loosened

itself around his neck.

"James?"

At that soft entreaty he paused and turned to face his mother. She was looking behind him into the darkened woods.

"No duchess of yours will be able to accept that you spend most of your time…there. You do not sleep in your bed or dine formally with your family!"

From the rough frustration in her tone, he surmised not even his mother accepted it.

"You will need to give up any sort of behavior that…that might give the impression you are…savage and…" Her lips tightened over whatever words she meant to say.

James gave no answer, merely turned back around, that dark wash of humor filling him once more. What did the world truly know of savagery? That amusement eased and an odd sort of bleakness filled him. A sense that taking a wife might be akin to placing himself in a tightly confined cage of expectation that he would never be able to meet scythed through him. He thought of this phantom creature who might swoon and wilt at his supposed savagery and unrefined manners. James frowned, but all thoughts of this wife he would need to pick crumbled as he ventured deeper into the woods, the scent of his wildflower reaching him and calming the tempest.

• • •

A couple days later the Marquess of Linfield took the duke and Jules out on the town. First they visited a popular drinking establishment for gentlemen. They tried the ale and Jules struggled to keep up with their drinking, making sure to swap tankards with James when Linfield went to the jakes, thus avoiding drinking too much. There were cards and dice being played at other tables but no heavy gambling as there would be in a gaming house.

"Are you going to play cards or dice, my lord?" Jules asked.

"The bit I experienced of gambling bored me. That is what I will tell Linfield if he wants to take us to a gambling den. Don't worry—I won't let you be fleeced by the sharpers in Town."

She jutted her chin and affected her most mincing drawl, "I am brilliant at gambling, my good duke. There is no need to worry I'll be taken advantage of."

James's lips quirked in a smile. "Are you?"

"Hmm, the lads at University thought they could defeat me many times. I took pleasure in correcting those assumptions. I must take you to the *Acolytes*, a very notorious gambling hell that only caters to the elites of London."

He lifted a brow. "A regular, are you?"

Jules laughed. "I was not lofty enough to gain admittance…but you…they will trip over themselves for their enigmatic and possibly feral duke to attend, and since I am your most loyal…erm, friend, how can I not take advantage and dazzle you with my skills at poker?"

"Poker?"

"Aye," she drawled, leaning back in her chair. "Many said it was our Queen who demanded to know the rules after hearing about it. It was introduced in the *Acolytes* only a few months ago, according to the scandal rags."

James's eyes gleamed with amusement. "You read the scandal rags. A creature of such interesting facets."

She took a sip of her ale. "An annoying love inherited from my mother. The stories can be rather titillating."

The marquess rejoined their table, and after a few more pints, Linfield suggested they move on to somewhere more exciting. Jules staggered a little as she stood, not having been able to avoid drinking more of the ale than she would have liked.

James pinned the marquess with a stare that appeared far too menacing when Linfield slapped Jules on his back, saying, "Come on, man, you have to learn to carry your drink, we're gentlemen out on the Town and we intend to have some fun before the night is over."

"Not foxed, my lord, just tripped over the table leg getting up. Lead on, my lord," Jules cried a bit too merrily. *Bloody hell. I* am *getting tippled.*

Over the marquess's head James arched a brow, Jules winked and he grinned, the raw sensuality inherent in that smile provoking a swirl of hot sensation low in her belly.

They all bundled into Linfield's carriage which stopped outside a house in Soho Square.

"What is this place, Linfield?" James asked, lifting an arrogant brow when they alighted from the marquess's carriage.

"Madame Laurent's, it's a nunnery...cunny house..." Linfield stopped as James clearly wore a bemused expression.

"A cunny house?"

The marquess tossed his arms about the duke's shoulder. "You have missed much in your years gone, my friend. Tonight we will start making up for it."

An arrow of shock went through Jules. Were they at a brothel?

James lifted a brow, a curious glint darkening his eyes.

A small sound of anticipation came from the marquess. "This is a very high-class accommodation house, a school of Venus and caters only to wealthy clients, but nonetheless a brothel."

Jules schooled her expression into what she hoped was a nonchalant mask, even as her heart jolted. She was curious, for even though she masqueraded as a gentleman, Jules had never visited a house of ill repute before. There was another part of her furious that James might be enticed to partake. Jules could not understand or explain the feelings seething inside her chest.

A pair of heavy-set men in livery stood stone-faced on either side of the front door. A footman with a healed but misshapen broken nose obviously recognized Linfield and promptly admitted them. The house was fashionably decorated but tended to the over-opulent, the salon that Linfield led them into featured many overstuffed sofas and an excess of gilding. On one wall was a large but relatively amateur painting of Leda and the swans, other classical nudes were clustered on the walls, although some of the subjects seemed to be of couples engaged in sexual acts.

Having taken in the somewhat exotic decor, Jules gazed around at the lush beauties on decadent display.

"There are women and dancing here on the first floor," the marquess said with a carnal smile. "Gambling on the second floor, and the private bedrooms are on the third. Indulge for the night, my friends. This treat is all mine."

A beautiful lady approached, introduced herself as Madam Vinnette, and greeted Linfield with carnal familiarity. Her eyes devoured James and interest sparked in the madame's gray eyes. When she looked at Jules, she considered her for only a brief moment, then said, "I know the perfect ladies for you gentlemen."

The madam sauntered scandalously close to Jules and trailed a manicured finger along her cheekbones.

"I do believe Jocelyn will enjoy you."

A spurt of humor shook Jules and she leaned away from the touch.

"I am sure Southby will be a nice surprise to her," the marquess said, a lustful twinkle in his eyes.

James winked at her above the madam's head, and Jules swallowed the groan, tugging at her neckcloth.

The madam who had witnessed the exchange arched a brow. "Allow me to escort you to some private rooms."

"Are you up for the experience, Southby?" Linfield murmured mockingly. "You seem a bit flushed."

"Linfield, you have no reason for concern. Our ladies can deal even with the most nervous of men. Young man," the madam said, turning to Jules. "Jocelyn will give you an education in the erotic arts that I am sure you will enjoy."

Jules affected an air of nonchalance, fighting the ridiculous blush climbing her cheeks. Thank heavens for the stage makeup. Still, a rough sound of provoking amusement came from James, and even the marquess laughed and said something to James about his important person being wet behind the ears and they should probably send him away in the carriage. Jules wished she could land him a bloody facer.

James stared at Jules, his gaze questioning her comfort and the tension unknotted from her belly. Jules nodded imperceptibly for somehow she knew he would never allow any harm to her person. The promise of it was naked in his eyes and her heart trembled with emotions.

The madam led them to the third floor, showing each to a private room. Once in hers, Jules groaned and leaned against the door. "This is a disaster," she muttered. "What am I to do with a bloody bird of paradise?"

Loud giggles sounded, and straightening, she glared at the connecting door in her chamber. Jules padded over, frowning when she recognized the marquess and the duke's voices. She opened the door, and to her credit Jules did not startle when she saw a scantily clad lady in the room with the two gentlemen. Nor did she growl, which would be perfectly permissible given the feral feel crawling through her at the suggestive looks the lady cast the duke.

"Are you to join us, Southby?" the marquess drawled with a sensual smirk. "The more the merrier, I say. Can you take all three of us sweetheart?"

"Oh yes," the Cyprian purred, sauntering over to Jules to run a finger over her lip. "I can tell you'll be the sweetest with me."

Almost amused by the absurdity of it all, Jules bit her finger and the cyprian darted away, gaily laughing.

Her eyes sparkling with wicked anticipation, the cyprian shifted to James. "I can tell you'll be the one to ride me the longest...and perhaps the roughest?"

She licked her lips, clearly anticipating that treat.

Something hot and dangerous burned inside Jules's throat, and she must have made a sound, for James glanced at her, a cynical humor burning in his gaze. Jules narrowed hers on his in ire.

*Good heavens, I am bloody jealous!* She had to take command of her emotions lest the marquess start to wonder why the hell she was out of sorts.

"Ah, sweetheart, I am wounded," the marquess said pressing his hand over his heart. "No thoughts on my prowess?"

The courtesan smirked. "You'll no longer feel so when I take your cock in my mouth, darling."

The marquess hummed his approval, grabbed her around the waist, and claimed her mouth in a deep kiss that had the Cyprian sagging against him. With shocking ease and skill, she undid the marquess's flap and sank to her knees. Jules contained her gasp when his manhood sprung forth and the lady sucked along his length. The marquess fisted her hair in his hand, tilting her head back.

"Are you to join us, James?"

Jules glanced at the duke. He was watching the display with an indecipherable mien. Was he curious about the pleasures the marquess experienced? Pinpricks of ice and heat stabbed at her chest, and jutting her chin forward she demanded, "*Are* you joining, Your Grace?"

# Chapter Fourteen

James wrenched his attention from the lascivious display to stare at his Wildflower. She stood by the connecting door, her hands fisted at her side, something wild and fiery in her green gaze. The soft question throbbed with an undercurrent of anger and something else James could not identify. It felt unquestionably dangerous. "Joining?"

"Are you to ride her while she sucks the marquess and I presumably drink brandy and watch?" Jules drawled.

He stared at his Wildflower, noting the pert bite in her tone. There might even be a hint of anger in those pretty green eyes. He smiled and she narrowed her dangerous regard. James padded over to her so that his words could not be overheard. Not that he thought Linfield paid them any heed. "If I should join, Wildflower?"

Her chin lifted in feminine arrogance, then she squared her shoulders. "I should indulge, too, of course. Very easy to find a room to change into one of those revealing dresses. I wonder if Linfield would know that—"

A feral hiss leaped from James before he could control

it, and he hauled her roughly against his chest, tugging her into the adjoining room. The door closed behind them, and he latched it. She whirled away from him, far more agile and graceful than he expected.

"Should the marquess or any other man touch you I would break them to pieces," he said with mild calmness, so at odds to with the raw feelings rushing through his veins.

A smile, bold and teasing, curled at her lips. "So you do not like the idea of another gentleman touching me?"

"No." *Not now and not ever.* His damn heart pounded at the emerging awareness.

She swallowed, and within a few steps stood before him, curling her hands around his neck. There was something soft and uncertain in the eyes that looked up at him. "I do not like the idea of you with another woman. Not while we are lovers," she said softly. "I cannot bear the idea of it."

James dropped his forehead to hers, then lowered even farther, his lips touching hers. "My loyalty and faith are yours, no one else's."

The words were pushed from him without conscious thought and echoed with a truth he knew with implacable certainty. His promise wrapped itself around their bodies like a tangible entity. Shock widened her eyes and he realized she had not expected it from him.

"James?"

"You heard me correctly."

He could feel the racing of her heart, and knew she was frightened before he even scented the change in her. James tugged her even closer against his body, and she immediately softened against him. He covered her mouth with his in a ravaging kiss, his tongue parting them, and he sank into bliss. His wildflower smelled like the fresh crispiness that lingered in the air on the breaking of a new dawn. The scent of the forest invaded his senses, the fragrance of snow. She surrounded his senses and burrowed deep under his skin. He smelled her hair, unable to stop the urge, trapping her wild flavor into his lungs.

He licked and sucked at her tongue, then groaned with desperate pleasure as she sucked at his. He fell into something he hadn't known had been missing from his life...from his damn soul. He fell into her taste, sweet and refreshing as the water droplets from the ice-laden branches in the mountain.

"I feel as if I never want to lose you," her breath whispered against his mouth, her eyes wide and searching on his. "I do not like this feeling of not being able to control the longings beating inside my heart, but I do know that my loyalty and faith also belong to you."

His Wildflower was asking James for an answer to whatever burned between them. He could give her none, for he himself had never felt chained to anything greater than surviving. This felt like...living. That hope he had buried so deep nothing would ever unearth it, pushed upward from its dark crevices, and reached for the woman in his arms.

James was not a man who thought of the future. Nothing mattered but the present. But as he cupped her cheeks and took her mouth once more with his, he thought that if he could do this tomorrow...and the next day and the next...the unexpected could be searched for.

"I want to do that to you," she said after pulling away from him. "Taste you as you tasted me."

James swallowed the groan rising in his chest. She danced over to the doors, ensuring each was closed and locked, before coming over to him. Holding his gaze, she reached between them and opened the flap of his trousers. His eyes were bright with mischief and sexual curiosity. His cock sprang forth, thick and hard, her delicate fingers barely able to encircle his girth.

She ran a finger over his length and a harsh breath pushed

from his chest.

"This feels good?" she asked softly.

"Yes," he hissed when she repeated the motion.

His Wildflower gracefully sank onto her knees before him, and without any hesitation sucked the head of his cock into her perfect little mouth. James almost snarled at the exquisite burn of pleasure. He wrapped his own hand at the base, squeezing so he did not release in her mouth like an untried lad. Her tongue curled over the head of his cock and exquisite pleasure bit at his nerve endings. He fisted the short strands of her hair, and she raked her teeth over his length. James hissed, trembling under the lash of pleasure. He could not last like this and he wanted to give her pleasure this night.

He hauled her to her feet and slammed his mouth against hers. She drew on his tongue, moaning that soft, feminine little sound of hunger that he loved. He tore his lips from hers, his teeth nipping at her jaw, her neck. James whirled her to face the wall, and she instinctively braced her hands. Snaking one of his hands around to her belly, he tugged her trousers open and shoved them down to her thighs. He glanced at the slender line of her exposed back, the taut curves of her rear. God, her arse was lush and rounded. The kiss James pressed into the curve of her neck was violent with restrained hunger. Following the instincts clawing through him, he bent and nipped the globes of her buttocks and sucked at the flesh there until there was a dark red mark.

James kicked her legs as wide as the trousers would allow, slid his fingers over her quivering stomach, and he found wet heat. Fuck, she was so damn wet. Soft, wanton sounds came from his lover, heightening his lust. Gripping her hips, he nudged his cock against her opening and pushed. Oh, the pleasure was exquisite.

"James," she cried softly, dropping her head back against his throat.

Her sex was narrow and tight, but he gripped her hips and with three hard thrusts, buried his length deep inside her wetness. She cried out, arching her back, her cunny squeezing and rippling over him. Hot, desperate pleasure crawled up the base of his spine and hardened his cock until it hurt.

"Hurt?" he managed to barely grunt out, ruthlessly holding back the need to spend like a callow youth.

"Yes…but a good kind of hurt," she moaned.

Her face was flushed with a delicate, rosy hue, and became a study in carnal pleasure. James kissed her shoulder blade before tenderly nipping the flesh. He felt like a damn starving animal. He wanted to consume everything about her.

He swiped his thumbs over her nipples before capturing the hard pebbles between his thumbs and forefingers, then rode her from behind. His Wildflower sucked him into a world of pure feeling and wonder, and he loved her until she convulsed in his arms, screaming her pleasure.

It took an inordinate amount of willpower to pull from her body without chasing his pleasure. James slowly removed her boots and undressed her until she was naked. He removed his clothes before lifting her into his arms and taking her over to the chaise lounge where he placed her. James blanketed her smaller frame with his, pushing his cock against her wet opening and gently entered her, their sighs echoing with the pleasure of joining.

The need burning through his soul was raw and insatiable, but he needed to be slow…to treasure and worship, to prolong their pleasure until they were wrecked with the need for release. And that was what he did, hooked her legs around his hips, kissed her over and over with deep licks and soft nips as he rode her long and deep.

"James, I need…!"

Jules's short nails raked his sweat-slicked skin, and she sank her teeth into his shoulder as her pussy rippled over his cock. Her release swept through her, and she convulsed, the clench of her inner muscles pulling his release from him before he was ready. With a harsh groan, he tumbled with her, withdrawing to empty outside of her body.

He turned with her, holding her against his chest. "Are you ready for a full night of wenching and drinking?"

A breathless laugh left her and she bit his chin. "Aye, Your Grace, I do believe I am."

"Well, I think Lindfield is fully occupied and we can leave him to his pleasures. He'll not miss us."

They dressed, kissing and teasing each other as they went about it with lazy ease. They checked their appearance in the mirror, prepared to leave the bordello. James unlocked the door to find the madam and another young lady framed in the doorway. The madam's discerning eyes missed little.

"I see," she murmured with a sly smile.

"Do you?" James drawled, understanding the madam assumed he was a molly. But something in her fascinated stare warned him that the madam suspected Jules Southby was of the female persuasion. He had seen the way she had assessed and touched his Wildflower earlier.

Jules choked when he tugged her to him and kissed her hard and brief. He then looked at the madam, letting the promise of ruination show in his gaze.

She dipped her head in a differential bow. "The bedrock of my business *is* discretion, Your Grace. I would long be out of business and chased from town if I had not practiced it."

James took Jules's hand and walked away. Once outside in the streets, Jules chuckled. He hauled her closer and touched the underside of her chin. "How and when did I get enchanted by you?"

A shaky breath left her lips. "Do recall I am here as a gent. Your stare is provocative."

"Let them see it and speculate. I do not care."

She smiled. "You are outrageous."

"I think you like it."

"I do, so very much."

Tenderness swelled through James. "Let's head back to my town house."

Jules canted her head. "Have enough fun for the night?"

"I find I want to sit with you by the fire...perhaps read a book or play chess."

"You are craving a quiet moment," she said softly, her gaze searching his. "If you wish for that moment alone, I understand, James."

"That's not it...I want to share that space with you, Wildflower."

Her breath audibly hitched, and an indefinable emotion filled her gaze before her lashes lowered. The air crackled and an odd sort of tension seeped between their bodies. Yet she did not say anything, and James did not wish to speak. Jules slipped her gloved hand between his and he squeezed her fingers, and they silently made their way to the street and to his waiting carriage.

# Chapter Fifteen

Late the next evening, James strolled through the halls of White's with an immaculately dressed Jules Southby by his side. The decor and ambiance of the famed gentlemen's club was as he remembered it. The marble floored club with its leather upholstered sofas and armchairs was as always a comfortable place to relax, and many gentlemen that James remembered vaguely from his youth were present. They all looked older but most of the faces were familiar even though he had not been introduced to most of the older men. A tight feeling entered his chest as he recalled the only time he had attended White's was with his father and he had smoked his first cigar with the old duke here.

"I have never been inside White's," Jules murmured, glancing around the common area. "It is impressive."

"Wulverton," the Earl of Summers greeted, a mixture of emotions gleaming in his brown gaze. "I cannot tell you how damn glad I am to see you. When I saw the news I..." The earl scrubbed a hand over his face, his feelings naked for all to see. "The news of your return was most welcome, Duke."

"It is good to see you, Summers," James said gruffly, the memory of their last time together heavy inside his chest.

He and the earl, who held the courtesy title Viscount Holland then, had been in the mountains hiking, rising to the challenge of scaling the winter landscape with all the exuberance of foolish youth. The rocks and ice beneath James's feet had fallen away and as he tumbled, the anguished cry of his friend had traveled with him for miles.

"I searched for you," Summers said, his eyes dark with remembered grief. "I did, I went back more than once with your father and I…"

"I know," James said. "I know."

A long silent stare passed between them, and his friend nodded tightly, his gaze shifting to land on Jules who stood only a few feet away.

"Mr. Jules Southby, I presume," Summers drawled, his eyes gleaming with speculation.

"You presume correctly, my lord," she said in that low, dulcet tone, dipping into a sharp, respectful bow. "A delight to make your acquaintance."

The earl's mouth hitched in a small smile. "Talks of your curious companion have been making the rounds about town, Wulverton."

"An oddity, am I?" Jules drawled, lifting a brow.

Summers pinned her with a stare. "I've never seen you in White's before. Your uncle is a member I believe."

Jules made a noncommittal sound low in her throat, and James hid his thoughts behind a cultivated facade of boredom, aware of the hushed whispers and many stares rife with speculation. They joined the earl at a table, and James took a healthy swallow of the brandy placed before him by the footman. Jules took a tentative sip, looking very much at ease in their surroundings. James realized then he could not imagine her in the traditional settings that ladies dominated.

"I hear congratulations are in order, Wolfe," the earl said.

"Enlighten me, Summers."

"You are about to select your duchess, are you not? There are already bets about the fortunate lady. Any insider information will go a long way, my friend."

A slight tremor went through his lover, commanding James's attention. She stared back at him silently, her expression unchanging, until he glimpsed her eyes. A powerful feeling shuddered inside the cage of his chest. His Wildflower was in pain.

"The intention is there," he said.

"Who is the fortunate lady?"

"It is yet to be decided."

The earl chuckled. "Come man, my lips will remain sealed. Is it Lady Emelia? The scandal rags all but have you two wedded."

"If it should be anyone...it would be her." The words stabbed deep inside him, and his Wildflower's scent changed.

Their gazes collided and he saw the naked pain in hers, and he understood some of the sensations tearing at her. This would end...and he could feel its inevitable demise looming and they might never see each other again. What would possibly happen for their worlds to collide? He felt a dark clawing sensation inside his chest, so raw and visceral it almost ripped a snarl from him. Jules looked away, and James noted that her fingers were gripping the glass of brandy far too tightly.

"Come, let's drink and then I will take you about town for a good time. You won't have much opportunity for such fun once you take a duchess."

From the earl's lascivious grin, James knew the kind of fun he implied.

"We shall drink this night," James said, "gamble and discuss politics if it suits, but I am not looking to bed anyone."

The earl seemed surprised by this, but he did not protest, he made a point of introducing James and Jules to other members and they chatted about politics, first discussing the Third Reform Act, which established a uniform franchise throughout the country, then they moved on to consider the planned Redistribution of Seats Act which would redraw the boundaries to equalize the districts.

There was some contention over the bill which caused some heated arguments, but James remained mostly quiet listening to the other men, calmy offering his opinion when needed, confident in his readings and understanding of the current political climate.

Jules articulated her views well on several matters to the point where Summers joked that she could become a member of Parliament. They had another drink before he departed with Jules. They spilled out into the chilled night air and James glanced at his pocket watch which showed it to be only minutes after midnight. A light, misting rain fell and Jules lifted her face to the sky, allowing the water to caress against her face.

"Your makeup will be ruined."

"I know," she said softly, her tone throbbing with an emotion he did not know.

"Look at me," he said gruffly.

Her throat worked on a swallow, and she took a deep breath before complying.

"I can see that you are in pain, Wildflower."

"I know, it is silly," she said with aching softness, pressing a palm over her chest. "But I hurt…right here…knowing this will end soon. You do not need me or my father, James, I doubt you ever did. You were so incredible tonight."

"I assure you a public ball is a different beast I will need to face," he murmured, his damn heart pounding. "Do not say goodbye as yet." *Not yet, Wildflower.*

They stared at each other, the emptiness of the night surrounding them. James did not know what words to offer or if he should offer any. "I do not want it...us...to end."

Her eyes widened, then she smiled even as her eyes remained dimmed, their soft luminosity shadowed. "So we are both being silly, hmm?"

*That we are, Wildflower.* "Do you regret it?"

"*Never,*" she said harshly, "I've told you I never regret once I step forward, and I will not regret anything with you."

The thumping torment rising inside his chest eased and James lifted his face to the rain. "The rain will come harder."

Her lips bravely curved. "I do not care, let's walk in it."

They strolled down St. James street, the only two souls about as the rain lashed down with more intensity. His Wildflower surprised him by starting to dance and sing in the rain, twirling and tapping her heels together in what looked like a Scottish jig.

James chuckled, and she tossed him a look over her shoulder, her lovely gaze gleaming with challenge.

"Will you join me, my good duke?"

"No."

Her shoulder rose in a shrug, she lifted her face to the heavens once more and shouted. Or was it a scream? The pain and agony in the sound scraped against his senses, raked at his belly, and dug deep like talons. He stood in silence, absorbing her emotions and understanding this was how she released the feelings that pulsed inside her at the thought of letting them go. James walked to stand beside her on the cobbled sidewalk, near a gas lamp. She took a heaving breath as the scream ended, and when their eyes met, he saw that tears glistened in her eyes.

"If I do not let it out...it will consume me," she said hoarsely. "I do not like feeling unmoored or as if I am not in control of myself."

He understood...there were days...nights...weeks, when the sense of loss would have cleaved him into pieces if he had not screamed it out to the shocking vastness of the mountains and caves. James lifted his face, tipped back his head, and howled.

• • •

The long mournful sound rippled across Jules's skin, raising the fine hair on her body. She had never heard a sound more beautiful and haunting from a human's throat, and she stared at the muscled column of his throat in awe. She understood then this must have been the sound he had learned from the pack who had kept him alive. The eerie note lifted even deeper before softly fading.

She stared at him, her heart pounding, a desperate longing welling inside her heart. A dart of hunger quivered through her belly, and she wanted so badly to step into his arms and hold him to her and never let go.

This evening James wore black, except for his snow-white shirt and cravat, and the deep burgundy silk waistcoat which fitted his lean frame to perfection. He wickedly wore his hair loosely caught at his nape, its length flowing over his shoulders and down to his back. As they had moved through White's, greeting old cronies and making new acquaintances, James had given the appearance of a gentleman in control of his behavior as he deftly avoided being touched, even in the barest of ways, by anyone.

A crack had formed inside Jules's chest, and with each moment spent in the company of the duke and his friends, it widened. James had prowled through the hallowed halls of White's, his gaze that of an arrogant and powerful duke certain of his privilege and position within the hierarchy of the *haut ton*. The few who dared whisper had met his steadily amused glare or perhaps it was indifferent regard. With his unflappable countenance and elegance of dress, James had silenced every skeptic and critic who'd thought they would see a man plagued by malady and nightmares. Those who had gawked at him had made deferential nods and respectful bows even if their gazes had remained cautious. It was James's indifference to their attention that perhaps convinced some that he was the duke.

If the duchess had been able to witness him, perhaps some of her fear would finally have abated.

*I will miss you so much, James. So very much.*

"You sound so beautiful, James."

He lifted one hand and lightly cupped her cheek. Jules held his hand against her face, a lump forming in her throat as they stared at each other.

"I am going to miss you, Wildflower."

A hollow sensation invaded her midsection. Unable to speak against the emotions tightening her throat, she nodded.

*Please, please* her heart cried, but she did not know what it asked or who it was asking, herself or the duke.

"I...bloody hell, I feel too much for you," he said, sounding once again like a wounded beast.

The feelings pulsing through Jules rose in a powerfully fierce swell, sensations she hardly knew what to do with until they encompassed her entire being. They crashed into each other, kissing for endless minutes, uncaring they stood in the rain, soaking their clothes where anyone might drive past in their carriages.

Her desperate madness was complete, for Jules knew then she had fallen in love with the Duke of Wulverton.

*Oh God, what a fool I am.*

• • •

A few hours after reaching his town house James was unable to sleep. Even after the three bouts of loving with his Wildflower. The first time had been hard and almost savage, then afterward they had read together and sipped whisky, before he had slowly made love to her. She had tumbled into sleep over an hour ago, but that dark, restless ache had been upon his soul.

James stared down at his lover as she nestled in the crook of his arms, running the back of his fingers over her cheek. She murmured sleepily, snuggling closer to his warmth, and instantly the emptiness closed and warmth filled his chest.

*My heart is only looking at you, Wildflower.*

Her lashes fluttered open, and her gaze ensnared him.

"You remain awake," she murmured.

He touched the corner of her mouth. "I have been wondering about your laugh."

Her eyes crinkled at the corner. "What about it?" she demanded pertly.

"It is low and husky. Have you ever laugh unfettered… high and tinkling like most ladies? Or is your laugh practiced and a part of your disguise?"

"I have never laughed freely."

He saw when the loss of such a simple joy hit his Wildflower in the chest as if she had been physically assaulted.

"This is silly," she murmured when her eyes burned with the ache of unshed tears.

His fingertip stroked lightly over her bottom lip. "Are you ticklish?"

Her eyes rounded. "*Ticklish*? You would not dare—"

James started to mercilessly tease the underside of her arm and side. She shrieked and laughter, free and unfettered spilled from her throat. It was a sound he'd never heard from her before, and James had never heard anything as beautiful…and free. She laughed for several minutes, dropping her weight against his chest and burying her face against his throat. Though her shoulders still trembled with humor there was a wetness on his skin. His Wildflower cried.

James shifted, easing her from his chest to peer down into her eyes.

"I have never laughed like this before," she said huskily. "I have never just spoken...without keeping my voice low and deliberate."

"With me you have no need to pretend."

"I know," she whispered.

She surged closer to him and mashed their mouths together in a desperate kiss. James groaned, took her face in his hands and kissed her hard, sucking them back down into ecstasy so they did not have to face those difficult decisions already beating at their senses.

James sprinted deep into the woods, running without slowing his steps until his sides ached and his muscles cramped. He had returned from London only earlier today to his mother's displeasure that he had not called upon Lady Emelia or her family while in town. His mother had not been pleased to hear the young lady had not entered his thoughts in the few days he had been in London.

Only Jules Southby had crowded his awareness. James slowed his running until he stopped, lifting his face to the night sky, closing his eyes as the memories washed over him. The wanton night of tupping in the brothel, visiting a gambling house, riding in Hyde Park in the early mornings, meeting old friends at White's, and then the wicked way they would come together in the nights when the household slept.

His Wildflower made him happy, and James knew she was also happy with him. He recalled the night in the rain, the pain in her eyes at the thought their friendship would one day end.

*Why the hell does it have to end?* he silently snarled.

Looking behind him at the great house in the distance, James could not imagine happiness to be found with any of the ladies his mother had invited to Longbourn Park hoping to become the future Duchess of Wulverton. The only woman he wanted was his Wildflower.

*Stop this. Jules does not live as a lady and could never do so.*

James had always known the freedom she enjoyed existing as a gentleman. Yet seeing her for those few days in town had powerfully reinforced how free and damn happy she had been with the life she had built for herself. He struggled to imagine parting from her. He could not envision never seeing her again because they did not belong to the same world. His Wildflower made him think of life beyond the present moment.

A wife, a duchess, was such a vague idea and took up no space within his thoughts other than fulfilling a duty that would see his family's position more secure within the *haut ton*. He did not imagine what that creature might look or smell or even taste like. He did not think about her, walking beside her or...anything. Yet whenever he thought of Jules, the future came to James in vivid dreams of her laughing and dancing in his arms and of her in his bed forever, the beauty of her smile as she peered down at their child snuggled in her arms.

A disturbing, ruthless need trembled inside.

*A mistress*, that ruthless voice whispered. His Wildflower could remain his mistress. *Yet she deserves so much more*, he silently replied. *She deserves to live the life she wants.* Asking her to give up even a part of that identity felt abominable. The images of her smoking a cigar, her green eyes dancing with liveliness, the way she had raced astride in Hyde Park, the way she had hollered when she beat him and Lindfield at Poker to the marquess's annoyance swam in James's thoughts. How free and happy she had been.

James stood there within the concealing darkness of the forest, knowing he could not marry anyone else when only his Wildflower commanded his heart. He scented Jules before he heard the soft whisper of her footsteps.

"You gave your Aunt Cecily a right fright racing across the lawns...naked," she drawled, coming to stand beside him. "I was sent right out by the duchess to ascertain what is wrong."

"I have on trousers," he drawled. "I think it is time my family depart for their own homes, then they would be less worried to see me running in the nights."

Her soft laughter curled through James.

"The duchess's ball in town is few days away...and that you have not conformed to their expectations is worrying."

He turned his head and watched her graceful approach. She had boldly removed her moustache before coming to him, the cravat was undone revealing the soft hollow of her throat, and the eyes that peered at him were bright with emotions and longing.

"Run with me."

They moved off together, away from the prying eyes of his family and deeper into the woodlands leading to the cottage. Jules stopped, panting, before tumbling to the earth, folding her hands behind her head as she peered up at the towering skyline of trees. James lowered himself beside her and hauled her to the top of his chest. Clasping her head between his hands, he ran his thumbs over her cheeks.

"Do not leave, Wildflower."

Her eyes widened. "What do you mean, James?"

"I will not marry any of the ladies that attended my

mother's house gathering."

Her lashes swept down across her cheekbones, hiding her expression from him.

"Do not hide from me."

She tried to move away, but he held her to him, and she trembled against his body, dropping her forehead to his chest. "Please let me go."

The soft plea cut through him like the sharpest blade. James opened his arms and she rolled off him, hurriedly standing. He pushed to his feet, frowning when he realized that silent tears trickled down her cheeks. The sight of them ripped a hole inside his chest. "Why do you cry?"

• • •

*Why do you cry?*

Jules's chest was so tight with pain she could barely breathe. *You know why, James!* His words just now had filled her with relief yet also pain. She, too, did not want him to marry, but after that...what? They could not be together beyond their brief affair.

"What are you saying?" Jules needed him to be explicit. "Are you asking me to remain as your lover?"

*Oh, please say yes and nothing more*, she silently begged.

His head jerked back. "No."

Jules was petrified to look at him. Her throat went tight, as too many emotions rippled through her heart.

"I know I should not ask it, but I want you as my duchess, Wildflower."

A dark, desperate feeling swelled through her.

"James—"

"Marry me."

Jules was so taken aback she laughed, only to abruptly sober up, dazedly aware the sound held the edge of shock.

"*Marry* you?"

"Yes."

"What are you saying, James?"

"You understand me, Wildflower, marry me," James said softly, taking a step closer to her.

"Why would you ask me this?" she whispered, feeling as if her heart would break into thousands of pieces.

"We are lovers."

She shook her head. "That we are lovers does not warrant a proposal!"

"Do you deny that we are made for each other? Do you deny the thought that we might end does not damn well cleave you in two? Do you deny it?" he snarled, almost frightening her with his intensity.

"James…you are a *duke*. We do not belong to the same world."

Something dangerous flashed in his eyes. "And it is because I am a duke I know I have the power to make us possible—"

She slapped her palm against his bare chest. "I am a woman *pretending* to be a man in this world." Jules's chest hurt with the effort to remain unaffected. "Are you asking me to give up on my dreams of being a doctor of the mind? Of one day inheriting my father's office?"

"I am asking you to love me as I love you."

For a long moment she did not reply, because she couldn't. *He loves me.* This was a man who did not give his emotions lightly, and when he gave them, she knew he would do so with his whole self. The pain that clenched her chest nearly took her breath. Jules loved him until her heart was breaking with it, yet what he wanted was impossible.

"I cannot marry you," she whispered.

A dark torment flashed in his eyes before his gaze shuttered. She could already see that protective wall building as he closed himself off from the emotions that tore at him. Jules wanted to scream for she knew that once he turned away, James would exile all traces of her from his heart.

"Do you love me?" he demanded rawly.

*I cannot answer you*, she silently cried, understanding why he did. If she loved him…and he loved her, they could fight to be together. Jules had to make him see that loving each other was not enough. Not when everything was so complicated. "Surely you know as your wife…your duchess, I would not be able to breathe and the person you know would no longer exist, James! Would I be able to race you in Hyde Park, to laugh and talk with you as I do now in public? Would I…"

He faltered into absolute stillness.

She pressed a hand over her mouth to still the wild words bubbling inside. "My God, I cannot even imagine myself in such a role. I know nothing about feminine wiles or comportment. What do I have to recommend me to the role of a duchess? Your mother said your wife must be your *anchor* in society. I have *nothing* to offer you in that regard, James. I would not be the thing that holds you afloat but weigh you down to your detriment."

Jules pushed to her feet, stepping away from him because she was within a second of leaning forward and putting her cheek against his chest. "The one you are to marry is Lady Emelia. If not her…despite all the gossips society loves you and half of the maidens are already in love with you. Anyone will be happy to be your duchess."

Her heart thumped in her throat, almost blocking words. Her tears blurred her vision as she stared up at him. "You and I both know that to be in this world as a wife…a duchess, I will not be allowed to study or pursue any passion that is mine. Marrying you would mean giving up…*everything*, James. Perhaps…perhaps we could be friends."

"No."

She flinched. "James—"

He cupped her chin between his hands and held her, looking down into her eyes.

James's eyes were dark and empty.

"It would not be fair to anyone I would eventually marry or take to be my lover if we are to remain acquaintances, for I will want you always," he said gruffly. "There is no force on this earth that can stop how I long for you. None."

He lowered his hands and stepped back. "I understand, do not believe I do not. I saw you in London...you glowed with fire and passion and purpose. I understood what I ridiculously asked you to relinquish even as I damned myself for wanting you so much as to ask."

His mask cracked, and naked pain was laid bare in his gaze. She cried out when she saw it, and she reached for him only to drop her hand when he stepped back. She understood then the controlled facade just now was to hide the anguish tearing at him. This was a man who felt...who loved...and he had laid his heart bare to her even knowing she might reject him.

*Oh God, James.* What would it be like to sleep in his arms every night? To be the person to listen to his fears, to smooth that deep groove in his brows and help him shoulder his worry? What would it be like to live as a lady with him, carry this man's child...and to learn alongside him how to love and laugh with that child? What would it be like to try and live as a duchess...understand such a role and power and bear the scrutiny of walking beside him.

Jules stared mutely at him, shocked at the dark anguish resounding inside of her chest. Such a life was not for her... it had never been her hope or dream so why should it now pierce her heart with such acute yearning?

An elusive emotion crackled through her, and she held

her breath until it burned the back of her throat, then Jules released it in a shallow rasp.

Everything felt too sudden and chaotic, there was not enough time for her to think or understand the emotions tearing through her. "James..." She bit her lip, for no other words would come forth.

At her silence James visibly slammed the door closed with his ruthless iron will, and she hated the fear that tore through her to see it.

It was the powerful and austere duke who dipped into a bow. "Goodbye, Jules Southby. I wish you only success in your endeavors."

With that, he turned and walked away.

Jules took several breaths to steady herself, to push down the swirl of emotions still trying to dig their claws into her. A sob tore from her, and she dropped to the ground, leaned her head between her legs, and wept. The sounds were raw and unchecked and went on for long minutes with only the sounds of the forest keeping her company. It took an incalculable effort to subdue the wild grief ripping through her heart, but she did it, whirled around, and made her way to the stables. She would mount her horse, ride away, and Jules knew she would never again see or speak with the Duke of Wulverton.

# Chapter Sixteen

Sleep eluded James, memories of his Wildflower chased his thoughts like a specter. Jules Southby and Dr. Southby had departed Longbourn Park hours ago. It had taken immeasurable will to maintain a facade of civility when everything inside him roared like the most feral of wounded creatures. Logically he knew he had to let her go. This was not the life she wanted, and it shredded his soul to even ask her to give it up to be with him. James damn well tried and had been working for hours to build up the walls around his emotions. Each time he thought he succeeded, a remembered scent, a taste, a smile, and the walls crumbled, and that terrible need for her came rushing back with brutal force.

Pushing out a harsh breath, he vaulted from the bed and strode to the open windows. A storm had unleashed over a couple hours ago, and the winds howled outside, tugging at the wild feelings beating through his heart. James put on his trousers, padded from his room and down the winding stairs, making his way outdoors.

"James?"

He faltered at the soft call of his name. "What is it Felicity?" he asked, without turning around.

"Are you also unable to sleep?"

He glanced over his shoulder, and his sister gasped, her hand fluttering to her throat at whatever she saw in his expression.

"I need…" His throat closed around the rough words. "Outside."

"The storm is raging, James!"

"It is what I need. Sleep well, Felicity."

"You are only clad in trousers! Surely you will catch your death should you venture out. Please let us retire to the music room together and perhaps we might play the pianoforte together?"

"Another time." He walked away, stepping out into the frigid night. James walked from the main house into the deep woodland of his home, then he broke into a run. He ran hard until the breath burned in his lungs and his muscles ached. Almost an hour passed before he skidded to a stop. Rain lashed down from the sky, the icy cold of the night penetrating deep into James's skin as he stood before the monument built in honor of the late duke, his father.

That sense of loss built into an agony he despised. He felt his resolve, moving inside like a living thing. *I am not damned weak*. This…this he had already conquered, and he would damn well do it again. Except, as the minutes trickled away and turned into another brutal hour where he stood still, allowing the elements to pummel him, James realized his Wildflower was not someone he could ever forget. James stooped on his haunches, tracing the words cut into the marble stone. Words of love and remembrance, words he'd not gotten to say to his father.

"I miss you, Father," James said gruffly. "I am damn sorry you died without seeing me again. I am sorry I will never be able to share any more of my thoughts with you. I feel like a damn fool talking to you when I know you are gone, but somehow it is you who I want to speak with, Father."

A clap of thunder sounded through the thick forestry, and he whimsically thought perhaps his father could hear him from an afterlife.

"You've taught me much about honor and duty," James continued, hearing his heartbeat in his ears. "Even lost in the icy mountains, I never forgot your lessons or love. I know I should put the family's needs before mine. Make an offer for a lady the family approves of and have an heir, securing the future of the dukedom. Yet I cannot. Fear and loneliness once held control over me, owned my thoughts, pricked at me day and night for months…years, reminding me that I have no power of my own, that I cannot control life or death or fate, yet somehow I conquered it. I returned home, and the only thing that mattered was living in the present, fulfilling a duty, and remaining sane in the emptiness. Yet I have felt hope again…this damnable fucking hope and dream for a life that should not belong to me. I want it…I want *her*. Her name is Jules Southby…and I love her. This…*creature*…a chameleon, a trickster…a sweet, genuine, kind, passionate enigma that has somehow taken a part of me, against my will, Father, and made it hers. I love Jules Southby…and I will not let her go even if it means relinquishing my duty, walking away from the dukedom and living with scrutiny and speculation for the rest of my days. Father…wherever you are, I hope you would understand that I do not wish to live without my Wildflower, and I *must*…by God, I must make it work at all cost."

James rose, tipped his face to the sleeting rain, and took a deep breath. *You damn well own me, Wildflower. Somehow in my eyes, there is only you and I don't want to forget anything about you…ever.*

...

A couple of days had passed since Jules returned to her parents' home from the duke's estate, pretending as if her world had not been indelibly altered. Each day she read the paper, devouring each mention of him, bracing for the day it would be announced he had chosen his duchess. The *haut ton* also waited with bated breath, each newssheet mention growing more outrageous by the day with their wild speculations.

Seated on the armchair near the windows, Jules curled her legs tighter and crossed her arms, hugging herself. *I want to be with you James...but it is impossible.* Jules closed her eyes, leaning back with her hands over her face, surrendering to the tears burning behind her lids. She was hopelessly in love with the Duke of Wulverton, and the joy she'd found being with him, Jules had never experienced the like of it and sensed she would never again.

*How do I be with you James, and not lose everything?*

"Yet when I think about never seeing you again, that is far more painful to contemplate than never working as a mind doctor, or donning trousers to drink a pint in a tavern," she whispered, leaning her forehead against the cool window pane. "In your arms James, I found..."

*I was free. Oh, I selfishly want it all.*

Perhaps she *could* be his duchess, and also moonlight as Jules Southby. Live a double life as his wife...and as a gentleman. Was that possible? She gave a faint, shaky laugh that turned into a harsh sob.

She'd known from the very start how foolish it had been to allow him close...to allow his kisses and his warmth to invade every inch of her body and chain her soul to his. She had known it...she had leaped...and now that she had fallen, Jules could not wrench herself from the depths of love that she had traversed.

Since their parting she had hoarded every precious memory, whispering his name in the dark night as she wept. For Jules knew that even as she craved him, he would be cutting her from his heart and memory. The duke would not allow her memory to live with him, for it had the power to hurt him. She would be a wretch to hope he would not be able to dig her free, but the selfish heart of her prayed he would never be able to forget her, for she would never be able to pry him from her thoughts or dreams. She tried to imagine a life without James in it, and it was simply impossible to envision it for a moment.

"He is a duke," she murmured in the silence of the room. "He said he is powerful enough to make anything possible… to make *us* possible." Jules bit into her lower lip until the flesh ached. She wanted to believe that promise with all her heart.

The door opened and she hurriedly swiped away the evidence of her torment. "Papa, I thought you had meetings for this afternoon."

He waved a letter in her direction as he ventured farther into the small parlor. "The duchess sent word that the queen was very impressed with His Grace when he visited her at Court yesterday. England is celebrating his return and she expects an announcement soon that he will marry Lady Emelia," her father said with a smile, folding the letter. "The duchess's ball is next week, and she is hoping it will cement his return in full and an announcement will be made of an alliance."

Jules parted her lips as she forced herself to breathe, forced herself to get control of the pain beating down on her.

"Jules," her father said, impatience ringing in his voice. "Did you hear my words?"

She sighed, gathering he had been speaking to her and she had been lost to her emotions. Jules raked her fingers through her hair. "Father, I—"

"You have been out of sorts since you returned from Longbourn Park," he said stiffly, a dark suspicion in his eyes. "This...longing you seem to have is unseemly."

Jules stiffened, staring at him in shock. "Longing?" *Is my hunger so evident for all to see and speculate?*

"Do you think I would not have noticed it? Even your mother is worried and tosses in her sleep at night." A frown pleated his brows, and he twitched in clear discomfort. "Are the feelings you own for the duke the reason you know that you have no wish to marry?"

A startled laugh jerked from her. "Father..."

Suddenly Jules could not bear to utter another falsehood. She looked away from him, toward her mother in the distance who directed a servant to set a table and chairs just so out in the gardens. A couple of guests would arrive soon, and they were meant to take a small repast outside while they conversed. As if she sensed her child's stare, her mother glanced in their direction and gaily waved.

Jules slammed her eyes closed, blew out a sharp breath, and whirled away from her father and his words that she should return. She hurried from the parlor and walked down the hallway, pausing when a maid hastened forward, holding out an envelope.

"Mr. Southby, sir, a letter arrived for you."

She took the letter, peering at the seal. "Thank you, Mary."

Jules went into the small parlor and pried open the wax sealing the letter with impatient fingers. She gasped, tightening her fingers on the paper until it crinkled. It was from the duke...no...James. Jules felt as if a boulder had been lodged against her chest. She closed her eyes briefly, only feeling dull despair. Almost afraid, she read his words.

*Dear Wildflower,*

*Exiling you from my heart is an impossible hope. More so because I do not want to. You once told me love bewitched, it healed, it was passionate, and it was what our souls longed for. At the time I thought you a fanciful fool, but I now know the truth of those words because this is the love I feel for you.*

*It was indeed wretched of me to ask you to give up a passion and dream that your eyes sparkle with when you speak about it. I tell myself I can live without you because I love you enough to hope only a happy, fulfilled life for you.*

*I deluded myself. It has only been a couple of days, but I know you will haunt me forever. You are like a thief in the night, entering my dreams and stealing my peace. I have seen the unsounded depths in your soul, and I hope you have seen mine. It is only you I love, and I am willing to live with you always in your disguise.*

Her surprise was so great the letter fluttered from her hand. James was willing to live with her as a gentleman? Jules dropped to her knees and scrabbled for the letter. She hurriedly devoured the words, her heart rattling inside her body with a bewildering mix of pain, relief, and surreal joy.

*Do not protest or deny my decision. It is mine and will remain unchanging. I've long surrendered to these emotions I own in my heart for you, and they will never be locked away again. Not by me, or you, our fears, or by society's censure. Some might wonder that we are lovers and frown on the closeness of two gentlemen, but it will be our lives and business. We will travel together, love and live and laugh. You can be my permanent guest at my home, and in the evenings we will sleep in each other's arms and love passionately. I do not fear society's speculation, nor do I fear never having children of my own. My cousin will remain my heir. I do not long for a duchess and children, Wildflower. What I long for*

*is you in my arms and by my side in this world.*
   *Yours,*
   *Wolfe.*
   *P.S. I will give you three days to read this letter, cry your denial and rage and laugh, then I am coming for you.*

Jules lowered the letter, a laughing sob tearing from her. *Oh, James, what are you thinking?* She read his letter again, her gaze lingering on *"I have seen the unsounded depths in your soul, and I hope you have seen mine. It is only you I love, and I am willing to live with you always in your disguise."*

Something inside her was breaking apart, shattering, and that very something also felt as if it was being reforged. "Live with me always in disguise. Oh, James." Jules put her hand over her mouth. She felt, absurdly, like laughing. She could feel herself shaking. Her duke was willing to endure scandal and lurid speculation for her. Society would indeed condemn him as addlepated and eccentric to live and travel with a gentleman friend always by his side while never marrying. Though James once told her he dreamed of children, legacies of his own to carry on his powerful family tradition he would eschew it all for her. Jules laughed and sobbed. She went to the windows, tugged aside the curtain, and peered at her father walking across their lawn with Matthew Crawford, another doctor he was hoping would join their team.

Jules pictured giving up this life, studying and working with her father to live with James and it felt...remarkably easy. Her breath hitched and she rested her head against the cool pane. While she could walk away from being a gentleman, striding toward a life where she live as a lady...a duchess was almost impossible to envision. The idea of being restrained petrified Jules, of allowing herself to be caged into the ideals and expectations that governed women of society. What was most painful, however, was the idea of existing in a world without James.

*It is impossible.* It couldn't happen. It wouldn't happen for she loved him.

The door opened and footsteps whispered over the parquet floor.

"My dear, your father and I are planning a small party to welcome—" Her mother jerked into stillness, her eyes widening. She closed the door and hurried over. "Jules, darling, whatever is the matter? You are crying!"

She peered at her mother through a curtain of tears.

"Please, what is it? Tell me!"

It seemed she had no choice but to provide an answer. "Jules Southby can no longer exist, Mama."

Her mother flinched, her face paling. She sat down heavily on the sofa, her slim shoulders shaking. "You are working beside your father, Jules," she said softly. "This is what you want, I can tell. Why are you saying this?"

She leaned over and kissed her mother's cheek. "I am leaving it up to you how and when you tell him, but when I leave in a couple of days, Jules Southby will no longer exist."

Her mother surged to her feet, her eyes flashing her denial. "How can you say this so casually? Have you thought of the scandal and the consequences? Have you thought of what this revelation will do to our family and…"

Her voice broke and she pressed a hand over her mouth, turning away from her daughter.

Jules stood, folding James's letter, and tenderly tucking it away in her pocket. "There is someone who loves me beyond scandal or consequences. Someone willing to sacrifice so much to call me his own."

Her mother spun to her. "*What?*"

"I have been home now for a few days, and every night I lie awake in deep despair because I know the first time I experienced true joy was when I was with him. Love bewitches, and it heals, and it is passionate, but it also so much more. Love never falters or gives up, and love sacrifices for true happiness. I cannot remain as Jules Southby, Mama, because I want to walk beside someone as their friend and lover. Even as I say this I am filled with fear because it will be immeasurably difficult, but I do not shy from the challenge, nor will I regret my choice."

Her mother's face crumpled. "I forbid you from doing this!"

"You would wish for me to deny my happiness to protect your heart from pain and censure?"

"You were only with the duke for a few weeks!" her mother snapped. "There is nothing you could have formed with him that is more valuable than this family."

Jules was not angry, seeing through her mother's anger to her fear. "So you do know it is the duke I speak about."

"Surely you know your father would have mentioned this aberrant connection between you both," her mother said, slashing her hand through the air.

"It is not aberrant," she said quietly.

"I cannot be selfish, I know this, Jules, but I need more time. Perhaps a few more months."

Jules went to her mother, brushed a kiss on her cheek, and walked away, disregarding her protests. She had her own letter to write, and somewhere Jules had to find the courage to face living a life she did not understand.

# Chapter Seventeen

The small announcement printed in the left corner of the newssheet was barely discernable, hardly worthy of attention. Yet, James saw it because there was nothing about Jules Southby that could escape his awareness, even if it was a post in the *Gentleman's Magazine* in the section of notices of deaths and causes of death.

> *Jules Southby, late of Derbyshire, perished in a carriage accident, the only son of noted Physician and Alienist Dr. Charles Southby.*

James read it for a third time, grappling with the flash of agony searing through his veins. A dark bleakness covered him. *Gone?* Jules Southby was dead? The torment that tore through James was unlike anything he'd ever felt. The sound that came from him had his mother and sister gasping, lurching toward him like marionettes.

"James! Whatever is the matter," his sister cried, all the excited chatter about the ball to start in a few hours forgotten.

He had always possessed a very determined will,

which had saved him more than once. Such weakness was abhorrent, and he would recover from losing her. He had to. Yet the crack inside his chest felt like it would never be made whole. A snarl hissed from him as anguish almost cleaved him in two.

"James," a voice cried behind him, "whatever is the matter? You are scaring us!"

He whirled to see his mother peering at him with wide, fearful eyes. "What is it?"

James ruthlessly drew on the cold he had used to help him survive the ten years alone and could not find it. "She is dead," he said harshly, "And I do not know if I can survive her loss."

His sister gasped, and his mother frowned. "Who has died?"

"Jules Southby." The words were scraped from the back of his throat.

Confusion pleated her brows, and she shook her head sharply. "What do you mean? Mr. Southby is dead?"

"An announcement was made in the paper. A carriage accident it seems."

"Good heavens!" She rushed forward and plucked up the crumpled paper, quickly reading it. "This is terrible news. We must send out condolences to Dr. Southby." She looked up at him and froze. "You are *anguished*. I can see it cut into your face, and it is frightening me."

"I cannot live without her. Not now. Maybe after years of happiness I could bear to part from her...but not now."

"*Her*?"

She stared at him for a long time, then slapped a hand over her mouth. "The mysterious lady you danced with at the ball. That was Jules Southby. *Good God*. This is...this is unfathomable. How is it possible that...that Mr. Southby was a woman? I cannot...this is shocking and *scandalous*!"

Felicity started to sob, and when she came over to James and hugged him, he allowed the embrace, somehow needing it to anchor him against the hole appearing in his heart. Had she even seen his letter? Had she known that she was loved endlessly? That rough, terrible sound once again hissed from him, and he closed his eyes as the burn of tears welled behind his eyes.

"Leave me," he said gruffly.

His sister stepped from him, wiping the tears from her cheeks. "What will you do?"

Roar his pain and drown it by drinking several glasses of whisky. As if she sensed his intention, his mother haltingly came forward.

"James, you must be presentable for the ball in only a couple of hours."

"Mama!" Felicity cried. "Surely James—"

"No," the duchess said, sorrow deep in her eyes. "I am very sorry for it, but I am begging you, James. The Prime Minister will be in attendance along with several of the most illustrious members of our society. You must be there…and you must show the world, which will be examining every action as if you are under a microscope, that you are the indomitable Duke of Wulverton. Then, in a few weeks, you must announce the selection of your duchess."

He leveled his gaze on his mother and she blanched, flinching from whatever she saw in his eyes.

"James, I am sorry she is gone but she would not have been suitable for—"

The duchess paled at the growl that leaped to his throat.

"Brother, please forgive Mama's thoughtlessness. She did not mean to be as callous as how she sounded. We would support whomever you love."

James did not answer her, for he understood his duty to his family. Yet it was the burning rage and pain seething in his gut that robbed him of the power to speak. His mother beckoned his sister, and with a regretful glance at him, his sister and mother departed, leaving him alone.

• • •

The night fell in soft whisper, the orchestra played their violins, and the finest lords and ladies of the *haut ton* flittered about, oblivious that their duke stood by the sidelines, an empty husk. He only attended at the entreaty of his mother. Tomorrow he would retire to the countryside and prepare for Parliament's sitting.

*And grieve.*

He would roar and grieve but he would not allow it to consume him, for once again he would need to learn to survive an impossible odd—existing in the world without Jules Southby. The laughter, facile chattering, and happiness in the palatial ballroom mocked his agony. James could feel a dark, hollow space inside his chest, and pain dug in its claws and widened that hole each second that ticked by.

His butler appeared in his periphery, in clear need of an audience. The duchess frowned and was about to make her way over when James walked away from the crowd and toward him.

"Is there a problem, Britton?"

His butler cleared his throat. "The duchess was very clear in her instructions, Your Grace. Only those with an invitation are allowed to enter the premises."

His mother had been very clear, not wanting any scandal rags or even the noteworthy reporters present. She had been very careful in whom she selected to attend his first ball as their returned duke, hoping for the influential support of noteworthy participants in this game that must be played.

"Is this a matter that needs our intervention?" he

demanded coolly.

"The lady is most insistent that she be allowed entry, Your Grace," Britton said, disapproval coloring his tone. "I fear the disturbance of a scene, yet I also fear for her safety as this Miss Southby is unknown."

A dart of shock went through James's chest. "What is her name?"

"One Miss Julianna Southby, Your Grace. She claims to be an acquaintance of yours and a cousin to Mr. Jules Southby. The young lady is suspect as she is clearly without a chaperone and her manner is rather bold *and* threatening."

James could give no name to the emotions beating inside his heart. "Let her inside."

Britton bowed sharply and departed to execute the order. James's heart pounded like a war drum as he waited, surrounded by a sea of laughing faces and glittering ballgowns, yet feeling that desperate aloneness. James could feel his mother's worried gaze upon him, yet he did not tear his gaze away from those steps, nor did he push himself to impatiently race to see who was this creature who presumed a connection and what was her purpose.

"Miss Julianna Southby!"

The announcement of her name barely created a ripple in the crushed ballroom. A vision of loveliness appeared on the landing, and the ground disappeared beneath James. She nervously scanned the crowd, and when she saw him, her lips parted on a wordless cry. She was breathtakingly beautifully garbed in a vibrant golden gown which clung to her upper body with mouthwatering sensuality. Her bustle was not as wide as others in the ballroom, and it accented the lush shape of the woman beneath the tightly laced corset and petticoats. Her arms were encased in white gloves, her delicate feet in golden silk slippers. The light from the chandelier played softly over her unfashionably short tresses, each strand seemingly on fire in the golden light. Her hair caressed becomingly around her chin in a riot of curls, bare of adornment except for a single flower tucked behind her ear.

It was indistinguishable, not a rose or an elegant stem anyone would recognize—a wildflower. She was enchanting, and as she descended the wide staircase James realized she had given up her entire world for him.

Equal joy and anguish clashed through James.

*Why, Jules? I would have made it work, damn it.*

Raw emotions burned his throat, and his hand holding the glass of champagne trembled. He could have found a footman to hand the glass or walk over to a table and set it down. James simply allowed it to crash from his fingers to the floor, uncaring of the gasps as the glass shattered.

Turning away from her was impossible, for he did not want to lose a moment of her. He vaguely became aware of everyone in the ballroom staring at him...staring at her. Silence fell in a wave, and his mother discreetly walked toward him, a panicked look on her face.

James moved forward to meet her in the center of the room, his gaze never leaving his Wildflower. Once he reached her, he glided his fingers across her temple, her brow, her nose, and her lips, uncaring of the scandalous gasps. "You are real."

Tears burned her eyes. "Yes."

"You are not dead."

Her eyes widened and she swayed. "I never thought you would see that mention, James. Forgive me for the pain I must have caused you. I hastened to town as fast as I could..."

"You are here, nothing else matters."

"I hurt you," she said, her voice cracking. "When I think of how you must have felt seeing that news...I *never* intended it for your eyes. I cannot even close my eyes and pretend that you are gone. The pain is too much to bear yet you believed I was gone... I...*oh God*. I could not have endured the thought for a minute, or I would have shattered."

She took another deep breath, peering at him with wide, luminous gaze. "The announcement to the papers was more for the professional acquaintances I have made over the years. I am sorry for it to know perhaps they will miss me, even if I was only a fleeting presence in their lives. My family will be told the full truth about it. My father...my uncle and my sister. My mother and I will reveal all to them, James, and they will help me exist as a cousin, Julianna Southby. I was never about much in society as Jules Southby to cause a ripple in the *haut ton*. I got your letter...and I had to come."

A stunningly powerful rush of tenderness went through him. "Dance with me, Wildflower."

"Yes."

He took her hand and led her to the center of the room.

"There is no music, James, and everyone is staring at us."

"Do you care?"

Her lips trembled and those tears spilled over. "No, I only care that I am here with you."

"Dance the waltz with me."

James took her into his arms, and glided her around the room, never taking his eyes off her. The orchestra hurriedly struck the notes of a Viennese waltz, but no one else joined, too stunned by his actions or perhaps eager to watch his behavior and speculate on it tomorrow.

"Why did you come like this, Wildflower?"

A soft breath hitched from her, and tears spilled down her cheeks and down to her neck. "You know why."

Emotions trembled through James, and he tugged her closer.

"We are scandalizing the world," she achingly whispered.

"Hang the world. While I will consider my family always, I will not be a slave to anyone's expectations. "

A smile shaped her mouth, then she laughed, the sound light and airy in the room. The sound real and honest. "I will lay the world at your feet," he vowed.

"I only want the piece you stand upon, James."

"You'll stand with me?"

"*Always.*"

"I love you," he said softly. "Will you marry me, Wildflower?"

"Yes!"

A breath of sensation pierced him like a well-aimed arrow. "I will build a hospital for you. One…a dozen, and you will work should you wish it."

Her eyes crinkled at the corner. "Oh, James, the scandal of that would be—"

His fingers tightened around her waist. "I cannot bear the thought of you giving up the freedom you've enjoyed, and the passionate pursuit of psychology. If we are to be together, they *must* coexist. You'll be the Duchess of Wulverton, my Wildflower. You can do whatever you wish with my full support and power. Even dress as Jules Southby and go to work if you wish."

She laughed again before it broke off into a sob. "You impossible man, I love you so very much, James. Jules Southby is no more. I do not wish to pretend anymore…to my family or the world. I want to exist as I am, and the world and society and my family must accept me with whatever eccentrics and intelligence I own. That I was given the privilege to study and graduate is something I will always treasure. *Always.* Will I leave it as a better memory of a previous life? *No.* You tell me that I will have power as a duchess."

"Yes," he said gruffly, tugging her scandalously closer, wanting to kiss her so badly his damn teeth ached. "More power and influence and wealth than you can ever know."

She smiled, her eyes glowing with that enigmatic passion

and mystery. "Your support and love means so much to me, James. The world is slowly changing, and while women are still not allowed to graduate from Cambridge or Oxford, those halls have allowed ladies to study. For so long I worried if my father knew the son he was so proud of was a woman he would be disappointed. No more. I do not wish to lie or deceive anymore. I will proudly show my intelligence and education and advocate for more distinguished studies for women, and study even further should I wish it. It might take a few years, but I believe there will be a day women will be freely permitted to study *and* graduate with degrees in medicine, psychology, arts, history, and I will lend my voice, passion, and status to that endeavor. Will I miss studying at university and the freedom to enter an inn and drink a pint or visit a gambling house? Yes."

Jules took a shaky breath, her eyes glistening with such emotions. "I can see in your eyes that you look sad…for what I am giving up, James."

"Bloody hell, Wildflower, you will not give up anything—"

"I do not feel as if I am giving up anything…for I am gaining so much. Loving you will not change the person I grew to be, nor will it change my experiences. That core of me is unshakable. My heart does not want to survive without you in my life, James, without the only person with whom I have been honest and vulnerable and real. Those days apart, knowing I might never see you or kiss you again, laugh or run with you in the woods, lie atop your chest and listen to your heartbeat, flayed my heart with torment. Do I long to live as a duchess and a lady? No. I do not long for such a life and restriction…but I am rather smart, if I might say so, and I will learn what is necessary so as not to shame you or cause any scandal for our family. What I hunger for James, is to be with *you*…to be your wife…your friend and lover. Being your duchess will not prevent me from devouring texts and theories, it will not prevent me from writing articles to our society for publication, and it will not prevent me from helping anyone I see in need."

A wide smile curved her mouth and her eyes sparkled. "I want to run in the woods and sleep in the tree house with you. I will continue learning and studying and I know you will never try to stop this passion of mine, James. And when I feel the walls closing in on me…I'll don trousers, a wig, grab my walking stick, and paint the town with you."

James laughed, ignoring that soft squeak as he tugged her closer. "God, I love you."

"We must not start a scandal," she whispered, humor glowing in her eyes as he twirled her away.

James danced with her, holding her in his arms like a treasure. When the waltz ended he continued gliding with her and the orchestra had no choice but to continue playing. By the time they came to a stop, they had toured the ballroom at least three times, dancing the waltz, all of society standing and staring at them in astonishment.

· · ·

*A couple of days later…*

Jules took a deep breath, opened the door to the drawing room, and stepped across the threshold. The letter she had sent her father a few days ago was still clutched within his grip, showing her he had read those words over and over. Words which had reassured him though he would have seen the notice of her death in the papers, she was very much alive and would provide an explanation upon her return to Hertfordshire.

"Papa," she said softly.

He surged to his feet and took a step toward her, only to falter into profound stillness. Jules held herself still as her father ran his gaze over the lady before him. He paled, then swayed, reaching out to grip the armchair.

Her mother entered the room and closed the door with a soft *snick*.

"My God," her father said, scrubbing a hand over his face. "Your mother...your mother told me only yesterday. I have been trying to come to terms with it but I...seeing you before me like this...I do not know what to say."

"I am the same person, Papa," Jules said, a tight lump in her throat.

"I know you are but..." He sat down heavily in his chair resting his face in his hand.

Shock darted through her when she realized he sobbed. She took a few steps over, but a light touch at her elbow arrested her movements. Jules glanced at her mother to see tears also coursed down her cheeks, and her eyes were so reddened it informed Jules her mother had spent hours weeping.

"Your father and I have many things to work out between us," she said softly. "My revelation has been a shock to him and...and he will need some time to..."

Her mother looked away.

Jules lifted her chin, tightly guarding herself against his rejection. "Do you wish for me to leave, Father?"

He snapped his head up and shoved himself out of the chair. "No. I...it was my lack of understanding that caused your mother to even think of such a scheme. If there is someone to blame for this it would be me, but Jules, I do not wish to blame anyone. You are a wonderful person...my son..." He took a deep breath. "My daughter. You are clever and beautiful and resourceful. But why did you...*why* did you announce your passing in the papers?"

"I am going to be the Duchess of Wulverton," she said, meeting his regard unflinchingly. "Mr. Jules Southby cannot exist anymore, Father, but I am still here, and I will continue assisting you should you wish it and will not be ashamed to have me with you."

Those words had her parents staring at her with varying degrees of shock.

"What?" her father said.

"A *duchess*," her mother gasped, a hand fluttering to her throat.

"Of course," her father said faintly, "now I understand what I observed."

Jules flushed and lifted her chin. "It will be a great shock to the family, and we will have to inform Uncle Albert and Sarah of everything…"

Her father walked around his desk, held out his arms, and Jules hugged him. As she squeezed him, she started to cry. Her mother came over, and her father enfolded them in his arms. Jules knew everything would take months for a sense of normalcy to find them once more, but knowing they were at the beginning of their acceptance filled her with peace and contentment.

• • •

*A year and a few months later…*

"James, James!" Jules cried, running from the library on the second floor along the hallway and down the grand staircase without any of the etiquette lessons she had absorbed over the past year.

She'd only started going through the correspondences their butler had delivered to her this morning because she had been too busy hosting a small garden party with only their close family as guests. It had been wonderful spending time with their family, and Sarah who was with her second child and gloriously happy. Her heart pounding with jubilation, she hurried down the hallway and shoved open the door to the library. "My research paper has been accepted for publication!"

Her duke was not in the room. A cool breeze wafted inside from the open windows, and a few sheets of paper fluttered over the desk to cascade to the carpet. Walking over to the desk, she lowered the letter received from the British Medical Association which had lauded the paper she wrote on the biological necessity of touch and how crucial it was from infancy. That they would also publish that paper as being written by Julianna St. Leo, the Duchess of Wulverton would cause a small ripple through those from the *haut ton* who might read it, but certainly a great uproar from those in the psychology field.

Jules padded to the open window, peering outside into the darkness. A sigh of pleasure left her when she saw James, walking half naked across the lawns. That he was outside at this hour meant he'd felt the walls closing in on him and had responded to the need to be outdoors.

Toeing off her shoes, then removing her stockings, Jules slung her foot over the very windowsill her love had escaped through and shimmied outside. She curled her toes into the wet grass, inhaling the varied scents around her. The earth smelled of moss and water, the air of roses, lavender, and gardenias. James had taught her so much about isolating all other senses and letting the sense of smell dominate. Heat curled through her as she recalled the carnal ways he had touched and showed her to appreciate the power of fragrances.

She sauntered over to him, smiling when his lips curved into a smile. He had smelled her already. James turned and watched as she approached. When he opened his arms, Jules laughed, ran the rest of the way, and jumped into his arms. Of course, he effortlessly caught her, and she easily wrapped her legs around his hips for she did not conform to the notion of wearing a bustle beneath her gowns, especially in the comfort of her home. Her hair, which she had not cut in over a year, rippled over her shoulders and settled around them in soft waves.

"You've been running," she murmured, cupping the underside of his jaw.

James gripped her hips and tugged her even closer, dipping his head to smell along the curve of her throat and cheek, a roughened sound of need rumbling from his throat.

"Let's spend the night in the tree house, my love," he said against her throat.

There was an undercurrent of something decidedly wicked in his tone. Heat sparked in Jules's veins when he bit her skin. "Yes."

Her duke took her lips in a passionate kiss, hotly gliding his tongue into the depths of her mouth. A sharp bite of pleasure gripped Jules as his tongue mated with hers. With a muffled moan, she clasped his shoulders, tightening her legs around his hips as he walked with her deeper into the woods where she knew he would make love to her over and over for the long night. They would laugh and talk, perhaps even spend a few days in the woods before retreating back to the main estate.

The staff would know they were in the woodland cottage, and they did not gawp at their eccentric duke and duchess but simply got on with their work, nor would they be bribed to discuss how their master and mistress conducted themselves at home. Jules considered that there would not be many more times they could sleep in the tree house together—at least for a while. Climbing the rope ladders would become difficult, as she was already putting on weight and suspected that she might be with child.

As he set her down before the ladder, she smiled up at him. "I have so much to tell you, my love, but first…"

Hauling him down to her, she swallowed his laugh and kissed him again.

# About the Author

*USA Today* Bestselling author Stacy Reid writes sensual Historical and Paranormal Romances and is the published author of over twenty books. Her debut novella *The Duke's Shotgun Wedding* was a 2015 HOLT Award of Merit recipient in the Romance Novella category, and her bestselling Wedded by Scandal series is recommended as Top picks at Night Owl Reviews, Fresh Fiction Reviews, and The Romance Reviews. Stacy lives a lot in the worlds she creates and actively speaks to her characters (aloud). She has a warrior way "Never give up on dreams!" When she's not writing, Stacy spends a copious amount of time binge-watching series like *The Walking Dead*, *Altered Carbon*, *Rise of the Phoenixes*, *Ten Miles of Peach Blossom*, and playing video games with her love. She also has a weakness for ice cream and will have it as her main course.

*Fall in love with more historical romance...*


### THE DUKE'S SECRET CINDERELLA
a novel by Eva Devon

Charlotte Browne could just kick herself. What possessed her to tell the Duke of Rockford that she is a lady? She's just plain Charlotte—with cinder-stained hands, a wretched stepfather, and no prospects. After one illicit kiss from the duke, Charlotte flees, leaving only a blue ribbon behind. The duke's touch may heat her skin, her very soul, but he can never know who she truly is...especially when even *she* doesn't know the truth.


### CINDERELLA AND THE DUKE
a novel by Lydia Drake

The Weatherford Ball is the last chance Julia Beaumont has to escape the clutches of her horrid stepmother. After one look at the refreshingly clever Julia, Gregory Carter, Duke of Ashworth, simply can't resist a stolen kiss—scandal be damned. Then the lady flees...leaving only a slipper behind. And it must have been one dandy of a kiss, because now Julia has proposed to him. After all, the lady needs a husband, and this roguish duke will certainly do. It's simply a matter of making him the perfect scandalous offer...

Made in the USA
Monee, IL
16 December 2023

49507287R00177